ROAD RASH

ROAD RASH

BY MARK HUNTLEY PARSONS

Alfred A. Knopf
New York

Text copyright © 2014 by Mark Huntley Parsons
Jacket art copyright © 2014 by Leonora Saunders (drummer) and Vitaly Krivosheev/ Shutterstock Images (background)

Grateful acknowledgment is made to the following for permission to reprint previously published material:

EPC Enterprises: Excerpt from "Layla," by Eric Clapton, copyright © 1970 by Eric Clapton. All rights administered by EPC Enterprises. Reprinted by permission of EPC Enterprises.

Alfred Publishing: Excerpt from "Brighter than Sunshine," words and music by Matthew Nicholas Hales, Kim Oliver and Benjamin Keeston Hales, copyright © 2003 by Warner/ Chappell Music Publishing LTD (PRS) and Benjamin Keeston Hales Publishing Designee (PRS). Administered by Warner-Tamerlane Publishing Corp. and WB Music Corp. All rights reserved. Reprinted by permission of Alfred Publishing.

Alfred Publishing: Excerpt from "So Far," lyrics by Josh Todd, music by Keith Nelson, copyright © 2005 by WB Music Corp., Cash and Carry Music, Dago Red Music, Lick the Star Music, Chiva Music and Numbsie Music. All rights administered by WB Music Corp. All rights reserved. Reprinted by permission of Alfred Publishing.

Sony ATV Music Publishing: Excerpt from "Something's Wrong," music and lyrics by Gert Bettens and Sarah Bettens, copyright © 1996 by Double T Music. Rights administered by Sony/ATV Music Publishing LLC. All rights reserved. Reprinted by permission of Sony/ATV Music Publishing.

Visit us on the Web! randomhouse.com/teens

Educators and librarians, for a variety of teaching tools, visit us at RHTeachersLibrarians.com

Library of Congress Cataloging-in-Publication Data
Parsons, Mark (Mark Huntley)
Road rash / by Mark Parsons.
p. cm.
Summary: "When teen drummer Zach signed up to spend the summer on tour with a rock band, he didn't realize the stairway to heaven was such a bumpy ride." —Provided by publisher
ISBN 978-0-385-75342-5 (trade) — ISBN 978-0-385-75343-2 (lib. bdg.) — ISBN 978-0-385-75344-9 (ebook) — ISBN 978-0-385-75345-6 (pbk.)
[1. Drummers (Musicians)—Fiction. 2. Rock groups—Fiction.] I. Title.
PZ7.P254Ro 2014
[Fic]—dc23
2013013578

The text of this book is set in 12-point Adobe Caslon.

Printed in the United States of America
February 2014
10 9 8 7 6 5 4 3 2 1
First Edition

For Wendelin, of course.
For all the right reasons.

PART I
HOME

1
"Start the Show"

Okay, so I was running late. Again.

I hauled the last of my cases to the ancient freight eleva-tor, slapped the button, and collapsed against the wall. And . . . nothing. No light, no hum of machinery, no opening doors, and no hope of not having to hump all my gear up three flights of stairs. That would be my kick drum, my snare, two rack toms and a floor tom, my cymbals, and all that heavy hardware.

Ouch.

Why does this crap only happen when you're late?

As I stood there, soaking in the wonderfulness of it all, the stairwell door next to the elevator flew open. Out swaggered Toby with two girls, and even though the place had a strict policy of not serving minors, it was clear they'd been drinking. Toby was so intent on laughing at what the girls were saying that I swear he was going to walk right by me. Just as I was about to say *Hey, how about a little help here?* he finally saw me and slowed. It wasn't a full stop, mind you, but it was better than nothing. For a lead singer.

"Hey, Zach. Elevator's out, mate." And he kept on walking, an arm around each girl. He turned to the hot little blonde on his right and said something into her ear as his hand slipped inside the back of her jeans. She giggled.

"Thanks a lot, *mate* . . . ," I said to his back.

At least Kyle didn't just stand there when I finally arrived upstairs, soaked in sweat. He grabbed my cases and started hauling them to the stage as he went off on me. "Dude! Where've you been? We're supposed to go on any minute."

"Elevator's dead," I said over my shoulder as I headed back for the next load.

"Whoa. Whatcha need?"

"I can get the rest of it. Can you unpack what's here?"

"Got it."

Now *that's* a friend. By the time I returned with the rest of my drums, I'd made a quick mental list of the gear I really needed for the first set, because I'd rather play with the bare-ass minimum than be the reason we were late getting started. Again.

Kyle had my stuff onstage and roughly positioned where it should go, near his bass amp. "Thanks, man," I said.

"No problem." He checked the time on his phone, then looked at the pile of equipment that, in theory, was a drumset. "Five minutes. Should I tell the manager we'll be late?"

"No way. I'm good. Maybe go round up the other guys?"

He nodded and headed off while I started bolting stuff together like a mad elf at 11:55 p.m. on Christmas Eve.

By the time the other guys were onstage, I had my kick, snare, hi-hat, and throne set up, and my sticks in my hands. The other half of my drumset could wait, and I hadn't even bothered hooking up my headset microphone—we could live without my backing vocals for the first set. Kyle and Justin had their axes strapped on and plugged in, and Toby said, *"Check, test, one, two . . ."* into his mic for like the hundredth time already. He looked over his shoulder at me and gave his best rock-star sneer. Which looks pretty dorky on anyone but a real rock star. "You *ready?*"

I glanced at the set list. "Holiday" was up first. Great. That was gonna suck without my toms. I almost changed it by calling an audible, but that'd be admitting that I really *didn't* have my shit together. "Let's do it," I said.

Justin started playing the opening riff on his guitar, loud and fuzzy. I kicked the snot out of it with what I had, trying to make up in attitude what I was missing in equipment.

Once I started playing, everything got a whole lot better. Nothing beats drumming for getting your aggressions out. . . .

We got through the song okay. And by the end of the first set—a dozen songs later—I was actually getting into the whole minimalism thing of playing with just the bare bones. Then Toby was his usual buzz-kill self as we came offstage for the break. "Hey, drummer boy," he said. "You gonna put the rest of your stuff together? 'Cause I feel pretty stupid standing up there in front of a baby drumset."

"Can't have that, can we?" Man, it was *always* all about him. . . .

"Hi, Zach." I turned around. It was Kimberly, Kyle's brainy little sister, with her friend Ginger.

"Hey, Kimber. What's up?"

"We thought we'd come down to check you guys out." She smiled at me. "You sound really good tonight."

"Thanks."

"What's wrong with your drumset? Did you lose some drums?"

"Uh, no." I explained it in Kimber terms. "It's a scientific experiment. You know—form follows function? Less is more?"

"I see. . . ." She held up her hands like she was about to take notes on a clipboard and assumed a scientific voice. "So, Professor Ryan, was your hypothesis correct?"

"Strangely, it kinda was. Helped me focus." I shook my head. "But on the downside, it sure pissed off the lead singer."

She nodded knowingly, still in professor mode. "Ah. Unintended consequences."

Ginger spoke up. "You guys are weird."

Kimber laughed. "Okay, we'll go." She grinned at me. "Bye, Zach."

"Later, Kimber."

As I was finishing getting the rest of my drumset together, Kyle came up to me. "Hey, a couple of the guys from Bad Habit are here. Including GT. I think Justin's a little nervous."

"I'll bet." Glenn Taylor had a rep as the best guitar player in town, and his band was definitely a couple of notches above us.

And when the second set started, I could definitely see it messing with *our* guitar player's head. Justin was trying too hard—instead of just keeping it solid, he'd go for something way over his head, and half the time he'd crash and burn.

It finally got out of control during that old Social Distortion tune "Born to Lose." When it came time for the solo, he started out okay, but he kept going. And going. And *going*. At one point he threw his guitar behind his neck and noodled away for like a minute straight. Now, that can look pretty cool if you can actually pull it off. With Justin it was a freakin' train wreck.

After the song was over, I called him back to my kit.

"Whassup . . . ?" he asked. "You like that solo?"

"Uh, yeah. That was incredible." In the literal sense. "I just wanted to tell you, GT and his buddies left during the last song."

"Oh. Um . . . thanks." He tried to look disappointed, but I could tell he was relieved.

"No worries." I gave him a thumbs-up and a smile.

It was complete fiction, of course—they were still there, sitting at a table back in a dark corner with some girls. That's one of the advantages of being the drummer. While the other guys are busy concentrating on their playing (or their *performance,* if you know what I mean), you're in back, watching everything. It's kind of like being the catcher on a baseball team—the pitcher gets all the glory, but you're really the one calling the shots and keeping an eye on the big picture.

There's this popular myth that drummers are the morons of the music world. *(Q: Why do guitar players keep a pair of drumsticks on their dashboard? A: So they can park in the handicapped spots.)* But to do it right, you've got to have two streams of consciousness going at the same time, where you're monitoring your playing *and* keeping an eye on what's going on around you.

On the one hand, you're thinking, *Okay, stay on the hi-hats . . . four-on-the-floor . . . make sure to hit those accents . . . good . . . now open the hats a little . . . yeah, build into the chorus . . . add eighth notes on the snare . . . crash! . . . over to the ride cymbal . . . more energy . . . go up to the bell . . . now ride the crash cymbal . . . not too loud yet—the chorus goes high and he can't sing as strong in that range . . . now drive hard going into the guitar solo, but don't get too excited and speed up. . . .*

On the other hand, it's like, *Good, people are starting to move to the dance floor . . . play solid on the kick drum—make it easy for them to catch the beat . . . this crowd seems to like the danceable mid-tempo stuff better than the fast punk-pop stuff . . . that hot girl in the white shorts can really dance—pull it back one percent and put a little something extra on the backbeat for her—make it sexy, man . . . catch the bass player's eye and nod so he'll get the groove and make it even funkier . . . now the floor's packed—signal the guys and keep the song going for an extra minute . . . sneak a peek at the list while you're playing and pick another tune in the same style—right now!—so there won't be enough downtime between songs for them to walk off the floor.*

Handicapped, my ass.

* * *

By the end of the gig I was back to feeling pretty good about being in the Sock Monkeys. Justin wasn't a bad guy, and he was a good enough guitar player . . . when he stuck with what he knew. And Kyle was more than just a solid bassist—he had become my best friend since I'd started school in Los Robles a year and a half ago. He was the one who'd asked me to join the group last summer, and hanging with him was the best part of being in the band. And I had to admit that Toby really was a pretty good singer, even if he did have a terminal case of LSD . . . Lead Singer's Disease. And when everything was working right, there was nothing like being onstage, driving the band. Especially now that we'd gotten good enough to go beyond the free parties and actually get some paying gigs. This felt real—like we could seriously get somewhere.

After we'd finished playing, I was walking toward the restroom when someone said, "Hey, good job up there, man."

I looked over. It was Glenn Taylor, sitting with two guys that looked semi-familiar and a couple of girls.

"Thanks."

One of the guys stood up, a little wobbly. I recognized him as Bad Habit's drummer, Nate. "Yeah," he snickered, doing some behind-the-neck air-guitaring. "I especially liked that pathetic Jimi Hendrix impression. What a joke!"

Glenn shrugged. "Okay," he said calmly, "but what did you think of Zach's drumming?"

To be honest, I was surprised he knew my name. The guys in Bad Habit were a couple of years older than us—they were all out of high school, and Glenn was the oldest by a few years. Kyle and I were juniors, Toby was a senior, and Justin was only a sophomore.

"I was too busy laughing at the rest of those clowns to notice." He snorted. "But I know this much—you lie down with dogs, you get up with fleas. . . ." He stumbled off, heading toward the door.

Glenn looked at the other guy at the table. "Could you give us a minute? No big."

The guy said, "Sure, GT," and he and the girls left.

Glenn nodded toward Nate's empty chair. "Have a seat."

I sat.

"Don't mind Nate," he said. "He's never been big on giving credit. And he's hammered, as usual." He paused. "Have you ever thought about expanding your horizons, musically speaking?"

"Uh . . . I'm not sure what you mean."

"I'm scouting around for someone more, um . . . *reliable*. I like the way you play—good mix of attitude and skill. Any interest?"

"Wow. I mean, thanks! But . . ." I saw Kyle and the guys across the room, joking around. "I'm pretty committed to my band." Man, that sounded lame.

"That's a good thing to be." He smiled and held out his hand. "Thanks anyway. And you really did sound solid tonight. Keep on it." I shook his hand. He wasn't a huge guy, but he had a grip like iron. "Well, take care," he said.

"See ya."

I finished my original mission, then walked back toward the stage. As I started taking my stuff apart and packing it up, I felt weird. Like, what if I'd just blown a great chance? Bad Habit were big on the local scene. Big enough to go somewhere . . . and believe me, I've got nothing against that. I mean, I've been playing drums since I was ten—I freakin' love music, and I've always dreamed of being able to do something with it.

But then I thought about the Sock Monkeys. We *had* sounded pretty good tonight—at least after Justin stopped showing off. And Glenn had probably just complimented me because he might need a temporary fill-in for his band sometime. I could hear my dad now. "Good networking skills," he would have called Glenn's pitch. "Never burn a bridge you might want to drive over someday." He was *full* of stupid sayings like that, but this time he'd probably be right.

Kyle grabbed one of my cases as I was loading out and fell in beside me. The elevator was still broken, but down was better than up, especially with two of us. He was pretty quiet as we navigated the stairs. Then he finally spoke. "I saw you talking to GT and those guys. What did they want?"

I almost told him, but what was the point? "He wanted your sister's phone number," I joked. We were always kidding about setting Kimber up, but she was evidently pretty picky.

"Yeah, right. . . ."

"Actually, we were just shooting some hoops. They thought we sounded good."

He nodded slowly, like there was no way he was buying *that* one, either. "Uh-huh . . . *sure.*"

"Okay, except for Nate, their drummer. He was less than impressed with Justin's tasty little solo."

"That's the first honest thing you've said. So, what did you think of it?"

"Justin? He was trying to show off and it sucked, big-time."

"Duh."

"But I get it. Glenn-Taylor-the-guitar-wizard walks in, so he feels like he has to prove something. He's only a sophomore, man—he'll get over it."

"Boy, you're in a forgiving mood."

"Look, he's one of us, so we have to cut him a little slack, right?"

"I guess. But I'm starting to worry that his insecurity might get in the way of us getting somewhere. This isn't the first time he's choked."

I shrugged. "I want a deal as much as you, but I'm not gonna sweat it—this is supposed to be about good times, too."

He gave me a strange look.

"Yeah. *Supposed* to be . . ."

2

"Kick Me to the Curb"

"Hey, Sleeping Beauty!" my dad said. "Nice of you to join us."
He held out a plate stacked with pancakes. "You almost missed
breakfast."

I snagged four or five. "I was up late last night, working."

"Hey, you pig," my little sister, Alicia, said. "Don't take
them *all*!"

"I'm making more," my mom called from the kitchen. "And
don't call your brother a pig."

Alicia's idea of complying was to pull her eyelids down and
push her nose up in a snout and snort at me.

Dad ignored her, as usual. "You were *working* last night?" he
said. "Then how come they call it *playing* in a band?"

That joke was getting old. "Just because parts of a job are fun
doesn't mean it's not work." I was thinking about that broken
freight elevator.

He nodded. "Yeah, maybe. But speaking of work, what are
your plans for the summer? School's out pretty soon and we're
not having a repeat of last year."

I rolled my eyes, but luckily he didn't see me. Okay, maybe last summer I'd kinda bailed on my promise to get a job, and I'd ended up spending most of my time with Kyle and the band. And to be honest we'd goofed off more than we'd worked, but the band had grown into something more serious now.

Mom tried to help. "Last summer was better than the year before, when he moped in his room all day."

"There's nothing wrong with him having friends," Dad said. "But he needs to learn how to work, too." He turned to me. "I was talking with Jerry over at Johnson's Yard Supply the other day, and he said he could use some extra help this summer, moving plants and loading trucks. I told him I'd send you down to talk to him."

Whoa—time to steer this bus in a different direction. "Thanks, Dad. But I already have a summer job lined up."

His eyebrows went up. "Really? Where are you working?"

"Land of Lights."

He pulled a face. "That laser-tag place?"

It was more than that—it was also like the world's biggest pizza joint, with a cool arcade attached, too. Probably the best hang in town—lots of people from school went there on weekends. And not just dudes, if you know what I mean.

"Yeah," I said. "Our band has a steady job there for the summer. Every Thursday, Friday, and Saturday night." What I didn't say was that they probably hired us because we charged less than other bands. This was our first real steady gig, and we were happy to have it at any price—it sure beat scrounging for parties and one-nighters, which were all we'd had until now.

"But if you're only playing three nights a week, you could still work at Johnson's during the day."

This wasn't going the way it was supposed to. I tried hard to seem businesslike about it instead of whining, because I knew from past experience *that* wouldn't fly. "Dad, besides doing the gigs, we need to rehearse. We're developing our original music too—we want to make a record this summer, and that takes a lot of work. We're serious about this."

Dad didn't say anything for a minute. I was waiting for him to call BS, but once in a while he surprises me. Like when I'd asked him if I could go to that big music fest in the desert last summer, and his answer was no . . . unless *he* took me. Kyle came too, and we had a blast.

But I was still surprised when he said, "Okay, Zach, I can tell you're serious. Sharla, what do you think?"

Mom raised an eyebrow at me as she spoke to Dad. "I think they should have some sort of schedule. So they stay on track."

"Thanks," I said. "To both you guys. We're definitely going to make things happen this summer."

Q: DID YOU HEAR ABOUT THE DRUMMER WHO FINISHED HIGH SCHOOL?
A: ME NEITHER.

Monday morning I looked for Kyle before school started—I wanted to talk to him about getting a schedule together for the band. What I'd told my folks about our summer plans wasn't *exactly* fiction, but I felt like I ought to try to get something more, uh . . . concrete arranged.

Kyle wasn't in any of the normal spots but I ran into Toby

holding court on the senior lawn. The dude's always onstage, whether he's fronting our band or hanging before school. Today he ignored me even more than usual, if that's possible, so I gave up and went to class.

In language Ms. Lovell continued with her painful dissection of *Huck Finn*. This cracked me up, because at the beginning of the book Mark Twain himself says, "Persons attempting to find a motive in this narrative will be prosecuted; persons attempting to find a moral in it will be banished; persons attempting to find a plot in it will be shot." But when I'd suggested that maybe he was directing this at language teachers, she didn't seem to see the humor. Still, her mostly-one-way discussion did give me a chance to sit in the back and get started on a band schedule, so it wasn't a total loss.

Next I had Spanish, where the groove wasn't as smooth. Mr. Arrez walks around the room as he lectures, which makes it difficult to get any "outside projects" done.

But in social studies we were watching a movie about the Great Depression, which was exactly as exciting as it sounds, so I decided to keep my mood elevated by working on my band stuff instead.

So by the time I was through my first few classes, I had a pretty detailed schedule hammered out, with times and dates. The basic plan: Mondays and Wednesdays we could practice in the evenings, probably at my place like usual. (If you're the drummer, it's worth hosting practice—beats hauling your stuff to someone else's place.) Then we could meet on Saturdays and have songwriting sessions—our gear would still be at Land of Lights through Saturday night, but we could just get together with acoustic guitars and a cajon and work on arrangements and stuff. And working on our originals was important, because on Sundays we would focus on that whole business of making a record.

That was really the big unknown. Sure, any nerd with a computer can "make a record," but it usually ends up sounding exactly like what it is: homemade crap. The trick is to make it sound pro. I've been playing around with recording for a few years now, and I've gotten to the point where I can make some fairly decent-sounding tracks, assuming the other guys do their part. Of course, it'd help to have a good tracking room and some better equipment, but we manage.

The *second* trick is to actually get your music distributed and not just buried somewhere on the internet, where no one even knows it exists.

The answer to that is to partner with someone. As in, a record label. Forget the majors—they're dinosaurs. But there are plenty of indie labels out there, and we're hoping to convince one of them that investing in the Sock Monkeys could be a win-win. Okay, that's not easy—you've got to be unique *and* good—but that was our goal. Which is why we need strong original material. Who wants to be in a cover band forever?

Anyway, I was feeling pretty good about my planning . . . right up to fourth period.

"Yo, li'l sis," I said as I walked into my next class. Kimber turned and made a face. Kyle and I are seventeen and she's still fifteen, and she hates it when I remind her of that. So of course I do, every chance I get. Not that she's a total kid—she's way smart, which is why she was in my math class as a sophomore.

"How's it going?" she asked.

"Fine. I didn't see Kyle this morning. Is he here?"

"Oh sure, we rode in together. I saw him talking to Justin by the cafeteria this morning."

That was weird—usually we met up before school started. But I didn't have time to think about it because we were neck-deep in quadratic equations for the next fifty minutes.

At lunch I grabbed a sandwich and headed over to the tables by the lawn, where I thought I saw Kyle talking to Toby and Justin. But by the time I got there, it was only Justin and Toby.

"Hey, guys, what's up?"

Toby just shrugged, too cool for school. Justin said, "Not much. What's going on?"

"Nothing. Where'd Kyle go?"

Justin tilted his head toward the science wing. "He went to see Mr. Jacouri about something, I think."

"Ah. So, we're on for practice tonight, right?"

Toby glanced over. "I want to have a band meeting instead of rehearsal. My place, seven-thirty."

"Cool. I have some things I've been working on—I'll bring them tonight."

✱✱✱

After school I fired up my computer and made my roughed-out schedule look good, with different colors showing rehearsal times and gig times and writing sessions. There was a semi-steady crowd at Land of Lights and we couldn't do the same songs in the same order every night. So I put together a spreadsheet with all the songs we knew and created different set lists for different nights, varying the songs between nights, as well as the order we'd play them in. While I was at it, I made a table tent asking people to follow us online. That way we could direct them to our band page and post announcements throughout the summer to try to build some buzz. Then I printed out four of everything, hole-punched them, and put them in folders so everyone had their own copy.

Okay, so that was totally anal, but I felt like I'd done an A job of it.

I pulled up at Toby's house at 7:20—it'd be pretty stupid to be late to a meeting about getting organized.

Toby's mom answered their massive stained-glass door and let me into the foyer. "I think the boys are in the garage," she said. "Just go on back, Jack." I let it go. It must be genetic.

I walked into the garage to find Justin sitting on an old exercise bicycle, just barely spinning the pedals, and Toby throwing darts at the board across the room.

"Hey," I said. "What's up?"

Toby spoke without turning from his darts. "What's *up* is you're out."

"Huh?"

"Out. As in, no longer in the band."

"What are you *talking* about?" I looked around. "Where's Kyle?"

"Kyle's been and gone, man." He threw another dart and spun toward me. "You're always late. You don't take it serious. We want to get somewhere, and you don't. So you're out."

"What the hell? Yeah, I was a little late getting my gear set up on Saturday, but we started on time." *No freakin' thanks to you,* I thought. "And I take this real serious. Look." I held out the folders. "I made a schedule for the band this summer. Gigs, rehearsals, writing sessions, set lists . . . How can you say I'm not serious?"

He ignored them. "Look, numbnuts, let me give you a clue. You're *not* the boss of this group, and we *don't* wanna see your stupid little schedule." He snorted. "You're out!"

I went from stunned to furious in about two seconds. "I don't believe this! Glenn Taylor asked me to join Bad Habit the other night, and I turned him down." I was yelling now. "I freakin' *turned him down*! And you know why? Because I was loyal to this band."

The second it was out of my mouth, I regretted it. Toby gave his patented sarcastic laugh. "Yeah, *right.* Nate Travis can drum circles around you. You're not just a screw-off, you're delusional."

"So that's it? No discussion, no vote, nothing?"

"We did vote—it was two to one, so you're gone."

Well, that made me feel a little better, to know that at least Kyle was taking my side. Maybe he and I could put something else together. . . . "So you guys are looking for a new drummer *and* a new bass player, then? Good freakin' luck!" Kyle and I were a rock-solid rhythm section, and these guys were going to have a hard time finding decent replacements in time to make the gigs at Land of Lights.

He gave me an exaggerated sigh. "God, are you like the retard from hell? Kyle's not leaving—we got stuff laid out for the whole summer. Shit, we're playing a big-ass party Friday night."

Friday night? *This* Friday night? Man, was I a mushroom or what? "So who's my replacement?"

"Don't worry about it. We found someone who can actually *play* the drums, not just play at them." He turned back to the dartboard. "See ya ... *mate*," he said over his shoulder as he threw. *Thwack.* Bull's-eye.

I walked out. Justin hadn't said a word the entire time.

3

"It's Not the Fall That Hurts"

I called as soon as I got home. Kyle didn't answer his cell, so I called his house. His sister answered.

"Hi, Kimberly. This is Zach. Is Kyle around?"

"Kimber*ly*?" she said. "Wow . . . what's wrong?"

"Nothing. Can I just talk to Kyle?"

"Okay, hang on. I'll get him."

While she went to find him, I tried to figure out what to say. I mean, beyond the obvious question of what the hell.

Kimber's voice came back on the line. "Zach?"

"Yeah . . ."

"Umm, Kyle's not available right now."

"As in, he's in the shower or something, or as in, he doesn't want to talk to me?"

She didn't answer, which was all the answer I needed. Finally, she said, "What's going on?"

"Not a freakin' thing, apparently." I hung up.

✳ ✳ ✳

The next morning, instead of looking for Kyle, I avoided him. If he didn't want to talk, that was fine by me. The more I thought about the whole thing, the more pissed I got. And confused. I mean, *WTF . . . ?* Where do they get off saying I'm not serious? Was all that from my offhand comment to Kyle about having a good time, with or without a deal?

No, this must have been in the works for a while. They already had a big gig lined up, and that doesn't happen overnight. Plus, they'd have to work the new guy in, and that takes time, too.

So I felt kinda . . . naked as I went to my classes. I'm not like a super popular guy at school or anything, but the people who *do* know me probably think of me as Zach, the guy who plays drums in the Sock Monkeys. And all the people I usually hung with were either the guys *in* the band or friends *of* the band. So who was I now?

I didn't feel like talking to Kimber, either, so I slid into my seat in math just as the fourth-period tardy bell finished ringing. Ms. Littleton gave me the eye, but she let it slide. She's actually pretty cool for a woman who spends most of her day solving for *X*. She saw us playing at an outdoor festival once, and the next day she said she'd enjoyed it and was impressed with my "percussive skills." She'd even told the class that drumming could be considered a great example of applied mathematics.

But now I was just another loser at school, trying to follow Ms. Littleton's discussion of polynomials. Then my phone vibrated. Someone was texting me. It couldn't be Kyle, could it? I mean, it was a total bust to use a phone during class, and Kyle was in history. Unless he'd cut . . . ?

I decided to sneak a peek. It was Kimber. She almost never texted me, and never in class. *I heard. Totally unfair!*

I glanced over at her. She was watching me. No smile, no wave. Just looking. I sent a quick *Thx* and looked up . . . straight into the gaze of Ms. Littleton.

"Well, Zach, what's the answer?"

Answer? I didn't even know the question. Hell, I didn't even know there *was* a question. "Um . . . I'm really sorry. I completely spaced. What was the question?"

Instead of repeating the question, she slowly said, "Mr. Ryan, I would really appreciate it if you could manage to *un*space yourself for the next forty minutes or so." I nodded. Whew . . . I got off easy.

Then she continued, still looking straight at me, "Ms. Milhouse, I'm sure *you* can answer the question." Crap. We were totally busted.

Kimber just shook her head. "I'm sorry. . . ."

God, Ms. Littleton was *still* looking at me. I tried to act normal and not squirm as I thought about how I was going to manage without my phone. Oh, I could get it back the next day, but only after my parents had been called down to collect it. And then *they* would take it, and for a lot more than a day.

Finally, she relented and turned to another student. "Mr. Ruiz, can you please answer the question?"

He could, and he did. And that was the last she mentioned it—until class was over.

"Zach," she said as I was packing up my stuff. "Can I see you for a minute? And Kimberly, you too?"

As the class emptied out, I looked over at Kimber and nodded toward the front of the room. "I don't want you to be late for lunch—go ahead." I hung back by my desk. When everyone had gone, Ms. Littleton spoke to Kimber for a minute, then Kimber left.

I made my way to her desk. "Look," I said. "No excuses. I'm sorry." I handed over my phone. "It wasn't Kimber's fault. I texted her, so it was my bad."

For some strange reason this made her laugh, then she sort of coughed and got serious. "Thanks, Zach." She looked at me for a second, like she was deciding what to say. "You've studied and practiced for a long time to get your drumming abilities where they are, right?"

"Uh, right." Where was this going? Had she somehow already heard about me getting kicked? God, did *Kimber* say something . . . ?

"So imagine you're in the middle of a show. They're paying you, and you're trying to do a good job. There you are, drumming away on a very challenging song, and people are listening and getting into it when all of a sudden a couple near the front starts talking, totally oblivious to what you're trying to do."

Oh . . . "Yeah, I've been there," I admitted, nodding. "Sorry. It won't happen again."

"I know it won't." She handed me my phone back. "I don't need this—I don't think that's really the issue here."

"Wow. Thanks."

She looked at the clock. "You'd better get going."

I started to go, then turned back. "Hey—how come you laughed when I apologized?"

"Remember what you said . . . 'It's not her fault, you can blame it on me' . . . ?"

"Yeah?"

She smiled. "Kimberly said exactly the same thing."

* * *

I did see Kyle a couple of times during the week, but we didn't really talk. The first time I ran into him between classes, he nodded and mumbled a quick "Hey, man—how's it going?" and kept on walking.

The next time I saw him, he tried that again, but I grabbed his arm. "Hey, you got a minute," I said. It wasn't a question.

"What's up?"

What's up? I wanted to say. *What the hell do you think is up?* But instead I said, "I want some answers on the band thing. So far, all I've heard is a load of crap. I mean, it's no real secret Toby's an asshole and likes to throw his weight around, and I guess Justin's pretty much a follower, but I thought you'd back me up a little more."

"Hey, I voted to keep you. And it wasn't even Toby's idea at first. Justin's the one who mentioned getting Josh in the band, and Toby just kinda ran with it."

"Josh . . . ? As in Justin's cousin?"

"Yeah."

"When did he start playing? And you're saying he's better than me?"

Kyle looked down. "I dunno. He's not bad."

"Yeah, well . . . Toby gave me some line that I wasn't 'serious' because I was late a couple of times. That's a load of crap, too. Do you think I'm a screw-off?"

"Naw, 'course not." He looked at the people walking by. "I've got to get to class."

I grabbed his arm again. "You said you voted to keep me. So I figured we could put a project together without those guys. But Toby says you're staying. I don't get it."

He shrugged. "They've got gigs lined up. . . . Look, I'm sorry, man. Really. There was nothing I could do about it."

"Yeah, *right* . . ."

He looked away. "I gotta go."

I held my hands up. "So who's stopping you?"

✴ ✴ ✴

Kimber said hi to me when I walked into math class, but all I did was nod and take my seat. I didn't really want to get into a discussion about her brother. Plus I've been keeping a low profile since the texting thing.

But when class was over, she came up to me. "Zach—how are you?"

"Freakin' wonderful."

"Have you talked to Kyle at all?"

"Yeah, this morning."

"And . . . ?"

"And nothing. I thought he and I might start a new band, but he's staying put, so I'm out of luck. End of story."

"That sucks."

"He told me about Josh being their new drummer."

She scowled. "Must be nice, getting a new drummer who comes with his own gigs."

"What?"

"His parents are loaded. They throw big parties all summer. Kyle and the guys are playing there tomorrow night."

Wow. "Hey . . ." I paused. "Do you know where he lives?"

"Josh? Yeah, up in Eastgate. I was with Kyle when he went there to drop off some gear yesterday. It's a mansion."

"If I drove, could you show me how to get there?"

"Sure." She smiled. "When—today after school?"

"No, I was thinking more like tomorrow night. . . ."

4
"Loser"

Kimber didn't get why I wanted to go. And I had a hard time putting it into words myself. Maybe just seeing what the hot fuss was all about . . . ?

"So are we going to, um, crash this party?" she asked as I drove us there in my dad's truck. To be honest, I was a little distracted by her. Her eyes seemed different somehow, and she was dressed . . . older? It was a great June evening, the kind Los Robles is famous for—the sun had just gone down but it was still plenty warm out—and Kimber had on shorts and this little strappy tank-top thing. "We'll feel pretty dorky if we get caught," she added.

"*Crash* is such a vulgar term, Dr. Milhouse. I prefer the phrase *surreptitious observation.*"

She didn't say a word, but I've learned what those raised eyebrows mean.

"Look," I said, "your brother's in the band, and it'll be a huge party, right? No one's going to notice. Really. Just act like you belong."

She was right about one thing—the place *was* a mansion. It took up half the block, with a low plaster wall around the perimeter. I got the impression it was modeled after one of the Spanish missions around here. And judging by the people going in, it wasn't just a party for the parents' friends—it looked like Josh had invited half his high school to come see him and his "new band." So no one gave us a second glance as we followed a group through a wrought-iron gate and into the yard.

Kimber stopped and looked around. "Talk about bucks up. All we really saw the other day was the inside of the garage—and that was big enough—but this place is stupid big."

She wasn't kidding. There was the house itself—which was like a castle—and then there were all these *other* buildings. Like a pool house, and maybe a guest cottage, and an office, and . . . what? Servants' quarters?

Anyway, there were people all over the huge lawn, and waiters in fancy outfits moving around with trays of snacks.

"I could get used to this," I said, giving Kimber a wink. "What do you say we go graze?"

So we mingled with the crowd, helping ourselves to these tasty little midget lobster things whenever a tray cruised by.

"You know, these are really good," I said after I'd had three or four, "but I want to check out the band."

She nodded toward an area behind me, across the yard.

I turned to look and about dropped my plate. "Holy . . . !" There was a full-on elevated stage set up next to one of the buildings. But what was more impressive was what was on it. The only gear that I recognized as actually belonging to the Sock Monkeys was Kyle's old bass amp. On Justin's side of the stage was a full Marshall stack, fresh out of the crate—I could practically smell the new-amp scent from here. Our old PA—a used Carvin rig—was nowhere to be seen. Instead, there was a big, brand-new JBL sound system set up, with subs and mains, as well as a beefy stage monitor for everyone in the group. Everything was miked up—not just the vocals, but all the amps and drums, too.

And the drumset ... whoa. It was a seven-piece Drum Workshop kit, with like a dozen gleaming Zildjian cymbals on a forest of chrome stands. The whole outfit was worth at least ten grand, and it looked like it had walked right off the showroom floor. Hell, his snare drum alone was worth more than my whole set. I just stood there staring, trying not to drool.

"So what are *you* looking at, mate?"

I knew who it was before I turned around. "Well, I *was* admiring all the nice new toys up there," I said as I turned, "but I got distracted because all of a sudden"—I sniffed the air—"wow, it smells remarkably like ass around here."

Kimber stifled a laugh.

"Uh-huh. So says the pathetic loser who just can't stay away," Toby replied. "Well, good! It'll give you a chance to see how a *professional* band plays." Then he looked Kimber up and down and gave her his bullshit smile. "*You,* on the other hand, should stick around after the show." He turned and walked away.

"Wow," Kimber said. "I guess I see what you mean."

"Yeah, and that's him being nice."

"In that case, seems like you're better off without them."

"Yeah, maybe ..." But as I glanced up at the stage, it sure didn't feel that way.

She studied me for a moment, then tugged at my arm. "C'mon! There's a waiter over there with a tray of those pink drinks with umbrellas. I want to try one."

I let her drag me along.

I got us two of them and took a sip. "Whoa, pretty dang sweet."

She tried hers. "I like it." She swished it around in her mouth like a wine taster sampling some rare, expensive vintage. "Hmm . . . Tastes like an afternoon on the beach. At Cabo San Lucas. Maybe on a Tuesday. After all the tourists have gone."

"So you've been to Cabo?"

"Oh, no. But this is what it would taste like. I'm sure of it."

I had to laugh. "You're weird."

"So they say," she said with a grin.

Suddenly we heard, *"Check, test, one, two . . . Check, testing, one, two, three . . ."*

I turned to Kimber. "Ever go bird-watching?" She shook her head. "That's the mating call of the fat-headed dork-meister."

She laughed and started to reply, but lights flooded the stage and Toby's voice came booming over the PA. "Hey, how're we doing tonight?"

There was a weak response from the crowd, and Toby spoke again, even louder. "I *said*, how're we doing tonight? Are you feeling all right?"

This time the crowd hooted and hollered a little more. "Good," Toby said, "because we're feeling pretty damn good, too. And we're about to rock your world. But first I'd like to introduce the newest Sock Monkey . . . the guy who's going to help us take it to the next level . . . drummer extraordinaire . . . Josh Dicenza. Give it up for Josh!"

It was pretty thick, even for Toby, but the guests responded with serious applause. Of course, everyone also knew that Josh's parents were hosting this blowout, so it was hard to say exactly who was kissing whose ass here.

I was a little surprised when I heard them start our usual opening number, but it made sense—there was no way they'd had time to learn many new tunes. Josh had probably been cramming just to learn the existing set list.

And apparently he'd done his homework. At least, he played the right parts. But it was like he thought his drums might break if he hit them too hard, and that song calls for the drummer to *slam* the toms and snare at the beginning. And the music seemed to surge ahead and pull back, like there wasn't a steady anchor under it.

I don't know what I was expecting, but this wasn't it. The production quality of the mix was good, and the tone from those beautiful drums was totally sweet. But . . . I don't know. It didn't have that tight, confident pocket that solid rhythm sections have. Okay, near the end he did this busy double-kick thing that I couldn't have played. Even if I had a five-hundred-dollar DW double pedal. Which I didn't.

Anyway, I thought that maybe they'd work the kinks out during their first tune, but the next song was more of the same. And the third one seemed downright weak.

But maybe it was just me. I glanced around and tried to read the crowd. The guests were paying attention, and there was polite applause after each song, but no one was dancing or even bobbing their head much. It was a tough call, so I looked to someone who wouldn't be able to hide the fact that it either *was* or *was not* happening—the bass player.

Kyle was up there doing his part, and he was trying to move with the music, but from where I stood, it wasn't flying. Whenever things were really in the pocket, he used to put one foot up on something—either a stage wedge or sometimes my kick drum—and he'd close his eyes and just freakin' *play*. But tonight he was looking from Josh to Justin, then down at his hands, then back to Josh, and his eyes were open the whole time . . . maybe a little wider than they should have been.

I caught Kimber's eye and nodded my head away from the stage like, *Let's get out of here.* When we were far enough away that we could talk, I looked at her and raised my eyebrows.

"They're a dog in a dress" was her reply.

"Huh?"

"Take a dog. Wash it, blow-dry it, brush it out. Spray French perfume all over it. Shove an expensive blond wig on its head. Put bright red lipstick on its muzzle. Then put it in a sleek little black dress. What've you got?"

"Hey, this is your kinky little scenario. You tell me."

"A dog."

I smiled. "I thought maybe it was just me. Uh, but Josh *did* do some stuff that was pretty technical on that first tune. Stuff that was beyond me . . ."

"You're kidding me, right? Is there any doubt that they sounded way stronger with you?"

I shrugged. "I thought we sounded better than that, but . . . but that's what the pathetic loser who can't stay away *would* think, isn't it?"

She grabbed both my arms and looked me in the eye. "Listen to me. You are *not* a loser. Not even remotely close, not in any way. And you totally kick Josh's ass on the drums."

I was kind of taken aback by her intensity. "Uh . . . thanks."

"I mean it." She let go of me and shook her head. "My brother can be such a moron."

I looked around. "I've seen enough. You ready to go?"

"Sounds good."

I suppose I should have been happy about what I'd just seen and heard. But really, it only made me feel worse. I mean, if my replacement had sounded totally pro, at least that would have made sense. But to get kicked to the curb for *this*? Was it really about Josh's parents being bucks-up and throwing a few parties where the band could play?

Whatever. It was clearly a permanent switch, so I needed to make some decisions. . . .

I turned to Kimber as I drove. "Hey, do you mind making a stop on the way home?"

"Sure, where are we going?"

"Land of Lights."

5

"Falling Slowly"

As we pulled into the parking lot at Land of Lights, Kimber asked, "Are we here because Kyle and the guys are playing here this summer? Not to play psychiatrist, but it seems like you're going out of your way to make yourself feel bad tonight."

"No, Doc. In this case, a cigar is just a cigar. We're here to kill that bad taste with some good music. That's all." I knew who was playing tonight but I'd learned my lesson—there was no way I was going to tell anyone else about the offer from Glenn Taylor.

And from the moment we walked in, it was apparent that Bad Habit wasn't going to make a liar out of me—they were rocking. The dance floor was already pretty full, and the people sitting around were getting into it, too. There was a raised section behind the dance floor, so we grabbed a table up there and I went and got us cokes.

"Sorry, they were fresh out of little umbrellas," I said as I sat down. "But I managed to talk them out of a couple of lime wedges, to give you that south-of-the-border feeling."

"Why, thank you."

As she took a drink, I had to ask. "So, what does *this* taste like? Cabo, too?"

She took another sip, deep in concentration. "No . . . it tastes like Bora-Bora, in Tahiti. In one of those huts raised on stilts out over the water. Sitting on the little deck at sunset, catching our dinner with a fishing line. And three more weeks of nothing to do." She looked up at me from her drink and slowly smiled.

"Whoa . . . I think you're a future Hemingway, li'l sis. I don't have a clue about Tahiti, but I like the way you paint a picture."

Just then the band launched into a pile-driver groove of wildly distorted guitar and pounding drums. People started pouring onto the dance floor as Bad Habit went into their own twisted update of "Are You Gonna Go My Way?"

Kimber gave me the look. I know the look, trust me. And as nice as it feels to be asked, it's better to show a little sack and step up.

I stood up. "C'mon, let's dance."

She gave me a big smile, practically yelling to be heard over the music. "Sounds great!"

Dancing with Kimber was sorta weird but also a good time, if that makes any sense. The floor was packed and the band was totally slammin' and we danced our asses off. GT took a couple of extended solos, and unlike Justin, he absolutely rocked. And he wasn't just shredding at top speed. That guy could play with feeling, stretching out a note until it howled like some demented coyote.

By the end of the song Kimber had a big sweaty smile on her face. "That was fun!" she said. "Let's stay for the next one. . . ."

So we did, and it was another good dance tune. And then they brought it way down, and I recognized the slow opening chords of "Landlocked Blues," by Bright Eyes. Kimber was still giving me the look, but I played dumb—*that* would have been too totally weird. "Uh, I'm thirsty," I said, nodding toward our table. "Let's go get a drink."

And actually, I was glad for the break. It gave me a chance to sit back and really listen to the band. Which was why I was there . . . right? They sounded more pro than we—I mean the Sock Monkeys—ever did. There was no getting around that. And I might have thought their equipment had something to do with it, but we'd just witnessed a graphic demonstration that gear does not make the band.

Okay, they did have five players—including a girl on keyboards who really filled out their sound. And their lead singer also played rhythm guitar on some songs.

But there was more to it than just numbers *or* gear.

Their lead singer had a really good voice and *huge* stage presence to go along with it. When he was singing, everyone was watching him . . . including the rest of the band. And while the bassist wasn't flashy, he was totally on the money. Their drummer, Nate, on the other hand, *was* flashy. Maybe even too much. He was all over his Mapex sunburst kit, even on the simpler songs. But apparently he hadn't been drinking that night, because even though he played some pretty technical stuff, he nailed it all. And the girl not only played keys, but she sang some, too, adding another dimension to their vocal mix.

But to me it was Glenn Taylor's playing that really put them over the top. It seemed like he'd been born with that beat-up black Strat in his hands. And the fat tone he got out of his amp—a Marshall Vintage Modern 2x12 combo—beat the pants off anything Justin could wring from his refrigerator-sized full stack.

God, what I wouldn't give to be in a band that had it together like *that*. But from the way they sounded tonight, I didn't see them making changes anytime soon. . . .

Suddenly Kimber leaned over and said in my ear, "Zach, you can adapt to new situations quickly, right?"

She sounded nervous, almost a little panicked. And what self-respecting guy's gonna say no to that one? I nodded. "I like to think so."

"I need a favor, and it's sort of an emergency." She was looking across the room as she spoke. "I need some serious, visible PDA. Right damn now."

I was deciding between asking more questions and making a crack when I realized she really meant it. So I scooted my seat around the table until I was sitting next to her and draped my arm over the back of her chair. "Okay," I said. "I'm your boyfriend for hire. What's going on?"

"I'm trying to avoid . . . uh, too late. Here he comes."

"Who?"

"Kevin Flanders. He thinks he's something."

Actually, there were three guys walking toward our table, but I had a pretty good idea which one she was referring to. The tall one in the middle had that smug thing going on that reminded me of Toby. Like he'd spent a little too much time trying to look like he hadn't spent any time.

"Hey, Kimmie, what's up?" he said loudly, to be heard over the music.

I looked at her and mouthed *Kimmie?* while trying not to laugh. She rolled her eyes.

"Uh, not much," she said.

"You here to listen to the band?" he asked. She nodded, then looked over at me with raised eyebrows.

So far, he hadn't even acknowledged my presence. As her rent-a-boyfriend, I was seriously insulted. And she'd ordered a plateful of PDA, not a side of sit-next-to-me. Okay . . .

So I pulled Kimber close, then scooped her up and hoisted her onto my lap. I put my nose in her hair, like I was going to nuzzle her. And *damn,* she smelled good.

"Don't say another word to him," I said quietly into her ear. "Don't look at him, don't talk to him, nothing. Okay?" She nodded. "Good. Now smile like you're having the time of your life, and talk to me. Doesn't matter what you say, just be cheerful about it. Trust me, he'll leave."

So she giggled like a drunk bimbo and said, "How long are we going to do this?"

"As long as it takes. But no worries—you're paying me by the hour."

"Oh my God, I think I'd rather go hang with Kevin."

"You got it, sister." I made like I was going to put her back down, and suddenly she clung to me like a kitten in a tall tree. That got me laughing for real.

"Smart-ass," she said.

"Hey, you asked for it . . ." But I held her even closer.

Kevin said something, but for a million bucks I couldn't tell you what it was.

"You know," I went on, brushing her hair out of her eyes, "I know this sounds weird, but . . . your hair smells great."

"Really?" Her eyes were shining.

I nodded. "Not part of the act—it won't even show up on your bill."

Kevin was still making noises, but finally, he spat out, "Whatever!" and left, his little posse in tow.

Kimber looked at me. "Wow—that worked perfectly. You were great."

"Thanks. So were you."

And then we just looked at each other without moving for like ten whole seconds. Whoa . . . major weirdness. I gradually became aware that someone, somewhere, was playing a hyper-kinetic rendition of "Sugar, We're Goin' Down Swinging."

"C'mon," I finally said. "They're playing our song. . . ."

6

"When the Levee Breaks"

I hated to admit it, but Toby was right. I must have been delusional to think that Bad Habit would really want me. Hell, after hearing how they sounded with Nate, I never even talked to GT at Land of Lights. Which meant that when Monday morning rolled around, I was still *el muchacho solo*. I spent my time between classes listening to "No One to Depend On." Funny how that works, huh? People listen to the blues when they're bummed, which only makes it worse, which sorta makes it better. . . .

Kimber was away at the state finals of Destination Imagination. Which was actually kind of a relief—Friday night had been . . . different.

Anyway, I was not exactly Mr. Happy that day, which might almost explain what happened at lunch. Not making any excuses, okay? Just looking for some answers.

The morning was relatively normal. When I walked into my Spanish class, Mr. Arrez said, *"Hola,* Zachary. *¿Qué onda? ¿Cómo estás?"*

I shook my head and gave him a line from my song of the day. *"No tengo a nadie . . ."*

"That I can depend on . . . ," he sang, finishing it for me.

"Something like that," I admitted.

"I know how that can be. It'll get better sooner or later, amigo. But in the *meantime . . ."* He held up a paper and spoke loudly to the whole class, like he was the ringleader at a circus. "Ladies and gentlemen! Is everybody ready? For . . . the great . . . the amazing . . . the one and only . . . *conjugation quiz!*"

At least he tried to make his class fun, as opposed to Mr. Langley's social studies class. I think Langley was secretly doing a psychology experiment, trying to see if it was possible to literally bore someone to death. So far we hadn't had any outright fatalities, but a few of us had been rendered comatose.

Math was also a bummer. Ms. Littleton had gone to the DI finals, too, and we had a sub who'd evidently learned how to teach at the Langley School of Death. The first two minutes were actually amusing—until I realized that it wasn't an act—and then the next forty-eight minutes were torture. I found myself looking for Kimber twice to pull a face.

I had to get out of there for lunch. I had to *move.* So I walked down the street to the 7-Eleven. I figured I'd get a sandwich and eat on the way back.

I never even made it inside the store.

Kevin Flanders was hanging out front with a couple of his friends, probably the same guys who were with him at Land of Lights the other night. He was leaning against what I guessed was his car—one of those little SUV-wagon-type deals . . . and brand-new, too. As a drummer I could appreciate the cargo space inside that boxlike thing, but what I really want to know is, where does a high school senior get the bucks for something like that?

Anyway, other than shooting a glance at his car, I ignored him. But of course, being the kind of guy he apparently is, he couldn't ignore me.

"Hey, look—it's Kimmie's little cuddle pal," he said loudly as I approached. What a jerk. I kept on going. "Hey, did you get any?" he said as I passed by him.

I stopped. "Shut up, dude."

"Or what?"

Good question. What did I care about this asshole? I shook my head in disgust and started back toward the store.

He took a step forward. "Hey, I'm just checking if it's worth my time before I hit that shit."

Something switched inside. It's hard to describe, but if it's ever happened to you, you know exactly what I'm talking about. Everything slows down, and your focus becomes real tight. Almost like tunnel vision.

I leaned in and spoke quietly. I didn't want the whole world to hear, because I didn't want it to look like I was calling him out. Just the opposite—I was warning him off. "Shut the hell up," I hissed, "or I swear to God I'll rip your freakin' head off. Got it?"

He swallowed and looked around. Maybe I'd been too loud after all, or maybe his buds were a little too close. Or maybe it was just the wonderfulness of his personality. Who knows?

"Yeah, *right*," he said loudly as he shoved me in the chest.

"Heck, if she'd give a lap dance to a loser like you, just think what she'd do for *me*. She'd probably suck my—"

I hit him. Hard.

You know how, on some songs, there's a big dramatic drum fill building into a climactic part of the tune? And inevitably it resolves with a huge cymbal crash on the downbeat? Where you stomp on the kick drum and you just *slam* into that crash cymbal for all you're worth?

This was like that—it was all about intent. I wasn't trying to hit his face. My goal was to drive my fist through his head and out the back of his skull.

And apparently it worked, because one minute he's standing there in all his immense jerkitude, and then *wham,* he's on the ground with his hands to his face and blood everywhere. I looked over at his friends. I guess I must have been seriously mad-dogging it, because man, they didn't *budge.*

So I turned without a word and walked back toward the school. It was probably a good move to leave before a crowd gathered, but I can't really take credit for it. I was in a daze—I'd never done anything like that before. What the hell had come over me?

As I made my way back to the campus, I slowly became aware of three things. One: My hand hurt. A lot. Two: I never got my sandwich and I was going to be hungry sooner or later, but right then I couldn't stand the thought of food. And three: For some strange reason, I had a big-ass grin on my face.

Q: WHAT DO YOU SAY TO A DRUMMER IN A THREE-PIECE SUIT?

A: "WILL THE DEFENDANT PLEASE RISE..."

I spent the rest of the day waiting to be called to the principal's office, but it never happened. Maybe Kevin just went home . . . or maybe because it happened off campus, the school couldn't really do anything about it? Whatever. When I made it to the end of sixth period unscathed, I was just relieved to get the hell out of there. I guess I was also pretty naïve to think that no one else would mention it.

I ran into Kyle in the hall on my way out. "Hey, man," he said. "I hear Kevin Flanders was mouthing off and you decked him."

"Uh, yeah . . . pretty much."

"Wow. What'd he say that pissed you off so much?"

Hmm . . . What I really wanted to say was *The jerk was dissing Kimber, so I came down on him like John freakin' Bonham on "Rock and Roll."* But that would have meant explaining why I had his little sister on my lap, and I didn't really want to get into it. So with a straight face I said, "He was putting down the Sock Monkeys. I guess he hadn't gotten the word that I was no longer in the band, but I didn't really care—it gave me a good excuse to hit his punk-ass face. And you know what? It felt great." I looked directly at him. "He reminds me of Toby." As soon as I said it, I realized it was true. And maybe the sincerity of that last line made him buy the whole story. I could see the wheels spinning in his brain, but I wasn't going to help him out. I turned and walked away.

✱✱✱

After I got home, Kimber texted me. *Kyle told me. Are you OK?*

Hmm. What exactly did he tell her? *I'm good,* I replied. Then

I thought about my hand, which still hurt. *At least, better than he is. LOL!*

I'm glad about that. GTG. Talk later.

Later, lil sis.

Speaking of little sisters, just then Alicia barged into my room. "Jody says you got in a fight today!"

Jody was one of her middle school friends. "And how would she know?"

"Well, did you?"

I got up and closed the door. "Answer my question, and I'll answer yours."

"Her older brother was at the store and saw it. He says you broke some guy's nose! Did you?"

"I don't know about that. But yeah, I hit him."

"Wow! How come?"

For once, I decided to treat her like an equal instead of a little kid. "Can you keep this just between us? Not tell anyone, even Mom and Dad?"

She seemed surprised. "Oh sure—I promise!"

"Okay . . . Basically, this guy was saying some really bad things—lies—about a friend of mine. I asked him to stop a couple of times, but instead he got worse. So I hit him."

"And then?"

I smiled. "He stopped."

"That's all?" She seemed disappointed.

"Pretty much, yeah. Since he was on the sidewalk bleeding . . ."

That cheered her up. "So who was he saying bad things about?"

"Doesn't really matter."

She looked at me for a minute, then raised an eyebrow. "It was a girl, wasn't it?"

I raised an eyebrow back at her.

She stared off into space for a second, then her eyes opened wide. "Kimber! It was Kimberly, wasn't it?"

Wow.

She must have read my face. "I was right!" she said. "Hey, if someone had said that about me, would you have hit them?"

"Naw, I don't think so."

She looked bummed. "Really?"

"Yeah." I paused for a minute, to let her stew. Then I wriggled my eyebrows in what I hoped was a sinister fashion. "They'd have to call the coroner."

"Wow . . . awesome!"

Sometimes she cracks me up, with the things she's impressed by.

Then she said, "Wait till I tell Jody . . . !" and turned to go. I was ready to unload on her about her promise when she turned back and pointed at me.

"Gotcha!"

7

"Summertime Blues"

I decided to go to the movies. There was only one more week of school, and homework was pretty much just studying for finals. Besides, ever since I'd been kicked from the band, my dad had been on me about getting a "real" job this summer, and I didn't want to hear about it tonight.

So I didn't even look up what was playing, and I didn't bother borrowing my dad's truck. I just hopped on my bike and headed down to the Creekside Complex. I figured with ten screens they had to be showing *something* passable sometime soon, and I didn't really care about the details.

Usually I'll go for an action film, but for some reason there was a romantic comedy that caught my attention. And since it was starting in fifteen minutes, I figured what the heck.

It actually wasn't too bad, except for one tiny detail . . . the plot. It was all about some guy who gets his first "real" job with some big corporation, but he secretly spends his evenings playing guitar in a band, and he really wants *that* to be his career.

And of course it all ends happy-happy—he dumps the nine-to-five, gets the dream rock-star gig, and gets the girl. The End.

Okay, so I was rooting for the guy to kick the stupid suit-and-tie job and start playing guitar again. But gimme a break. It was so far from reality—at least from *my* reality. And the few parts that were fairly realistic—mostly the scenes at the early gigs—only bummed me out.

I didn't feel like going home after that, so I went next door to Starbucks for a while. I got myself a coffee and managed to snag a tiny little table in the corner. I was lucky to get that—the place was totally crowded, probably with people like me who didn't really care that it was a weeknight because school was almost over.

So I sat there and watched the crowd from back in the corner, kinda like watching the audience from behind the drums at a gig. After a while I borrowed a pen and a piece of paper from a girl behind the counter and started working on a song idea I'd had for a while. It was only half formed, but basically it was about loyalty and loneliness and feeling like you didn't fit in. It wouldn't take a PhD in psychology to see where this came from, but I worked on it anyway because sometimes good lyrics come from bad places.

Anyway, I'd been there for half an hour, writing and then scratching out clichéd lines, when someone sat down in the other chair at my little table. I looked up. It was a girl from school that I barely knew. She'd been in one of my classes last year, but I couldn't quite remember her name.

"Hi," she said. "You're Zach, right? You play the drums?"

I put down my pen and nodded. "Uh-huh. What's up?" I was wondering if maybe she couldn't find a seat and was asking if she could share my table. If that was the case, I was going to say, *Take it, I was just leaving,* because even though it's sometimes cool to write in a public place, it's a totally different story with someone sitting two feet in front of you sharing a table the size of a floor tom.

But that wasn't it. "My name's Maria?" she said. I swear, that's how it sounded, like a question. "We were in the same social studies class last year? Remember?"

"Sure, I remember. How's it going?"

"Fine. I'm here with my friend Shannon? Sitting over there?" She pointed toward a girl at a table across the room.

"Uh, okay . . ."

"Well, we've been here for a while, watching you write or whatever you're doing and, well, Shannon said she thinks you're cute? So I told her I sort of knew you? Which was, like, a big mistake because she's been, like, bugging me to come talk to you ever since?"

I glanced over at Shannon. The funny thing was, she looked like the absolute stereotype of a rocker's girlfriend—jet-black hair, dark eyeliner, red lipstick, black nail polish, the works. She smiled at me. I smiled back and turned to Maria. "Tell her I think she's hot," I said, "but I have a girlfriend. Thanks."

She got up from her chair. "Well, she can't say I didn't try. See ya around."

She went back to deliver the news while I sat there, surprised at myself. Again. Things like that did *not* happen every day. Not to me. And she *was* hot, in a skanky sort of way. And I'd just told her thanks but no thanks. WTF was up with that?

I looked at my watch: 10:15. Whoa. I tried to remember if I'd told my parents where I was going, but then I figured if they were worried, they would have just— *Oops.* I looked down and sure enough, my phone was silent. I'd silenced it when I went into the movies and forgot to turn it back up. There were four missed calls and two messages. Uh-oh.

I punched up the first message.

Hey, Zach, it's Glenn. Glenn Taylor. Listen, we're in kind of a bind and I was hoping maybe you could help us out. We have a gig tonight and Nate is . . . well, let's just say he's in no condition to play. Let's see . . . it's about seven o'clock now and we go on at nine. His drums are already at the gig, so you wouldn't have to bring yours. So if you wouldn't mind, please give me a call back at this number when you get my message. I'd really like to work with you, but I've got to get a drummer for tonight one way or another, so I'm going to keep looking. Take care, man. . . .

Beeeeep . . .

Hey, Zach. It's Glenn again. It's eight-fifteen and I've found someone who's available to do the gig, so I'm going with him. Thanks anyway. Take care.

Holy crap. . . . When I was at the movies watching the fictional life of some fictional guy in some fictional band, living in a *totally* fictional world, I could have been getting ready to do a real gig with one of the best real bands in the area.

For a drummer I sure had lousy timing.

So I left Glenn a message saying I was sorry I missed him

and I hoped we could get together to play sometime, and then I went home to sulk. At least, that was the plan. My dad had other ideas. . . .

"Where were you?" he asked as soon as I walked in the door.

"The movies."

"You need to let me know where you're going if you go out at night. You know that. Anyway, someone called and I wasn't sure where you were, so I gave him your cell number."

"Thanks. It was a guy named Glenn. They needed a drummer tonight."

"That's what he said. So what happened?"

I sure wasn't about to tell him that their regular drummer was too drunk or drugged to make the gig. That groove would definitely *not* be smooth. . . . "Not sure, but it doesn't really matter. I had my phone off in the movie, so I missed his call."

"I know your phone was off, because I tried to call you, too. More than once." He took in a deep breath, then slowly let it out. "Look, Zach. I know it's been hard since your friends found another drummer. And to tell the truth, I think that stinks. But school's almost out and you have to do something."

"I know."

"Good, because you start at Johnson's Yard Supply on Saturday. At seven a.m."

Boom . . . Sometimes the biggest bombs don't make any noise falling. "But Dad, I never even talked to him. I haven't filled out an application or anything."

"I know. But Jerry called me over the weekend and asked if you were still interested. One of his guys quit and he needs someone right away."

No doubt he could tell from my expression that I wasn't thrilled at the prospect of working at a yard-supply place all summer.

"Hey, you should be glad—I told him you had finals and couldn't start until Saturday."

I just hung my head. *"Great . . ."*

"Look, I know this isn't exactly how you planned to spend your summer, but opportunities like this don't just fall into your lap every day. Think of the money you'll make. You could save for a car, or maybe college, or—"

"Dad," I interrupted. "I appreciate you trying to get me a job. Really." And that wasn't complete fiction. I did. In a theoretical way. Sort of. "And yeah, I could use the money. But I would rather make it by playing music than hauling sacks of fertilizer out to old ladies' cars." By like a thousand times.

"Well, like it or not, I don't think the first option's available to you right now. And you're *not* doing nothing all summer. So be ready to start at Johnson's first thing Saturday morning."

Maybe it was a good thing I didn't hook up with Shannon after all, because there was no getting around it—I was quickly going from Zach Ryan, Rock Drummer to Zach Ryan, Manure Boy.

8

"Should I Stay or Should I Go?"

Bzzzzzzzzzzz! God, already? I rolled over and looked at my alarm clock: 6:00. As in a.m. On a Saturday. On the first day of summer vacation. That's just *wrong. . . .*

The last few days of school had gone by fast. Nothing but study-test-study-rinse-repeat. And with the way things were, it wasn't like I even cared about summer. I hummed a bastardized version of that K's Choice song, "Something's Wrong." *If you can't look forward to summer . . . something's wrong. If your whole world is a bummer . . . something's wrong.*

"Zach . . . *Zaaaaach* . . . Are you up? Breakfast is ready!" It was my mom. How could someone be so cheerful at six in the morning? Well, if you weren't going off to become Manure Boy, I guess I could see it.

I pulled on my jeans and a faded black Ramones T-shirt, laced up my kicks, and headed downstairs to the kitchen. There was my mom, scrambling eggs and burning toast.

"Wow. You don't have to do all this. I could have grabbed a bowl of cereal."

"I know. But it's your first day of work, and I wanted you to get a good start."

"Thanks. Is Dad up yet?"

On cue he walked into the kitchen. "Hey, big guy—how's it going?"

"Fine." *I guess.* I tried to act reasonably happy, because I knew he thought he'd done me a huge favor by getting me this stupid job. But what I really wanted was to go back to bed for three or four hours, then maybe get up and play my drums or go shoot some baskets or cruise downtown on my bike.

"You going like that?" he asked.

No, I'm changing into my suit and tie as soon as I'm finished eating. "Uh, yeah. Is there a problem?"

"Well, it just doesn't seem like the best thing to wear on the first day of a new job. Don't you have something else you can put on?"

"Dad, this is an entry-level, manual-labor-type gig. It's okay. Really."

"You never know where it can lead. . . ." God, like my dream is to be *head* manure boy or something. "And by the way, I need the truck this morning."

Well, I was going to get my bicycle ride in after all. Oh, joy. . . .

* * *

Jerry Johnson was actually a pretty cool old guy. Even though he owned the place, he still took the time to show the new kid around. When we were done with a quick tour of the store and had made our way outside, he introduced me to the yard supervisor. "This is Chris," he said. "He'll get you squared away. Anything you need, you just let him know. I'm sure you'll do great, Zach, and we'll be seeing you around."

I looked at Chris. He was a large guy, maybe in his late thirties. "Jerry seems like a nice guy to have as a boss," I said.

Chris squinted at me. "Let's get one thing straight right now. *I'm* your boss here." He looked at me like I was a homeless guy who'd wandered into a fancy restaurant, then threw a shirt at me. It was a fluorescent turquoise polo shirt with JOHNSON'S YARD SUPPLY written over the pocket. Stunning. Well, at least they could find me in the dark. . . .

"You got any earrings? Tongue stud?" I just shook my head, half expecting him to check my teeth like I was a horse. "You work Thursdays through Mondays. And I know what you're thinking, so forget about asking for a Saturday or a Sunday off. Ain't gonna happen." He pointed to a supply shed. "Okay, go change out of that stupid T-shirt and put your crap away, then hustle back here and I'll put you to work."

I shouldn't have worried about carrying fertilizer out to customers' cars. That sort of easy stuff must have gone to the higher-seniority yard boys. Yeah, that's what they call us—yard boys. Even the older guys.

I spent most of the day unloading delivery trucks in a warehouse, and I swear, it must have been a hundred and twenty degrees in there. I got two ten-minute breaks and half an hour for lunch. Other than that, it was go-go-go. And even that might have been bearable, because I suppose you could look at it as getting in a good workout while you got paid.

But Chris seemed to think his mission in life was to make

us miserable. Most of the other guys were pretty cool—one of them was even someone I knew from school. So we talked as we worked. About school, about girls, about music . . . whatever. Made the time go faster.

Apparently, Chris did not approve. He wandered by while we were working and said, "Can the chitchat! I'm paying you to work, not talk. That truck should have been unloaded by now!"

So after that we didn't talk so much. But I saw a radio on a table next to the watercooler. "Anybody want some music?" I asked. A couple of the guys said yeah sure, so I turned it on and set it to the local rock station.

The DJ was yakking away but then he actually got my attention. ". . . so get your original songs in *muy pronto,* guys, because the entry deadline for this year's annual Wild 107 *Best in the Rockin' West* compilation CD is the middle of July. That's when the area's very best local bands get a big boost in the butt, but remember—only the best make the cut. Last year we had over a hundred entries for twelve spots. So get your act together and submit. MP3 . . . CD . . . YouTube . . . I don't care if it's by carrier pigeon, just get your tunes in here by July fifteenth! This is Dandy Don Davis, saying stand by for a smokin' new song by local faves Refuge. But first . . ."

I was just starting to think how cool it would be if I were still in the Sock Monkeys, because I'd made recordings of a few of our originals, and some of them were actually pretty killer songs. But then I realized that they'd probably just redo them with Josh and submit them. *Great.* Just then Chris came back to check on us and had a freakin' cow. He stomped over to the radio and ripped the plug out of the wall.

"This ain't a damn party!" he yelled. "We got work to do—I need that stuff unloaded . . . now!" He put his fists on his hips and glared. "If you guys would rather screw off than work, I got a whole list of people who'd love to have your jobs." He turned and stormed off.

I looked at the guy next to me—he was one of the older workers who'd been there a few years. "Sorry, didn't mean to get anyone in trouble."

He kinda smiled. "Not the first time. And I reckon it won't be the last."

"You know," I said, "I just met him today, but Jerry seems like a pretty nice guy. And he's the owner, right?"

He nodded. "Yeah. Good guy, no doubt about it."

"Then how did a jerk like Chris get to be a supervisor?"

The guy looked at me funny. "Uh . . . he's Jerry's son." He looked around at the other guys and sighed. "Well, I guess we'd better get going. . . ." So we got back on the chain gang. No talking, no music, no nothing. And we probably got less work done during the next hour than any other time that day.

While we were unloading the next truck, my phone vibrated—someone was texting. I looked around before I checked it, just in case Chris was somewhere nearby—how sad is that? Anyway, it was Kimber.

You got a minute?

Chris was nowhere in sight, so I replied. *Only for you, lil sis. What's up?*

Want to talk later. Face to face. No big. Buy me coffee? ☺

OK. *$ @ 7?

Great. See you tonight.

See you.

After that it was back to the thrill of unloading more trucks for the rest of the afternoon. We'd been sweating away for quite a while when Chris walked in. "Hey, everybody—listen up! We've got another delivery coming tonight, so I need two guys to stay late."

The place went graveyard. Was he kidding? It was Saturday night.

When no one spoke up, he looked at me. "Okay, then, it's the noob and Trent. You're the lowest guys."

I thought about meeting Kimber at Starbucks. And I'd definitely need a shower first or I'd knock people over when I walked in the door. "Uh, how late are you talking about?" I asked. "I've got plans . . ."

"You work until the truck is unloaded, so how late is up to you. And I don't want to hear about your—"

Just then my phone went off, and I don't mean it silently vibrated because someone was texting. My ringtone at the moment was the intro to "Can't Stop," by the Chili Peppers, and it cranked through several bars of pounding sixteenth notes. *Duh-duh-duh-duh-duh-duh-duh-duh . . .*

Chris's eyes bugged out and his big fat head whipped around, trying to see where the sound was coming from. "Turn that garbage off!"

Oh, crap. I took out my phone to silence it, but out of habit I glanced at it to see who was calling. *G. Taylor.* And Chris was still raging away, only by now he'd figured out that it was *my* phone that was making the hideous noise. "Didn't you hear me?" he bellowed. "I said turn that off, right now. *Now . . . !*"

I'd been planning to do exactly that. I swear. But I guess my hands had a life of their own. I answered it and punched up the speaker.

"Hey, Glenn, what's up?" I said casually.

"Hey, Zach. To make a long story short, Nate is out and we're auditioning for another drummer. I heard you were between gigs, so I thought I'd ask if you were interested."

I figured I'd better cut this short, because Chris was turning red in front of my eyes. "Yes, I sure am."

"Great. Are you free tomorrow, around noon?"

Whoa . . . Suddenly I felt like the guy in that stupid movie, only this wasn't some film, this was real life, right here in front of me. It was like I was weighing my options, one in each hand: How do I see myself? As a yard boy, or a rock drummer? *Yard boy . . . ? Or rock drummer . . . ?* It was no freakin' contest. I looked right at Chris as I spoke to Glenn. "I'm totally free; noon would work great for me."

"Cool."

"Thanks. Hey, I've gotta run. Can I call you later for the details?"

"Sure. See ya."

I put my phone away and stripped off my dirty, stinky, sweat-soaked polo shirt. "Here," I said to Chris. "You can give this to the next lucky bastard on your list."

And I threw it in his face.

9

"A Little Less Conversation"

"You *what?*" Kimber couldn't believe it.

Over coffee I told her all about the wonderfulness of my one-day career at Johnson's Yard Supply. Okay, I skipped the part about the audition. I was dying to tell her, but I'd already been burned once by that. Plus, the last thing I needed was for Kyle—and Toby—to hear about it. But otherwise I hit the high points, and pretty soon we were both laughing at the whole thing.

"Plus," I finished, "if I'd stayed there, I'd be unloading trucks until God knows how late, instead of hanging here with you."

"Sounds like a horrible place to work. What do your parents think about all this?"

"I haven't told them yet."

Her eyes widened. "Uh . . . aren't you a little concerned?"

I didn't even want to *think* about what my dad's reaction was going to be, so I switched gears. "How'd the Destination Imagination thing go?" I asked.

"Let's see . . . Sacramento was really hot, the pool was closed at the motel, one of the girls on our team got food poisoning and we had to perform our skit without her, and we lost out to a couple of teams where most of the props had obviously been made by their parents."

"But other than that?"

"Oh, other than that, it was great." She laughed.

"So . . . what are Kyle and the band up to?" I tried to keep it casual, like I didn't really care.

"Actually, that's what I wanted to talk to you about." She looked serious all of a sudden, like she had some bad news. "They've been spending a lot of time recording."

"I bet they're trying to get on that Wild 107 "Best in the West" thing, huh?"

"I don't know about that. All I know is, they're spending a lot of time in the studio, making a record."

"Making a full-length? In a studio?"

She nodded. "Remember Josh's house?"

"You mean the royal estate?"

"Right. Well, Josh's dad has a recording studio in one of those outbuildings that's *totally* pro. It looks like something out of a magazine."

"And Josh's dad built all this just for him?"

"No, apparently he's had it for quite a while. Kyle says Mr. Dicenza made his bucks as an entertainment lawyer in LA. I guess he's pretty well connected in the industry—knows people at all the labels and stuff."

Whoa . . . Talk about a lightbulb going on, big-time. I shook my head slowly. "You know, that connects a lot of dots."

She grew quiet for a minute. "I feel awful even telling you

about it, but I figured you'd hear it sooner or later." She paused. "Look at it this way. At least you know it didn't have anything to do with your playing."

I nodded. "Thanks . . . I guess."

"Well, just for the record, I think they're jerks and this whole thing totally stinks."

I was grateful for the support, but I didn't really want to think about being sold down the river for thirty pieces of . . . well, whatever it is you get sold down the river for. So I changed the subject. "What does that taste like?"

"This?" She held up the white chocolate mocha I'd bought her. "I'm not sure yet. I'll let you know when I figure it out." Then she looked at me kinda funny. "So, what else is new with you?"

"Uh, not much," I said, feeling a little guilty about not mentioning the audition.

"Hmm . . ." She paused. "I heard through the grapevine that you had a girlfriend."

"Oh, really? And where did you hear this?"

"From Ginger, who got it from Kelli, who sits next to Maria in history."

I nodded slowly, the light dawning. "Oh, Maria? Maria Delgado? The one who, like, speaks in questions?"

No laugh. Not even a smile. And my impersonation was right on, if I do say so myself. "Yeah, that Maria" was all she said.

"She sure has a big mouth," I said. Okay, I was making her work for it, but can you really blame me? After all, I've been dealing with a real little sister most of my life.

"And . . . ?" she said.

"And what?"

"Who is she?"

"Hard to say."

"In other words, you don't want to tell me?"

"No. In other words, I don't *know* who she is. I just needed one—I wasn't required to attach a name to her."

"Huh?"

I cut her some slack. "It was like you with Kevin Flanders. I needed a rent-a-girlfriend to fend someone off, so I just whipped up this imaginary girlfriend." I grinned. "Pretty good, huh?"

"Sure, but . . . why'd you want to fend her off? Did she bark and wear a collar?"

"Actually, no." Well, I wouldn't be surprised if she *did* have a collar somewhere in her wardrobe, but that wasn't what Kimber meant.

"Then . . . ?"

I shrugged. "Not my type."

"And speaking of Kevin Flanders, what the heck happened between you guys?"

"Didn't Kyle tell you?"

"Not in detail. He said Kevin was dissing the band or something?"

What to say? It didn't bother me not to fully disclose to Kyle—especially after the way he'd treated me the past few weeks—but I hated to spew full-on fiction all over Kimber. On the other hand, she was the thing I was lying *about*.

"Uh, something like that," I finally said.

She leaned in. "What could he possibly have said that would have gotten you that mad?"

God, she was asking all the hard questions tonight.

I stood up. "It's a long story, but I've gotta roll—you want a refill before I go?"

✳ ✳ ✳

"You *what?*"

My dad couldn't believe it, either. He started to go off on me big-time, so I jumped in quick. "Let me explain, okay?"

"I just don't see how the hell you could quit the first day. You didn't even give it a chance. And after Jerry did me a favor by hiring you."

"Yeah, and *Jerry* seems like a great guy, who I'd be *happy* to work for."

That made him back up the bus a little. "Okaaaay. . . ."

"But I wasn't working for Jerry. . . ." So I explained the whole story all over again, pretty much the same as what I'd told Kimber but I included the audition call from Glenn. (All right, I left out the part about me throwing my sweaty shirt in Chris's face, because I didn't want my dad going off on a tangent about burning my bridges. And I didn't just burn that particular bridge—I freakin' *nuked* it.)

"Look," I finally said, "you agreed that I got a bad deal from the Sock Monkeys. I'm a good drummer and I should be playing in a band, not just spinning my wheels at some dead-end job. But the *good* news is, I got a call to audition for Bad Habit. That doesn't happen every day. So when I get the chance to try out for the best band in town, what am I supposed to do?"

I thought he'd see my point for sure on that one, but the groove wasn't quite that smooth. "Honestly," he said, "I don't think that's such great news. Those guys are a couple of years older than you. Are any of them going to college?"

I didn't say anything. College was a big deal to my dad. And my mom. And Kimber—she talked about it all the time. And maybe even to me . . . when I thought about it. But what did that have to do with playing music?

"I think it's important who you associate with," he went on, sounding like Nate with his dogs-and-fleas speech. "And I think you're slanting this whole thing—if you really wanted to, I'm sure there's a way you could do the audition and still keep the job."

God, wasn't he listening? "That's exactly my point! Any *normal* boss would at least try and work something out—it's only an hour or two. But no, this guy is like the Yard Nazi. He *enjoys* the tiny amount of power he has, and he gets off on pushing those poor guys around."

"Let's get one thing straight," my dad said. "Even if you join another band, you're still going to find a real job this summer. Period."

10

"Dazed and Confused"

One good thing about the audition was I didn't have to deal with all my gear. They already had a drum kit in their practice room—a converted garage at their singer's house—which made it easy. It was your basic five-piece set, pretty similar to what I had—all I had to bring was my stick bag.

"Hey, man, how's it going?" Glenn said when I walked in. "Glad you could make it." He introduced me to the other people in the room, starting with the guy who'd opened the door when I'd knocked . . . the lead singer. "This is Brad Halstead."

He looked like the epitome of a Cal Coast surfer dude—tall, tan, and blond—except that he seemed to prefer leather jackets and skinny jeans over board shorts and sandals.

Brad nodded. "Hey."

"This is Jamie Davenport."

She smiled. "Hi, Zach."

You know how you'll see some girls onstage and they look hot, with all the lighting and makeup and hair and stuff, and then you see them up close after the show and it's, uh . . . not so much? Jamie was the exception. Yeah, she looked good up onstage, with her Hayley-Williams-as-a-brunette thing going on, but it didn't fade as you got closer. It got stronger. Especially when she was smiling at you with those bright blue eyes. Like now. I found myself smiling back, until Glenn got my attention with the last member of the band.

"And Daniel Mendoza," he said.

"Call me Danny," Daniel said. He looked more like a motor-cycle mechanic than a musician . . . which meant he looked like what he was: a killer bass player. Ponytail, beard, tats, and all.

"Why don't you take a second to get the drums the way you like 'em," Glenn said, "and then we'll blow through some tunes."

"Sure." I sat behind the kit. Whoa . . . the last guy to play these sure sat a lot higher than I did. I adjusted the throne and moved a couple of the cymbals. I tapped the toms—they had pretty good tone. The snare was tuned a little low for my taste, so I grabbed a key out of my stick bag and cranked up the pitch to give it more of a crack. The kick sounded fine. Fine enough, anyway—there was no way to really dial in the sound I wanted quickly, so why stress about it?

I'll admit I was a little nervous. No—I was a *lot* nervous. Usually I was relaxed once I was behind the kit, but I wanted this gig bad. Hell, my hands were shaking, and that never hap-pened. Okay . . . relax . . . deep, slow breath . . .

"All right, I'm good to go," I said.

"Good," Glenn said. "Do you know 'Are You Gonna Go My Way?'"

"Yeah, I've seen you guys play it."

He nodded. "Great." He counted it off, and we jumped into it. What immediately popped into my mind was that intricate thing Nate had done on the toms, so I tried to do something similar. It kinda worked, but it was a struggle to make it fit. Definitely not as solid as it could have been. When it was over, Brad and Danny looked at each other but didn't say anything.

"Okay," Glenn said. "How about 'Times Like These'?"

I nodded. "Sure." I'd heard it on the radio, but that was it. He started it on guitar and I jumped in where I thought I should. Oops—too early. As I started to stress about that, I realized that this little opening section was in 7/4. By the time I figured out that it was in an odd time signature, I had the beat backward. Not the end of the world to fix, and at a gig probably ninety-five percent of the people in the audience would never realize something was wrong, but it freaked me out. So I tried to make up for it by putting in some flashy stuff to show them I had skills. I made it to the end of the song, but it was pretty rough. And Danny never even came close to putting his foot up on the monitor cabinet, if you know what I mean.

"Sorry about that," I said when it was over. "I got kinda lost there at the top."

"No big," Glenn replied.

Danny came over and started showing me how the pattern was supposed to go for that last song. I was trying to pay attention, but out of the corner of my eye I could see Brad talking to Glenn. I couldn't hear everything, but I could tell he wasn't real happy.

Glenn said something to Brad and walked over to me, and Danny went to go adjust his amp or something. "How's it going?" Glenn asked quietly.

"Okay. . . . Well, maybe I'm trying a little too hard," I admitted.

"Man, I'm glad to hear you say that, because that's exactly what's going on." As he talked, he started pulling the cymbals off the stands. Holy cow—was this his way of letting me know that my audition was over? "You're overthinking it. . . ." There went the crash cymbal. "I've seen you play. . . ." He pulled the rack toms from their mounts. "And I know you're a real solid drummer. . . ." He stacked the small toms on the floor tom and pulled it aside so that none of them were playable. Nothing left but the kick, snare, and hi-hats. "So . . . ," he finished, "just play a solid groove. That's all. Chops are cool in the right place, but a band lives or dies by its pocket. *Comprende?*"

"Got it."

"What do you want to do?"

"How about we try 'Go My Way' again?"

"Sounds good."

This time I figured the hell with it—I'd approach it like I was just doing another gig with the Sock Monkeys. No more trying to channel their old drummer, no more trying to impress anyone. Just lay it down, like always.

I started clicking my sticks loudly in time, and everyone looked over. Hell, I was the drummer—it was my job to set the tempo and count it off, right? "One! Two! One . . . two . . . three . . . four . . ." On the *four* I slammed my snare and dove into the song, just hammering it out. I looked at Danny, watching—and listening to—what he was doing. He started nodding back in time. I could feel the vibe—much better. Jamie was smiling, and Brad wasn't exchanging worried looks with anyone—everyone was too busy getting into it. *This* was how it was supposed to be—all of us working together in sync, like a team.

When it was over, Glenn nodded. "Exactly."

We did three or four more songs, and I approached them all with the same attitude. That's not to say I just played a bone-head simple beat to everything. I threw in some cool kick and snare syncopation when it fit, and I tried to hit all the accents with the rest of the band. But I didn't worry about showing all my chops at once. I just tried to lay down the fattest, most danceable, most in-the-pocket groove that I could play. I felt like I'd won a moral victory when Danny spent most of the last couple tunes in front of the drumset, locking eyes with me and rocking hard. When we were done playing, he leaned over the drums and bumped fists with me.

After I'd packed up my sticks and was doing that awkward stand-around-not-knowing-what-to-do-next thing, Glenn came over. "So, what do we think?" he said.

"I think I owe you, man. Thanks."

"There's nothing I told you that you didn't already know." He looked at me. "You're you. And that's a good thing. So be you."

I was in the middle of trying to decide if that was stupid or brilliant when Brad walked up. "Thanks for coming by," he said. "We're glad we could hear you play." He stuck out his hand. "Take care, Zach."

I shook his hand. "Thanks for having me," I said.

He smiled. "We'll call you when we decide something."

And the next thing you know, I was out the door. Boy, *that* wrapped up quick. Talk about mixed signals . . . I wasn't quite sure if I'd blown it big-time at the beginning or if I'd managed to pull it out of the fire. But knowing my luck lately, I figured the odds weren't good.

Q: WHAT DO YOU CALL SOMEONE WHO HANGS AROUND WITH MUSICIANS?

A: A DRUMMER.

My dad was waiting for me when I walked in the house. Did he even bother to ask, *Hey, how'd it go . . . ?*

Nope. The very first words out of his mouth were "I went down and talked with Jerry Johnson about your job."

That did it. "It's *not* my freakin' job, and it's never going to *be* my freakin' job again, thank God!"

Wrong move.

Instead of yelling back, he spoke pretty quietly, but I could tell he was really pissed. Or worse, disappointed.

"So like I was saying," he continued, "I talked to Jerry. I explained everything you said about Chris. No one wants to hear those kinds of things about their son, but to his credit he heard me out. Then he said, 'Well, that explains a lot,' and he told me a few things you left out of your little narrative. Like the way you left."

Uh-oh. "He deserved it. He—"

He cut me off with a chopping motion. "No excuses! When you've done something out of line, the worst thing you can do is try to justify it—that only digs you in deeper. The bottom line is, no matter how mad you get, the way you win is to act professional. If you'd gone to Jerry and explained the situation, I bet he could have straightened it out. And even if you'd quit, if you'd done it calmly and professionally, you'd probably have the job back now that Jerry understands the situation." He softened his tone a little. "Why did you feel like you had to act the way you did? That's not really like you."

I thought about it. . . . Getting kicked. Toby. Getting bailed on by Kyle. Seeing the Sock Monkeys at Josh's. Punching Kevin Flanders's lights out. The choked audition with Bad Habit. Hearing about my replacement's dad *just happening* to have a pro studio and *just happening* to have connections in the business. And of course, having to deal with a flaming asshole like Chris.

"Dad," I finally said, "I'm full." I held my hand up to the bottom of my raised chin. "Up to here."

He didn't say anything. He just nodded and waited.

"Okay," I grumbled, "maybe I overreacted. I've just had so much bullshit flung at me that I couldn't take any more—I had to get the hell out of there."

He considered this, then surprised me by saying, "Okay, I guess I can see that. And don't tell your mom I said this, but I might've done the same thing at your age." He took a deep breath. "But you need to understand that kind of stuff doesn't fly in the real world. If I treated my business associates like that, we'd be living in an old shack somewhere, eating beans out of a can."

I nodded. "I get it." It was a long shot, but I had to try.

"So now that you understand where I'm coming from, does this mean you're dropping the requirement about getting a job?"

He smiled, and for a second I held out hope. But only for a second. "No *way*, dude!" Then he cracked up, like that was funny as hell.

11

"Get Out the Door"

After a few days I still hadn't heard from Brad or Glenn, and with each day my hopes sank lower. I'd assumed they were going to listen to a few more guys, sure, but they must have heard them by now—there weren't *that* many drummers in the area. And along with everything else, I really missed playing! Just getting together with other musicians and blasting out some tunes—there's nothing like it. Sure, I practiced solo in my garage to keep my skills up, but it's not the same. . . .

So by Thursday I figured they'd found someone else and just hadn't bothered to call me. I mean, you call the winner, right? Why call someone to tell him he lost?

And of course, none of this solved my job situation.

The obvious place was our local music store (maybe I could meet some other musicians and join a group) but they weren't hiring at the moment, so I applied at every Burger King, McDonald's, and Taco Bell in the area. But it seemed like every other guy in town had done the same thing, only they were smart enough to apply for their summer job *before* summer started. Who woulda thought?

So the going was slow, but I kept after it. Partly because I had to give a report to my dad every night about the efforts I'd made toward gainful employment. Other than that, I worked on music, rode my bike around town, and played b-ball.

Kyle and I used to go shoot around. Did you ever notice that you can talk better if you're also doing something else? So we'd shoot or play a little one-on-one, and we'd also talk about our band or whatever at the same time.

Shooting hoops usually made me feel better, but now I ended up thinking about the whole band thing and the whole job thing. Yuck. I had to face it—Bad Habit had gone with another drummer, likely someone older and more experienced. I'd probably only gotten a chance to audition because I'd met Glenn recently. I bet he said something like *Hey, let's give the kid a try—can't hurt.* So they spent an hour humoring me, but that was that.

I also had to face the fact that I'd exhausted my fast-food options and I was still unemployed. So I was going to have to scrape around and take whatever I could find.

With that happy thought in mind, I went home to shower. As I was drying off, my phone let me know that I'd just missed a call: *G. Taylor.* Oh great . . .

I went to call back, then I stopped. Yeah, I'd been telling myself that I didn't land the gig, but I still had this little one percent hope that I might get it. And I'll admit that it wasn't rational, but once I actually talked to them, that one percent would be zero. *Nada.* And somehow there's a world of difference between *one* percent and *no* percent.

Okay, enough of that. I made myself pick up the phone and call.

"Hey, Glenn, how's it going? My phone says you called."

"Yeah. I wanted to know if you were available to come over, so we could talk about a few things."

"Uh, sure. When's a good time?"

"We're getting together tonight, at Brad's place. Can you make it around seven?"

"Yeah, that'd be good. Anything I need to bring?"

"Naw, we're just going to talk."

"Okay, see you there."

"Thanks. See ya."

Wow.

✳ ✳ ✳

Jamie answered the door. "Hi, Zach," she said. "Come on in. Can I get you some coffee?"

"That'd be great. I mean, if it's already made. I don't want you to have to go to any trouble. . . ." God, I sounded nervous.

She smiled. "It's no trouble. And I wanted to tell you, you sounded great when you were here the other day. Real solid."

"Thanks."

She handed me some coffee. "Come on back—the guys are already there."

As we headed back, it occurred to me that she seemed pretty at home here. I heard myself say, "Do you live here, too?"

She kinda choked for a second. "Uh . . . no. Why do you ask?"

Suddenly I felt stupid. I shrugged. "I don't know . . . sorry."

Man, I have *got* to learn to engage my brain before my mouth. . . .

We ended up in the same room I'd auditioned in, but no one had their instrument out. They were just sitting around, drinking coffee and hanging. Well, Brad had a beer going, but you get the idea.

Everyone said hi, then Glenn grinned. "Hate to keep you in suspense, so here it is—we'd like you to play with us."

I tried to stay cool, but I could feel a big-ass grin break out. "That's great."

I had the sense that Glenn was going to say something else when Brad leaned forward and cleared his throat. "We would have called you sooner, but we had some business we had to nail down first."

"What Brad means," Jamie said, "is we're going on the road this summer. We just finalized it with a booking agency."

Wow.

"Yeah," Brad added. "There just aren't enough good-money gigs around here, but if we tour, we can play four or five nights a week all summer."

"So . . . when are you going? And when are you getting back?"

"We leave tomorrow, get back sometime in October," Danny said matter-of-factly.

"Uh, but . . . there's no way I can . . ." I looked at the others—they were all trying not to laugh. Except Danny. He had a poker face on.

"You'll have to get used to Danny," Jamie said. "That's his idea of humor."

He looked at me, palms up. "Hey, bro—just joshin'."

I grinned. "No problem . . . you had me going there for a second." I turned back to Brad. "So, when *are* we leaving?"

"We're outta here the week after next and returning late August," he said. "Does that sound doable?"

Okay, on the one hand, I could stay around Los Robles all summer and scramble for a job making french fries. On the other, I could get paid to play music and see the country. Boy, *that* was a tough one.

I nodded, trying to sound calm. "That sounds like something I could swing."

"Cool," Brad said with a nod. "We've got a little shakedown gig next weekend at Paisano's. Do you think you could make it here a couple of times during the week so we could rehearse?"

"Sure. Could you get me a set list ahead of time? That'd make things easier."

"How about a live recording from a month ago, pretty much all four sets?"

Man, that was about as helpful as it gets. "Perfect. So, where are we going?"

"Mostly the Rockies. We open in Bozeman, Montana, in twelve days."

✱✱✱

"No," my mom said.

"What do you mean, no?"

"What don't you understand about *no*?" my dad said. "*No* means negative. As in no-how, no-way, ain't-a-gonna-happen."

God, he could be so annoying. "I *know* what the word

means!" I shot back. "What I don't understand is why you're saying it. You don't even know the details yet."

"I know enough," my mom said. "I know you want to go traipsing across the country in a van or a bus or something with a bunch of older kids you don't even really know. What else do I need to know?"

"There's a *lot* more you should want to know before you make a decision like that." I glared at them. "But you know what? I don't even want to talk to you about it—you guys are way too close-minded right now. . . ." I turned and left. They called me back, but I ignored them and went up to my room.

I sat on my bed, totally pissed. I mean, is it that freakin' hard to just *listen* for once before jumping to conclusions? Don't answer that. . . .

In the middle of thinking all this, my phone rang. I didn't really want to talk to anyone right then, but it could be Glenn. Or maybe Kimber. I looked. Kyle. What the hell did *he* want?

"Hey, what's up?" I said, not real friendly.

"Not too much. How about you?"

Well, I got the best job offer of my life, but it just got shot down. I didn't *even* want to go there right now. Especially with him. "Same-same."

Then I just waited. After all, he'd called me, right?

He finally cleared his throat. "Well . . . You remember 'No Life to Live' . . . ?"

"Duh." That was one of our original tunes. I'd helped write the damn thing—it had some wicked off-beat sections that Kyle and I had come up with.

"Uh, do you think you could still play it?"

"Of course." Where was this going?

"Well, um . . ." I could hear him take in a breath, then let it out. "Look. We're trying to do some recording, and Josh is having a hard time really nailing some of the songs. And I was wondering . . . actually, *we* were wondering . . . if maybe . . . well, if you could help us track some of the tunes?"

The word of the day for today was definitely *wow*. "So you want me back in the band, then?"

"Well . . . you could play on a lot of the tracks. You'd get a credit on the record. And you'd get a chance to record in a real pro studio."

"But I wouldn't actually be *in* the band?"

"Uh, not exactly."

It hit me. If I'm in, then Josh is out. And if Josh is out of the band, then the band is out of the studio . . . and they're also out of his dad's contacts and everything that went with all that.

"Sorry. I can't do it."

"You mean you don't want to do it."

"I actually don't know if I want to do it or not. But it doesn't matter, because I've got other plans."

"Look, man, I'm sorry we can't officially put you back in the band. It's not my choice—"

"You know, I've gotten a lot of that from you lately," I interjected.

He kept going like he hadn't heard me. "—but if that doesn't work for you, just say so. You don't have to make up some bullshit story about 'other plans' or whatever."

That did it. "No fiction on *my* side, man! You're the one

that's spewing the bullshit. Sorry dude, but I can't bail out you and your spoiled-ass drummer boy right now . . . because I'll be on the road with Bad Habit all summer."

"What . . . ?"

"You heard me," I said, and I hung up.

God, me and my mad mouth . . .

PART II
ROAD

12

"Magic Bus"

Danny came up and tapped me on the shoulder. He spoke quietly so he wouldn't wake the others. "Hey, bro, you doing all right up here? Need anything?"

"Thanks, man, I'm good."

"Ten-four. Let me know when you need a break."

"You got it."

Driving a motor home is like driving a car once you get the hang of it. It's just that getting the hang of it takes a while, and it was "earn while you learn" in my case. When they'd asked if I could take a turn behind the wheel, I'd said sure, like I piloted a thirty-foot motor home down the interstate every day. Or make that every *night*, since my turn came after we'd stopped for dinner at a Subway outside Vegas.

I figured it couldn't be all that different from driving my dad's pickup. *Wrong.* Especially when it came to getting up the on-ramp and back onto the freeway—that damn thing was *big*, and changing lanes was hairy-scary. It didn't take me long to figure out that the best strategy was to pick a lane and stay in it.

At first that was the slow lane, but as we got out into the middle of nowhere and I got more used to the beast, I migrated into the fast lane and just tooled along at seventy-five or so. My plan was to try to make it to Salt Lake City before stopping to swap drivers. So far, the glamorous life of being on tour was a lot like being a long-haul trucker. . . .

* * *

Amazingly, my parents had been pretty reasonable once I'd actually talked with them. They didn't care that Bad Habit were the hottest act in town, or that I'd improve my drumming skills by working with them, or that it was a feather in my cap that they'd picked me at all. And they couldn't have cared *less* about what I'd flung in Kyle's face. Nope. What convinced them was the fact that they'd replaced their old drummer because he was a druggie. Pretty funny, considering I'd done everything I could to *not* mention Bad Habit and drugs in the same sentence. And my mom was actually relieved when she found out that two of the people going were girls. . . . Jamie was bringing her friend Amber—I guess so she wouldn't feel weird being the only girl. Mom somehow thought that having them along would make the guys more likely to "behave." Whatever—it worked.

After we'd hashed it all out, my dad said, "I have a couple of things I want."

I would have shaved my head and dyed my eyebrows pink for him at that point. "Sure."

"I want you to call or text or email on a regular basis. I'm not talking every day, but do it when you can, okay? Just to let us know you're alive?" I nodded. Easy. He went on. "Your mom worries about you, probably more than you know. My main objection to letting you go was about the stress it might cause her, more than anything to do with you. Letting her know you're okay will help with that."

"Sure, I can do that. No problem."

"Thanks." He grinned. "If I were in your shoes, I'd be wanting to go, too. In a big way. So behave, but enjoy yourself. I think it'll be a good experience for you."

"Thanks, Dad. What was the other thing?"

"This is going to sound dumb, but humor me. . . ." God, was he going to ask me to wear a chastity ring or take some drug-free vow or what . . . ? "I want you to send postcards. I'll get you a roll of stamps before you go. Buy a postcard at every town you visit, scratch something on it, and send it home. That's all."

I didn't get it. "Dad, I've got my phone. I can send you pics anytime I want."

He cleared his throat. "I was actually aware of that. Just work with me on this, okay? I don't expect you to understand now, but you'll be glad you did it later. And besides, Alicia loves getting old-fashioned postcards. So if nothing else, do it for her. Okay?"

He was right—I totally didn't get it. But considering all the weird things I could imagine my parents asking for, it was the least I could do. "Okay."

Once all *that* was straightened out, I spent the next week rehearsing with Bad Habit and woodshedding the songs on my own. I had a lot of tunes to get a handle on, but it felt good to be playing, and it was also nice to be learning different material. . . .

The guys in the Sock Monkeys liked the more garage-y,

pop-punk stuff (even though their set lists were all over the map), while Bad Habit had more of an indie and modern-rockish vibe going on. There was still some overlap—they both did "Lonely Boy," by the Black Keys, for example—but even then their versions were different: the Sock Monkeys did it as a straight-ahead, four-on-the-floor, guitar/bass/drums thing, while Bad Habit changed it up a little, with Jamie's backing vocals and cool piano part adding more dimension.

So yeah, I was happy being in a band again—things started feeling almost normal.

One thing that *was* weird, however—and I'm not really sure why—was Kimber. The night after I'd talked with Kyle, she texted me.

Kyle told me you're going on tour w/ Bad Habit???

That's the truth, lil sis.

:-(

Then a second later she added *JK!* ☺

I hope so, I wrote. *I'm stoked about going.*

Yeah, me 2. GTG. Talk later.

Later . . .

She showed up at the gig at Paisano's. I don't know—maybe it was the stress of playing new songs with a new band—but the whole thing was strange. . . .

I saw her during the first set, standing near the back with her older sister, Sarah. I guess she'd gotten a ride from Sarah—who must have been home from Cal Poly for the summer—because Kyle was nowhere in sight.

Kimber came up during the break and we sat at a table and had a couple of cokes.

"God, you sound good," she said, looking at me. When did her eyes get so big?

"I think it's the company I keep. Those guys are pros."

"Maybe. Partly. But that's you and no one else up there playing the drums, and I know what I see."

"Thanks." She still had that big-eyes thing going on, and I swear I almost let fly with *Hey, you got any annoying jerks you need scared off? The first one's free tonight.* My face must have given me away.

"What's with the grin?" she asked.

"Nothing." Okay, besides that whole hop-on-my-lap image, what I was really thinking was how nice she'd been since I'd gotten kicked from the band. I shrugged. "You've been a good friend. That's all." That came out sounding dorky, but she didn't seem to mind.

"Thanks, Zach!" She smiled, but then she looked up at the gear onstage and got kind of quiet. "So you're really going on the road with these guys? Kyle said all summer?"

"Yeah. Northern Rockies."

"Why do you have to go all that way? There's got to be plenty of clubs in California. . . ."

"Yeah. But there are also a lot of bands here, so clubs don't need to bring them in from the outside. They don't have as many local acts up there, so there's more work for touring bands. We start in Montana next week. Then Wyoming, Idaho, and a couple of weeks up in Canada. We'll be back a week or two before school starts."

She didn't say anything. Maybe it was like someone telling you all about the great vacation they're going to have in Hawaii or whatever, and you're stuck in town all summer. I was about to tell her that it wouldn't be all play and no work when she held up her drink.

"This . . . ," she said quietly, staring into the glass like it was a crystal ball. "This tastes like . . . like I'm sitting alone at two in the morning in an all-night diner in Barstow. There's no one in the place but me, some smelly old drunk at the counter, and a burnt-out waitress with blond hair and black roots. The flickering fluorescents are giving me a headache as I suck down my third cup of lukewarm coffee." She set the glass down and stood up. "*That's* what this tastes like." She came around to my side of the table and gave me a quick hug, then turned and walked away.

＊ ＊ ＊

The signs go flashing by in the night. SALT LAKE CITY—82 MILES. I almost wish they weren't there at all, because you see that your destination is three hundred miles or whatever, then you drive for*ever,* and the sign says it's still 209 miles. (If you wanted to inflict some real Langley-type torture on someone, you could have a road sign every mile. God, that would be the worst.)

Man, it was going to be almost two a.m. when we got to Salt Lake. I'd thought about getting someone else to drive, but everyone was asleep by then and I hated to wake them. Plus, they'd trusted me to take my turn, and I wanted to show I could carry my weight.

By the time I got to Salt Lake, we needed gas, I was burnt, and I was about ready to pee my pants. So I pulled into this big-ass gas station right off the highway, used the bathroom, got a large coffee and a power bar, and filled the tank. I'd had the radio on while I drove, turned down low and tuned to a talk station to keep me awake. I left it on at the gas station, and sure enough, everyone stayed asleep. I'd learned that trick when we were kids. We'd be on some long drive and Alicia would wake up every time we stopped until my dad started leaving either the radio on or the engine running. Funny how the *absence* of noise can wake you.

So I paid with money from the band fund and pulled back on the freeway. After I'd finished the coffee and the power bar I felt a lot better, so I kept on cruising along as I listened to some goofballs debate the likelihood that aliens were responsible for a bunch of dead goats in New Mexico.

I made it as far as Idaho Falls and had to give up—it was almost five a.m. and I was toast. I pulled off the freeway, found an empty parking lot next to a shopping center, and shut it down. I have a hard time sleeping sitting up so I climbed in back and looked for somewhere to snooze. The girls were up in the little loft above the driver's seat, two guys were on the little fold-out dinette benches, and someone was sprawled out on the seat across the aisle. The heck with it—I found someone's sweatshirt to roll up and use as a pillow and I just crashed on the floor.

* * *

I was having this bizarre nightmare about Mr. Langley torturing his students. He had us tied up in the classroom, and he'd say, "That's one minute out of the day. Only one thousand four hundred and thirty-nine left." Then sixty seconds later he'd say, "That's *two* minutes out of the day. Only one thousand four hundred and thirty-eight left. . . ." Then Kimber walked into the classroom and I told her to run and get help. She sat down and said no, she was going to drink cold coffee instead. . . .

Suddenly I woke up. Where the hell was I? I sat up and . . . *whack*. I looked around. No wonder I'd banged my head—I was up in the loft. Through the funky plaid curtains I could see scenery going by—we were back on the highway, and somehow they'd managed to hoist me up there without waking me. Well, at least they hadn't stripped me or tied my feet together or any of the other things the guys in the Sock Monkeys might have done if I'd fallen asleep on the floor.

You'd *think* there'd be enough room for all of us to sleep semi-comfortably in here. And I suppose in a new motor home this size, there is. Every year at the Golden State Fair they have a huge display of RVs, and sometimes I wander through and look at them. Some of them are pretty impressive—water beds, hot tubs, big-screen TVs . . . whatever you want.

Well, the ol' Bad-Mobile was *nothing* like that. It was probably okay when it was new . . . which was way before I was born. Apparently, Brad's family had used it on vacations when he was a little kid, but since then it'd spent most of its time sitting under a tarp next to their garage, home to bugs and birds and wayward squirrels—not even worth the cost of having it hauled away.

But to the guys in the band, it looked like the perfect road warrior. They gutted the whole back half and built a plywood wall cordoning the rear section off. Never mind that this eliminated little details like the bedroom, kitchen, and bathroom—it made a great cargo compartment for all their gear. So all that was left for the passengers was the front half—the dinette, this little vinyl-covered bench that was probably called a sofa in the original sales brochure, and the two seats up front. Oh yeah, and the tiny loft. In theory everyone was supposed to be in a real seat wearing a real seat belt whenever we were moving, but in reality you do what you have to do to make it work.

I climbed down from the loft and looked out the window. "Where are we?"

Jamie turned and glanced at me from the passenger seat. "Hey, everybody—looks like Baby Brudder's awake!"

Danny gave me a big-ass grin and a thumbs-up from the bench seat, where he was sitting next to Amber. "Yo, little bro, what's up?" he chimed in.

Great—that's all I needed. I figured the best thing was to ignore it. I nodded at him and sat down at the dinette across from Glenn. There was a map of the Western states on the table. I spun it around so it faced me and looked at it. "So, are we in Montana yet?" I asked.

Glenn looked at me like there was something really amusing about the question, but he gave me a straight answer. "Just barely—we're almost to West Yellowstone. Should be in Bozeman by noon."

"Cool."

Brad spoke up from behind the wheel. "Is anybody hungry? My phone says there's a pancake house up ahead."

There was a chorus of yeahs, so pretty soon we were pulling into the parking lot. As we walked toward the front door, Glenn fell in next to me. "How late were you up driving last night?" he asked.

"Maybe five."

He looked up, like he was doing a calculation. "Yeah, that seems about right. Thanks for sticking to it and making such good time." I was about to tell him it was no problem when he continued, "But don't be a hero. You ever pull dead bodies from a car wreck?"

"Uh, no . . ."

He nodded slowly. "We can't play the gig if we don't get there alive, right? So don't be afraid to wake me or one of the other guys, or just pull over and sleep." He looked at me and suddenly grinned, which totally didn't make any sense, considering the subject.

"Uh . . . okay. Thanks."

"No big. Hey—betcha I can eat more pancakes than you."

"No way." I was starving.

Turns out he was right, but I made a valiant effort. Once in a while, I'd catch someone at another table glancing at me, but they'd look away as soon as I noticed. *What?* Did I have food stuck between my teeth? Was my bed-head hair poking up funny? I mentally shrugged. Whatever . . .

Pretty soon we were all kicked back in our corner booth, having a last cup of coffee and making small talk after the busboy had cleared our dishes. I'd just asked Danny a question about the set list, since tonight would be our first official gig as a touring act, when Amber caught my eye. Which was easy for her to do—she had big brown eyes, a head full of wild dark curls, and skin like a perfect Starbucks mocha. The two things I'd never seen her without were gigantic hoop earrings and this total troublemaker grin.

Except now the smile was gone. She was sitting there staring at me, toying with an earring, when she announced from across the table, "Man, you sure do look sexy first thing in the morning. . . ."

The whole table suddenly went silent. Whoa. What do you say to that? Talk about feeling like a little brother—I could actually feel myself start to blush. Then she slowly continued, totally serious, like she was mesmerized or something. "Especially with that mustache. *Yum* . . ."

What the . . . ?

Jamie joined in. "No kidding. But what really does it for me is the beard—*totally* hot. . . ."

Huh? "I don't have a—" Suddenly I got up and went into the restroom and looked in the mirror.

Someone had taken a big felt-tip marker and drawn a large bandito-style mustache on me while I'd slept, complete with curlicues on the ends. And a pointy black beard. Give me a big hat with a plume in it and a sword and I'd be one of the Three freakin' Musketeers.

Okay, I laughed a little. Until I went to wash it off. It must have been a permanent marker, because soap and water didn't budge it. Not one bit.

I went back to the table to congratulate them. But they were gone. All that was left was the check. And a note next to it, with each line in different handwriting . . .

Dear Baby Bro—Thanks for picking up the tab, we really appreciate it. ☺
PS Damn, you look good!
PPS Dee-Lish!!!

PPPS The bus leaves in 30 seconds. It's a long walk to Bozeman—get your ass out here.
PPPPS Welcome to Bad Habit!

There was a horn blaring outside. I looked out the window—they were heading out of the parking lot, windows down, arms waving, honking, hooting, and hollering. I glanced at the check. Fifty-two bucks. Damn! I threw three twenties on the table and ran out the door. Even then I had to chase them halfway down the block before they pulled over, but when they finally let me in, there were hugs and grins all around.

I guess I was in the band. . . .

13

"A Sound That Only You Can Hear"

Dear Mom, Dad & Alicia—

Greetings from Bozeman. This postcard shows it in the
snow, but the weather's perfect now—sunny & warm. Mom,
you'll be glad to know the guys are all taking good care of
me. Alicia, you'll love this—they treat me like their little
brother! (Remind me to be nicer to you when I get back—ha
ha!) Gotta go now—have to set up the gear for our first gig.

No worries!

Zach

We found our first club right after lunch. Hard to miss a place
called the Dog & Pony when there's a huge neon sign out front
showing, well . . . a dog and a pony. We pulled around the back
and Brad and Jamie went inside to check it out while the rest
of us started unloading gear from the rear of the Bad-Mobile.

That's one thing I like about this band—everyone works until everything's done. None of this *Well, I've got my harmonica*

packed, so good luck with those drums crap. We had most of the stuff staged in the parking lot and I'd just picked up a PA cabinet when Brad came back out. "Well, you can put that back in the bus," he said to me.

Suddenly I had visions of the gig being cancelled at the last minute, or maybe the agent had given us the wrong date? Then Glenn spoke up. "House system?"

"Yup," Brad said. "And it's sweet."

Glenn and Danny bumped fists. "Yes!"

So we loaded the PA back into the motor home and carried the drums and guitar amps inside. *Whoa* ... Brad wasn't kidding. The place had a great sound system—speaker cabinets flown overhead, dual subs on either side of the stage, monitor wedges for everyone plus side fills, the works. The stage was wide and deep and raised three feet off the floor, with light trees on either side. It was a nicer setup than anywhere *I'd* ever played before.

I was still staring like a wide-eyed tourist when a big guy walked up to us, wiping his hands on a bar towel draped over his shoulder. "You guys the band?" Then he laughed like he'd just told a hilarious joke. "Duh, huh?" He stuck out his hand. "I'm Jake, the owner." We all shook hands. He reminded me of Chris from the yard-supply place, at least in appearance, but personality-wise he turned out to be the anti-Chris.

He motioned us over to a table near the bar. "Have a seat— you guys came a long ways. California, right?" We nodded. He spoke to one of the waitresses. "Hey, Rachel, can you get these guys whatever they want? Thanks."

So we sat around and had cokes—well, Brad asked for a

Corona and they served him, no questions—while Jake gave us the scoop on the gig, explaining about times and breaks and stuff.

"And the rooms are upstairs," he continued. "There are three of them—that enough?" We all nodded. After sleeping on the floor of the motor home I would have been thrilled with an old couch in a back corner of the bar.

"Good," he said. "What else . . . ? Oh yeah—food. We'll comp dinner for you every night while you're working here. Just tell your waitress you're in the band and it'll be taken care of. After the first day you'll know each other anyways—they're all real friendly."

Jamie leaned her head sideways and batted her lashes at him. "Can't we just stay here and be your house band all summer?" she asked. We all laughed.

"Hey, gotta take care of the band—that's what brings in the people, right?"

"I wish all club owners felt that way," Glenn said. "Some of them treat a touring band like they're a bunch of escapees from a carnival."

Jake grinned. "Well, some of them *are*. But you can smell those guys coming a mile away, and we try not to book them here."

He glanced at his watch. "It's been nice meeting you all, but I'd better get back to work or the girls'll accuse me of slacking. You need anything, you let ol' Jake know. I'm sure you guys'll do great—Corey said you were top-notch people." He got up and headed back into the restaurant area.

That last comment was interesting. The guys had told me

about Corey—he was our rep at the agency in Spokane, and he'd booked us for the summer based on a YouTube demo and a photo the band had sent him a few months ago. He'd never heard Bad Habit in person . . . or even *met* them, for that matter—it'd been all emails and phone calls. I mentioned this and Danny just clinked his glass on mine. "Welcome to the music biz."

"But on the other hand, occasionally you run into someone like Jake," Glenn said. He looked at Brad. "What did you think of him?"

He shrugged. "He seems like a nice guy."

"I agree. So I think the least we can do is not drink in his place if we're not legal. If he finds out we're drinking underage in here, he's probably not going to be thrilled, and it's a huge bust for him if we're caught."

Made sense to me, but apparently Brad didn't see it that way.

"How's he gonna find out—you gonna tell him or something?"

Glenn shook his head. "'Course not. That's not the issue."

"Look, just because you're a couple years older than me doesn't mean you can treat me like I'm your 'little bro,' too."

"Dude, you're missing the point," Glenn replied. "I don't give a damn what you do on your own. You want some beer, go down the street and drink all you want, if they'll serve you. And if they won't, I'll buy you a sixer at the store and you can take it up to your room. I just don't want to cause any problems for the clubs we play in." He looked at Brad. "Okay?"

Brad didn't answer right away. Finally, he stood. "Yeah, sounds good." He tilted his head toward the door. "I could use a break—I'm going to walk around for a while."

Glenn just shrugged without saying anything, and Brad left. I sat there, not really sure what to think. It was weird, like your parents fighting right in front of you or something.

Jamie looked at Amber. "So, do you feel like putting our stuff away and maybe looking around a little bit?" Amber nodded, and they left, too.

Q: WHY DO BANDS HAVE BASS PLAYERS?
A: TO TRANSLATE FOR THE DRUMMER.

"So, what was *that* all about? I mean, the whole Glenn-and-Brad thing?" We'd finished doing a sound check—well, at least as much as we could without our singer and keyboard player— and Danny and I were sitting at the bar having cokes while Glenn was up on the stage, putting new strings on his guitar.

"Don't sweat it—it's just their way of sorting things out."

"Uh, I didn't see much sorting going on."

"Yeah, I know. But I think it's that old singer-guitarist creative-tension thing. Nothing to worry about."

"Oh yeah," I said. "Like Axl and Slash?" Okay, that was kind of a cheap shot. . . .

"Well, let's hope not." He laughed, then paused for a minute. "Politics are everywhere, bro. No exceptions."

"You sound like my dad."

He grinned. "See? The old man ain't so dumb after all."

It occurred to me that being in a working band is a strange gig in itself. It's like a big family vacation where some of the people are opinionated about what to do and others are happy to go along for the ride. But it's also a business, and you're all in it together. Some bands are democracies, and others have one guy that runs the show. I suppose either one can work, but when you blur the lines . . .

"So, what *are* the politics of this particular ecosystem?" I asked.

"Well, it's a little complicated. GT's like the musical director of the band. But Brad is sort of the manager."

"I'd figured Glenn was the ringleader, period."

He nodded. "Yeah, I can see where you might think that. But the band actually started as a duo, with Brad and Jamie doing coffeehouses and stuff. Then I joined and we got some guy on drums and started gigging as a band. But the drummer was sort of whatever, so we got Nate and we rocked a lot harder—we were pretty good. But Brad was never a wizard on guitar and he wanted to focus more on singing, so we scrounged around for another guitar player."

"And you got Glenn?"

"Well, we had to go through a few other guys on the way. But when GT joined, all of a sudden we were at the next level."

"Yeah, he's a smoking player."

"No doubt. But he also knows arrangements, he knows about running sound, he's been on the road . . . The dude has been around."

"But it was Brad's band," I added.

"And in theory, it still is. But in reality, it's not so clear-cut anymore."

Just then Brad walked in the front door. He went up to the stage and said a few words to Glenn, then they hugged and laughed.

A few minutes later Jamie and Amber came in. Jamie went

over to Brad and Glenn and talked for a minute, then came back to where we were sitting.

As she approached, Danny spoke up. "We all good?"

She nodded. "We're golden. I think Brad just needed to blow off some steam."

"Cool."

She turned to me and winked. "Nice 'stash. You gonna keep that as a permanent fixture?"

"Yeah, why not? I think it adds to my stage presence." Actually, I'd decided to just stop shaving until it wore off. "In fact, I was toying with hanging a sign around my neck saying FREE RIDES, since you and Amber seem to think the look is so hot. Think I'll get any takers?"

"Sure." She laughed. "Sooner or later some old barfly who's half blind and hammered out of her mind is bound to take you up on it."

"Ouch!"

Brad joined us. He seemed to be in a much better mood. "What's so funny?"

"Jamie's giving me romantic advice," I said.

He snickered and shook his head. "Talk about the blind leading the blind . . ." She slugged him in the arm. "Ouch!"

Danny pointed to me. "That's what *he* said."

"So if you guys are ready to quit goofing around," Jamie said, "maybe one of these days we could actually, like . . . play some *music*?"

"Sounds good," Danny said.

"Yeah," Brad said. "And thanks for setting up, guys. I owe you."

We all got up, and as Brad and Jamie made their way to the stage ahead of us, Danny turned to me. "See? No worries . . ."

* * *

The full-band sound check went surprisingly well, considering. These guys were all business when it came to the music. After that we got our personal stuff out of the motor home and went up to our rooms.

I hadn't really thought about it, but I guess I'd figured I'd end up rooming with Danny. After all, we had that whole bass 'n' drums thing going, and we seemed to get along pretty well. But when I got upstairs, I saw that Brad and Danny had one of the rooms and the girls were in another, so that left me and Glenn. Which made sense once I thought about it. I mean, I suppose a little of that "creative tension" stuff was cool, but putting Brad and Glenn in the same room? Why push your luck. . . .

Anyway, I threw my duffel on one of the beds and grabbed some stuff out of it, then took a shower. When I came out, Glenn was sitting on the other bed playing his guitar through a little practice amp. He had this killer riff going—it was basically a driving 4/4 rhythm part, but it had this cool little melodic twist after each line that made it really interesting. I could hear a syncopated drum part in my head that could fit it real well. It sounded like some tune off the radio, only I couldn't recognize it.

"Hey, what is that?" I asked. "It's great, but I can't place it."

He barely looked up from his guitar. "It's just something I'm working on."

Whoa . . . "That's *yours?*"

"Yeah."

"Wow. Nice." He just nodded. "No, seriously," I added. "That's a totally killer riff. . . . Is there more? A chorus?"

He stopped and looked up at me. "Thanks," he said. "Yeah, I've got a chorus. I'm still messing with the bridge, but it's about there."

"Lyrics . . . ?"

"Yup."

That was it—just *yup*. "Well . . . ?" I finally asked, with my hands held palms up in that universal let's-have-it gesture.

He didn't say anything. Hmm. Even though he freakin' smoked on guitar, maybe he was insecure about his singing. I'd seen him sing behind Brad and he sounded fine, but some people just didn't like to sing solo. Or maybe he had lyrics, but no melody yet . . . ? "Hey, that's okay," I finally said. "You can play it for me whenever you want. Or not. No big." I turned around and started unpacking my stuff. And as I was placing my clothes in the little dresser on my side of the room, he started playing.

He played the original riff a couple of times before he stripped it down to a simple, chugging eighth-note thing that made up the body of the verse. Then he started singing. . . .

> *You go north*
> *and I go south*
> *every day.*
> *You hear words*
> *that don't come from my mouth*
> *every day.*

I'd guessed wrong. He didn't give the impression that he was insecure about his singing. It was more like the song might have been a personal thing to him.

His voice was actually pretty damn good. Well, a better word might be *effective*. To me, if it's convincing on a gut level, then it works, no matter what technical skills the singer has. He didn't have that big rock voice that Brad had—it was a little leaner, a little more intimate. But it worked perfectly for that song. The tune was about communication problems between a guy and a girl—hardly a new topic—but the sincerity of the delivery, along with the guitar riff and the overall vibe, really worked.

After a couple of verses and a chorus, he stopped. "That's most of it, so far. Like I said, there's a bridge. Probably half time. Then a solo and a couple of repeat choruses and an ending."

That all made sense—that's probably how I would have arranged it, too. But what was more interesting was what he didn't say. Like, *So, what do you think?* Or, *Do you like it?* He just went back to trying some different chord voicings on the guitar.

"Hey," I interrupted him. He looked up. "Dude, that's a freakin' great song. I can totally hear the drum part, the bass, backing vocals. Hell, I can hear that on the radio."

"Thanks."

"You got more originals?"

"Yeah."

"So why aren't any of them in our set list?"

He didn't say anything for a long time. Finally, he looked at his watch. "We'd better get going—it's almost time to meet everyone downstairs for dinner."

14

"My Best Friend's Hot"

The waitress turned to me. "And what will the drummer boy be having?"

Jake was right—the staff was really friendly. "The trout sounds good," I said.

"It is," she promised. She looked at Glenn. "Okay, guitar hero, what'll it be?"

"Do you have sushi?"

"Just California rolls," she admitted.

"Wasabi and ginger?"

"I think I can scare some up for you."

Glenn thought about it for a second. "Okay, sold."

"You're jonesin' bad, huh?" She pointed up the street. "When you get a chance, head a few blocks that way. There are two places. One right here on Main, and one a block off it, on Bozeman. The real deal, flown in fresh."

"Thanks—I'll remember that."

Brad snickered. "I'll eat fish," he said, "but not bait."

"Whatever floats your boat, honey," she said. She winked at

Glenn, finished writing up the order, and left. It was like she was right out of the old-school-waitress academy, but in reality she was maybe twenty-five, max, and kinda cute. Cracked me up.

As we ate, Brad and Glenn were joking along with the others, and I realized Danny had been right. And they all seemed so relaxed, shooting hoops and kidding around with the staff. To be honest, I was nervous. Not like I was at the audition, thank God, but still . . . It was our first real gig as a road band, in a big club that was totally new to us, so yeah, I had butterflies. Plus, I'd had to learn like fifty new songs in the past couple of weeks, and I'd be lying if I said I had all of them totally nailed.

Danny must have caught my mood, because he kicked me under the table and made a goofy face. "*Smile,* man. You look like you're going to the gallows." He grinned. "Look, here's how it's supposed to work—we storm into town, we rock their socks off, we have our way with their women, then we roll on to the next port o' call like postmodern pirates. What better way for a young buccaneer such as yourself to spend his summer, right?"

I laughed. "Well, now that you put it that way . . ."

He nodded. "Relax, bro. You're rock solid."

I almost said *Aaaargh, matey!* but *matey* reminded me of *mate,* which reminded me of *Toby,* which of course reminded me of the Sock Monkeys and Kyle and the wonderfulness of *that* whole thing. So I just said, "Thanks," and let it go.

Brad got up and stretched. "I'm gonna go back to the room and chill," he said. "Meet back here at a quarter till for preflight?"

The others agreed, and one by one they took off, until I was sitting by myself. I was finishing off my water when our waitress came by. "Looks like they ran off and left ya, huh?" I nodded. She sat down and said, "So tell me, honey. The hot one—does he have a girlfriend or anything?"

I honestly didn't know who she was referring to. I mean, it's not like we have this one obvious total-stud guy and the rest are all slobs or something.

She misread my hesitation. "Hey, I didn't mean you were chopped liver, sweetie," she said. "You're a cutie-pie. But you're a little young for me."

Whoa . . . The food metaphors were coming too fast for me. "No, that wasn't it. I just didn't . . . Never mind. You're talking about Brad, the singer?"

"Naw. He's a pretty boy all right, but I'm talking about the gunslinger—he's what I call interesting. And I saw you guys rehearsing. That guy can *play*." She kinda shivered. "So . . . ?"

Oh yeah, her question. I was about to say no, he's not hooked up, when I thought about the tune he'd just played for me in our room. And about what happened this afternoon in the club. And I realized I really didn't know these guys very well.

"You know, this is going to sound lame, but I'm kinda here on the tourist plan and I really don't know. I suppose I could ask for you?"

She laughed and I swear, I thought she was going to reach over and ruffle my hair. "You really are sweet, you know that? But that's okay, don't worry about it."

She went back to work and I went up onstage, where I sat behind my drums and fiddled with them, making sure everything was adjusted just right. Then I glanced at the set list taped to the stage next to my floor tom and mentally went over the songs in the first set. It lowered my stress a little when they all came back to me—the groove, the tempo, the arrangement. Sometimes I "practice" songs in my head, just by letting them run on my internal playlist. Especially with new stuff—it makes me feel like, *Okay, I know what I'm doing.*

As I was going through the set, Brad walked in and came over. "Hey, you seen Jamie?" he said.

I shook my head. "Sorry, I've been here since dinner." He nodded and walked off.

I checked tuning real quick . . . everything sounded fine. I would have played a little to loosen up, but people were starting to come in and I hate to noodle in front of strangers. It was almost eight—another hour to go. It was starting to dawn on me that road life was twenty percent onstage and eighty percent off. I was getting ready to do my usual pre-gig thing and grab a coke or a coffee and read a magazine or something when I realized I had a room right upstairs—*duh.* I guess I *am* a newbie tourist.

When I walked into my room, Jamie was there, talking to Glenn. They both looked up when I opened the door.

"Hey, Zach, how's it going?" she said. "You ready for tonight?"

I wondered if Danny had said something to her, but then I realized that if my nerves had been obvious to him, they probably were to her, too. "Yeah, I'm good," I said. "How about you?"

"I'm fine. I just hope there's a decent turnout."

"Me too. But I suppose one good thing about not being local is, if there's not a great turnout, they can't really blame it on us."

"At least not the first night," Glenn said. "After that, they sure *can* blame it on us—and believe me, they will—because a lot of it's word of mouth, especially in smaller towns."

I grinned. "So I guess we'd better not suck, right . . . ?"

Glenn hit himself on the side of the head. "Wow! Why didn't *I* think of that? I *knew* there was a reason I wanted to hire you. . . ."

"Okay, I'll leave you comedians alone," Jamie said, getting up.

"See ya, JD-girl," Glenn said.

At the door she turned. "Bye, GT. Bye, ZR." She laughed like that was the funniest thing in the world, then left.

I plopped on my bed and started reading the latest issue of *Modern Drummer*. I was getting into this feature on recording drums using a minimal miking setup when I heard music. Glenn was playing something on guitar. Not on his Strat—he was playing this little beater acoustic that he'd packed along. The tune wasn't a rocker like the other one. It was slower, almost a ballad, but it had a really nice melody and these haunting, minor-key chord changes.

I didn't say anything, I just kept on reading. When he finished, I looked up. "Let me guess—that was yours?" I asked.

"Actually, yeah."

"Lyrics?"

"Not much yet. Just starting on it."

"Hate to sound like a broken record, but man, that's nice. What do you call it?"

He just blinked at me, then shook his head. I wasn't sure if that was *I don't have a title for it yet* or *I don't want to talk about it,* but I guess it didn't really matter.

"Do you have any recordings of your stuff?" I asked.

"Well, just some rough demos of a couple of things."

"You got them with you?" He nodded. "Can I have a copy?"

He shrugged. "Sure, I suppose so."

"Great." I dug through my stuff and handed over a thumb drive. "Just dump them on here whenever you get the chance."

He laughed, like he didn't really get why I wanted to bother, but he took it.

"Thanks," I said.

"No problem." He looked at his watch. "We'd better get rolling. . . ."

"Yeah." I got up, then stopped. "Hey—I almost forgot . . ."

"What?"

"That waitress at our table tonight?"

"Yeah . . . ?"

"She wants you."

Now *that* made him seriously laugh. "Figures . . ." was all he said.

15

"Communication Breakdown"

The Dog & Pony had a large movable wall between the restaurant and the club area, keeping the stage and the dance floor—and the surrounding seating and the bar—separate from the dining area. But by nine p.m. the dining side was cleared out and mostly served as a quiet place where the band could hang before the gig.

We all met there a few minutes before showtime. The band had done something before the show at Paisano's that was a little, uh . . . different, and at the time I figured they'd done it because it was the first time with the new guy. We'd all gotten into a huddle and sort of went around the circle and said positive things. Kind of a cross between a group hug and a team getting psyched up before a game.

But apparently it was a regular thing with them, because they did it again here. We wandered into the dining room one or two at a time and ended up sitting at a table just shooting stuff around. Brad was the last to arrive. He sat near me, and I thought I could smell beer on him. "Is the PA hot?" he asked.

"Yeah, it's all fired up and ready to go," Glenn said.

"Cool," Brad said. He looked at his watch. "Time for pre-flight."

We all got into a huddle—Amber, too. Brad said, "These guys are gonna see what a band from California can do, 'cause we're gonna kick ass tonight!" and Danny said, "Can't wait for 'Go My Way,' 'cause I love the way baby bro hammers it!" I've gotta admit, that made me feel good in spite of the nickname, and I said, "I'm just happy to be here, and I'm going to do my best to keep up with all of you." GT replied, "You're good, man . . . you don't have to keep up with anyone but yourself." Jamie laughed at him and shook her head. Then she turned to me and smiled. "Zach, we're really glad you're here with us . . . facial hair and all."

Everyone laughed, and Amber added, "You guys are going to do great tonight! Anything you want me to listen for?" There was no sound guy running the PA, so we were going to have to rely on our sound check to set our mix, plus whatever info we could get while we played.

"Thanks," Glenn said. "You can tell us about small stuff during the break, but if anything gets really out of whack, let us know right away. I may get out front with my wireless, too—the more ears, the better."

"It's time," Brad announced.

We wandered through the bar and up onto the darkened stage. . . .

Q: HOW CAN YOU TELL WHO REALLY RUNS THE BAND?

A: WHY DO YOU THINK THEY CALL IT A THRONE, BITCHES!

I freakin' *love* drumming . . . There's something about playing the drums that's different from any other instrument. Maybe it's the physical part. I mean, you're generating sounds by *hitting* things. You're the guy with his foot on the gas, driving the whole thing. You're the one making people get up off their asses and dance. You're the one setting the vibe—is the groove gonna be hard and mean, or maybe a little slower and sexier?

It's just so . . . primal. Imagine you're dancing in a room full of people, only every time your foot hits the floor, the whole room goes *boom!* And every time you clap your hands, the room goes *pow!* And when you shake your ass, the room *shivers.* Everyone feels it and everyone moves with you. Drumming is exactly like that—you're sitting at your instrument, dancing to the music. Only your dancing *makes* the music, instead of the other way around.

It's the coolest thing ever. . . .

★★★

Brad stomped on a foot switch, and the stage was flooded with colored lights. "BOZEMAN, MON-FRICKIN'-TANA— *YEAH. . . !*" he boomed into the mic. Some cheers started up, but he didn't wait. "We're-Bad-Habit-and-we're-from-California-hope-you-like-the-show!" Without missing a beat, Glenn fired up the grinding guitar intro to "So Far" and I started laying down a slammin' pile-driver beat as Brad jumped into it.

> *I'll tell you how the story's told*
> *I always wanted so much more*

And way on down the road
I caught a glimpse of the sunlight . . .

And just like that we were off and running with our plan to take the Northern Rockies by storm. We followed that song with another strong one, and another. My nerves had vanished after the first thirty seconds, and we were in the pocket and rocking through song after song. *Except . . .*

By the end of the first set—after a dozen-plus killer tunes—it was apparent from the lack of audience response that something was wrong. If we'd sucked, I could see it. But what are you supposed to do if you're at the top of your game, really nailing it, and you *still* get a lukewarm response from the crowd . . : ?

It was weird, like telling hilarious jokes to people who don't speak your language. The others chalked it up to being the new guys in town, and we jumped on the second set after a short break, just going on down our set list. But by then I had a hunch about what was wrong, since the Sock Monkeys usually played to a less exclusive crowd than these guys did. We'd been like a mutt band, where Bad Habit was more of a purebred, and we'd had to do a little bit of everything to keep people happy. Well, looks like things hadn't changed as much as I'd thought . . . but I was *way* too new here to start throwing my opinion around.

Luckily, someone else did it for me. . . .

* * *

"Hey, guys—Corey was right. You sound great." Jake was talking to Brad and Glenn and me during our second break.

"Hell, you think *this* is good," Brad said. "You should see—"

Glenn held up his hand. "But what?" he asked.

"Well . . ." Jake paused. "My feeling is, people pretty much like to hear what they're familiar with. Especially when they go out to have a good time. If I had to guess, I'd say about three people in the room tonight have heard most of the songs you've played so far."

"Hey, man," Brad said, "these are pretty happening, for the most part. Good tunes. Don't you guys listen to what's goin' on?"

I thought Jake was going to get pissed, but he seemed to take it in stride. "Sure we do. But it's a big country—things might be a little different here than in California. I'm just saying."

Glenn spoke up. "Can you give us some examples of what they might like to hear?"

"Hey, I'm just a glorified barkeep," Jake said, "not a music expert."

"Well, what do most bands play here?" I asked.

"Hell, I don't know . . . I've heard a hundred bands play here, and they're all different. But I can tell you one thing our best bands all have in common—when they play a song, you've probably heard it before, and you probably like it." He took a sip from his coffee. "Look, guys. I'm not trying to be a pain or tell you how to do your job. Like I said, you sound real good. I just think you'd get more people out on the dance floor if you'd drag out some of the songs from your Saturday night set and mix them in. That's all."

"Uh, *Saturday night set* . . . ?" Brad asked. "What are you talking about?"

"Corey didn't tell you about Saturdays here . . . ?"

Glenn was shaking his head. "Nope, he didn't mention anything special about it. What's the deal?"

"Every Saturday during the summer season we host Club Classic. It's a big thing around here—happy-hour prices all night and free snacks, and whatever band we have that week plays classic rock all night. We get a great turnout—probably more money comes in that night than the rest of the week." He took in a deep breath and slowly let it out. "But from what I'm hearing, it seems like you guys won't be able to cover it."

"Yeah, classic rock . . . I don't know—" Brad said.

Glenn interrupted him again. "We'll make it happen."

"Maybe I'd better try to book another band for that night instead," Jake suggested. "Might be hard this late in the game, but I could probably scrounge someone up."

"You won't need to," Glenn said. "We'll do it, and we'll do a good job." He looked at Jake and nodded. "I promise."

Jake looked at him for a minute, then finally nodded back. "Okay. But you let me know if you need anything."

"That's a deal. And thanks." Then he added, "When's the best time for us to get in here during the day without disturbing your customers?"

"Well, we open for lunch at noon, and the lunch crowd's gone within a couple of hours at the latest. Then we open the bar when we start serving dinner at five."

Glenn nodded. "Thanks."

"No problem," Jake said. "I've got to get back to work. You guys take care."

After he left, Brad turned to Glenn. "Why'd you tell him we could do it?"

"I've never bailed on a gig in my life, and I'm not going to start now."

"But it's only one night, so why are we gonna kill ourselves over it? He said he could get someone else to cover it."

"It's not just one night—it's the whole summer."

"Huh?"

"You think these guys don't talk? If we shit the bed on this, the first thing Jake'll do is complain to Corey, who's going to swear on a stack of *Billboard* magazines that he told us all about it. Then Jake's going to call all the other managers on the circuit and let them know how 'difficult' we are to work with. Sounds like the perfect way to kill a tour—get your agent mad at you and get a bad rep with the other club owners before you even get started. No thanks."

"So, how are we supposed to morph into a classic-rock band overnight?"

Glenn raised his eyebrows at me. "What do you think, Zach?"

I shrugged. Why me? "Well . . . I'd say get down here first thing and woodshed until they open for lunch," I said to Brad, "then put in a few more hours in the afternoon. Same thing for Friday and Saturday, too. I'm up for it if everyone else is—it's the only option I can see if we're gonna cover this thing." I felt a little weird telling him how to run what was supposedly his band, but that was how I saw it.

Brad thought about this for a minute, and you could almost see him switch hats. "Okay, that'll work. We'll meet at ten tomorrow morning. I'll tell the others." He looked at his watch. "Time to play."

For the rest of the gig they dug out the most popular tunes they could recall from their overall repertoire and we worked them into the set. It was probably hardest on me—almost none of them were on the list I'd practiced, and many of them I'd never actually played before, period. I kept a close eye on Danny and he helped me out with cues, and I managed to get through it without causing a train wreck.

We even took a few requests along the way. At one point someone yelled out, "Play some Clapton!" Damn, I guess Jake was right—they really did go for the old stuff out here. . . .

I looked at Brad. "You know 'Layla'?" I figured that was the ultimate Clapton song.

Brad looked up at the ceiling and nodded his head in time as he sang the words to himself. "Yeah, I know it."

"Cool." I looked at the others as I started tapping the tempo on my hi-hats. "We good with that?"

I was waiting for the opening riff when Glenn shook his head. I was surprised—I knew it wasn't the easiest song on guitar but I would have bet my snare drum he could nail that thing in his sleep.

He let out a breath. "Sorry, man. Let's do something else." And without waiting he fired up the opening lines of "Crossroads." Luckily, I'd heard it enough to fake my way through it.

I finally realized that if you don't really know a tune too well, it only makes it worse if you approach it all careful-like. No matter what, you have to play it like you freakin' *own* it. Sure, once in a while I guessed wrong or missed a cue or something, and if anyone was really paying attention, they probably noticed, but I learned to recover and just keep on driving, full speed ahead.

And the funny part was, Jake was right . . . at least partly. The songs we pulled out of the hat were the ones that got people out of their chairs in the first place. But I took pride in the fact that once we got them on the floor, we kept them there with our regular material by sheer force of groove, if nothing else.

It wasn't exactly the most *relaxing* gig I'd ever played. But by the end of the last song—after the applause had stopped and Brad had said, "See you here tomorrow night, and bring your friends!"—I realized it might have been the most satisfying.

＊＊＊

From: Zach Ryan [ZR99@westnet.net]
Sent: Thursday, June 24 2:42 AM
To: Kimberly Milhouse [kimmilhouse@cencast.net]
Subject: Road life

Yo, Kimber—
What a day. (Or maybe it's two days. Uhh . . . would you believe three?) The highlights so far:

I drove all night the first night. Pretty surreal, flying down the road in the Bad-Mobile at three in the morning with five people I barely know sleeping in the back. Lots of time to think, mostly about Kyle and the guys. I was totally bummed about the way things turned out—maybe even more than you know—but I think I have a handle on it now. Maybe. I hope things work out for them and their big recording plans, but all in all, I'd rather be here right now.

So I went to sleep last night as Zach Ryan, newbie touring drummer, and I woke up as some kind of Musketeer. (Kind of a fraternity initiation. Uh, don't ask . . .)

Anyway, here we are in Bozeman. And after a few bumps in the road, our first night at the first club went pretty well. (Basically, you don't bring a knife to a gunfight and you don't bring a modern-rock band to cover an oldies gig. But we figured it out and we're still employed. For now.)

So far I feel like I'm in school, getting a degree in improvisational stagecraft with a minor in political science. If I make it to the end of this, I'll have a freakin' PhD . . .

Speaking of PhDs, how's my favorite little professor doing? Are you enjoying summer school? Okay, dumb question. But hopefully it's not too painful . . . You and Ginger staying out of trouble—or at least not getting caught? And has Kevin Flanders been leaving you alone? If not, just tell him I'd be happy to re-peat our pleasant little exchange, free of charge. (Just kidding. I think.)

Well, I hope you're having fun this summer. I'm sorry I didn't get a chance to talk with you more at Paisano's, because obviously you were a little bummed. I'm sure it seems like this on-the-road stuff is one big vacation for me, but believe me, it's work, just like any other job. (Okay, it beats the hell out of being a yard boy, but still . . .) And since you'd asked about the "when & where," attached is our travel schedule.

Well, I've gotta get going. We need to do some serious (unpaid and unplanned, but totally required) rehearsing in the morning.

Talk soon,

Z

PS—Hey, one more thing. Sorry for calling you little sister—I'll try not to do it again. Explanation to follow at a later date . . . ☺

JUNE 21 DEPART LOS ROBLES, CA
JUNE 23–JUNE 26 BOZEMAN, MT
JUNE 29–JULY 3 BILLINGS, MT
JULY 6–JULY 10 HELENA, MT
JULY 13–JULY 17 BUTTE, MT
JULY 20–JULY 24 W. YELLOWSTONE, WY
JULY 27–JULY 31 JACKSON HOLE, WY
AUGUST 3–AUGUST 7 COEUR D'ALENE, ID
AUGUST 10–AUGUST 14 MEDICINE HAT, ALBERTA, CAN
AUGUST 17–AUGUST 21 LETHBRIDGE, ALBERTA, CAN
AUGUST 24 ARRIVE LOS ROBLES, CA

16

"Poker Face"

Glenn woke up around nine, probably because of me ticktacking at my computer.

"What are you hacking away at?" he asked, one eye open.

I looked over. "Trying to save your unblemished reputation."

"She said she was eighteen, Your Honor. I swear."

"Not that reputation. I'm talking about you never bailing on a gig." He gave me a blank look, so I nodded toward my computer and the headphones that were plugged into it. "I've got tons of tunes in here, old and new. I'm going through them for stuff that might work for us, building a Jake-worthy playlist for us to woodshed."

"Cool." He yawned and stretched. "And thanks for the help last night." He must have seen *my* blank look. "I meant with Brad, about the Saturday thing."

"Yeah, why'd you have *me* explain to him what we should do? I'm pretty sure you'd already decided on everything I said."

He didn't say anything for a second. "Maybe," he finally replied as he started pulling his clothes on, "but I think it's good for him to hear it from someone besides me." He came over and looked at my screen. "So what's the plan for the songs?"

"Well, I took some of the older stuff we faked our way through last night and I found thirty or forty more that fit the same mold and saved them as a big playlist. Now I'm going through it and breaking it into four sets and putting them into order."

"Wow. Did you do that for the Sock Monkeys?"

"Yeah, sometimes. Or I'd keep the master list by my kit and call them on the fly. Depends on the gig."

"Sure," he said, nodding. He paused. "But before you go too far arranging sets . . . You know how you can get through a tune with just a few clues?"

"Yeah . . ."

He pointed to one of the oldies at random. "Take this one— 'Hot Blooded.' Let's say you were raised in a cave and had never heard it. I could tell you, 'It's just a four-on-the-floor straight-ahead rocker . . . maybe a hundred and twenty beats a minute . . . has a few accents during the verse, but no sweat—you'll get it after the first four bars, and even if you just play right through it, you'll still be okay.' Would that work for you?"

"Uh, I hope so. That pretty much sums up last night."

"Right. But now let's assume you're going to have to *sing* this song that you've never heard. . . ."

Whoa . . . If I were a character in a manga, there would have been a little lightbulb going on over my head. "Oops—good point. So what do you think?"

"I think . . . that I've said enough." He grinned. "Me, I'm going to go find some breakfast before practice. Most important meal of the day, right . . . ?" He grabbed his stuff and left.

"Thanks for all the help . . . ," I mumbled as the door closed behind him. Speaking of breakfast, I'd been thinking along the same lines. But instead I dug up a power bar and took a bite as I got out my little printer. . . .

✳ ✳ ✳

Brad and Jamie came in together, each holding a Starbucks. Venti, no less. *Man, you're killing me,* I thought.

Jamie must have seen my look. She held up her cup. "You want some coffee?"

I figured she was just being polite. "I'm good. But thanks."

I must have paused a little too long. "Amber's still there," she said as she took out her phone. "What do you want?"

"Just a coffee. Cream, no sugar. That'd be great."

"No problem," she said, texting away. "You eat yet?"

That power bar was just a lump in my stomach. A very lonely lump. "Uh, not really."

She nodded. "Okay." She hit a few more keys and put her phone away.

Glenn walked in. "Hey, guys," he said. He looked around. "Does anyone know where Danny is?"

"He'll be here in a few," Jamie said. "He's with Amber, getting some coffee."

Looks like I had some time. I turned to Brad. "Hey, do you have a minute?" I held up some papers. "I have a few questions about some songs."

"Sure." He headed to a nearby table. "Let's do it."

We sat down. "I've got a bunch of classic-rock tunes on my computer," I said, "and I put together a big list of the ones that kinda fit what these guys seem to be looking for."

He nodded real slowly, like he wasn't sure about this. *"Okaaay . . ."*

"But you have to sing them, not me." I took out the master list I'd just printed. "So, anything on here look doable to you?"

His mood lightened. "Let's take a look." He took the list from my hand and started running down it. "Hmm, let's see . . . I know this one . . . and this one. . . . God, I *hate* that one. . . ."

I gave him a pen. "Here, why don't you mark all the ones you already know. And maybe also mark some of the other ones that you like and you think you could learn pretty easy."

"Dude! You're like a den mother. Are you always this organized?"

"Hey, just trying to save us some time." I probably came off a little defensive, but I guess I expected something more for trying to help. "You're not the only one who'd like to get out and see something other than the inside of this club." Oops . . . I guess I *had* been cooped up too long.

He looked at me for a second and I wasn't sure what was going through his head. Then he finally grinned. "I hear ya."

He started marking the list. A few minutes later Danny and Amber walked in, laughing.

Danny held out a bag to me with a flourish. "It's *Coffee Boy,* at your service!"

"Thanks, man." I looked inside. There was a venti coffee and some sort of enormous muffin with nuts and berries and, I don't know—small winged creatures?—sticking out of it. I glanced up from the bag and saw Amber looking at me. She was standing there with a receipt in her hand. Oh, yeah . . .

"Um, it's fifteen twenty-two. Let's call it fifteen bucks even." She was serious.

Fifteen dollars? For *that*? So far this road thing was more rash than riches. But I'd ordered it. Sort of. I reached for my wallet as I swore that this was the last time I got on this particular bus.

Right when I got my money out, I noticed Amber was busting up. "Just kidding," she said. "And thanks for breakfast yesterday."

Danny held out his hand for her to slap. She did, but at the last second he closed his hand and snagged hers. "Damn, you're good," he said to her. Then he turned to me and winked. "Don't ever play poker with her, bro—you'd lose your Underoos."

"Hey!" Jamie said to the room at large. "Are we gonna make some music or what . . . ?"

We got down to business. . . .

✳ ✳ ✳

"According to what Jackie said, it ought to be here somewhere," Glenn said.

"Jackie?"

"Yeah. That trippy young-old waitress . . ."

I let it go.

We were walking up the main drag, looking for a bite. I'd figured we'd eat in the D&P's dining room like yesterday, but after practice Glenn had said, "C'mon, let's get out of here—I know just what you need." I literally hadn't been out of the club since we'd arrived, so I jumped at the chance to stretch my legs and see a little bit of Bozeman, but we ended up in a restaurant that wouldn't have been my first choice . . . Yamaguchi Sushi.

The place was a lot busier than I would have expected a Japanese restaurant in Montana to be. And different. Meaning it was clean and comfortable, but there weren't any bamboo screens or whatever in sight. More like some of the nicer Southwestern places we have back home. And there was disco music, of all things, coming from the ceiling, and a big screen above the bar was showing a ball game with the sound turned off. Kimber would have called it "eclectic," in her professor voice.

"You okay with this?" he asked.

"Uh, sure . . ."

"You like sushi?"

I shrugged. "Don't know—never had it."

When the waitress came over and said, "Hi, what can I get for you?" Glenn looked at me. "Okay if I call it?"

I nodded. "Lead on . . ."

He ordered a few different things, and I just figured, *What the hell, bring on the bait—I'll choke it down.*

After the waitress left, I said, "You know, I was way impressed by how fast you guys made the new stuff sound totally pro today. I mean, on the first run-through some of those songs sounded like a record. That was like magic."

"You were there, too."

"All I did was pay attention."

"Exactly. You've got big ears." He saw my expression and

laughed. "Not on the sides of your head." He tapped his fore-head. "Up here. You *listen*. That's the big secret."

"That's it?" I was kinda hoping for something more.

"You know who Eddie Bayers is?" he asked.

I'd read that name somewhere recently . . . maybe in *Modern Drummer*? I shrugged. "Is he a drummer?"

"Oh yeah. An A-list Nashville studio drummer. Played on tons of sessions—you've probably heard him on hundreds of songs on the radio. Anyway, I was at a big music convention in LA and I wandered into a clinic he was giving. He'd brought some other session guys with him and they were set up onstage. The clinic was called Anatomy of a Session, and the guys on-stage were looking at charts. They'd handed out copies of the chart at the door also, so the audience could follow along. And here's the brilliant part—this was the first time Eddie's guys had ever seen the song, so we were going to get that fly-on-the-wall look at what really goes down at a pro session."

"Wow, that's totally cool."

"Yeah, they sat there talking about the tune, and Eddie's saying, 'The feel is like this . . .' and he sort of hums the basic groove, and the bassist says, 'So I come in after four bars, then?' and the guitar player asks about one of the chord changes, and so on."

"Sounds pretty normal, so far."

"Yup. So far. And then after a couple minutes of this, Eddie looks around and says, 'We good?' and everybody nods, and he counts it off. And that's where 'normal' went right out the window. Man, those guys *nailed* it, first take, cold. I don't mean they got through it without a disaster. I mean it sounded like a polished record. Even the guitar solo—perfect. I'll never forget it."

"And they had those 'big ears' . . . ?"

He nodded. "Yeah. *Huge* ears. That was really the lesson for me. When those guys played, they weren't about themselves. They were all about listening to each other and playing for the music. It wasn't a chops fest at all—nothing to prove. We're trying to do the same thing now, only instead of charts, we're using tunes off your playlist." He paused. "Remember your audition?"

"Huh?" I deadpanned. "Did I audition for this gig?"

He laughed. "As painful as it might have been, in an hour you put together some concepts that took me a whole lot longer to figure out. I was as impressed by that as much as anything. . . ."

Just then the waitress returned with our food. She set three plates in the middle of the table, along with a few small dishes of sauces and something that I swear was a big gob of green Play-Doh.

"Can I bring you anything else?" she asked.

"No, it looks perfect," Glenn said. To me it looked like logs of rice and fish and veggies—with more raw fish on top—cut into slices.

"That one's spicy," he said after she left, pointing to the one in the middle as he snagged a piece of it with his chopsticks, "but good. The others are mild." He put a thin slice of some pink stuff on top of it, followed by a small chunk of the green Play-Doh. "That's ginger, and this stuff is wasabi. It's great, but it'll clean out your sinuses."

Spicy, I can hang with. I did the same as Glenn and used

my chopsticks to shove a big bite of raw fish, rice, ginger, and wasabi into my mouth. *Whoa.* He wasn't kidding about the sinus alert—my nose burned and my eyes started to water, and then *bang* . . . it was gone. Wild.

As I tried different things on the table, I took up where we'd left off. "So, that clinic," I said. "It sounds pretty amazing. But I have one question. All those songs he recorded? The ones that made him a top player? The records and the concerts and the hit singles on the radio?"

"Yeah . . . ?"

"Were they cover tunes?"

"No, of course not. Ninety-nine percent were someone's orig—" He suddenly stopped, then slowly smiled. "I think I'm being Zach-attacked."

I shrugged. "Sorry. I just don't get why we're not doing your originals. You know way better than me that it's the only way to get to the next level. And they're freakin' *good.* At least what I've heard so far."

"Thanks. But you didn't ask why we weren't doing originals. You asked why we weren't doing *my* originals."

That little manga lightbulb went off over my head again. "Oh . . . Does Brad write?"

"A little."

"And . . . ?"

It was his turn to shrug. But other than that, it was strictly no comment. I had to give it to him—he had the perfect chance to bag on a bandmate who probably had no reservations about returning the favor, and he let it go. Man, I knew a couple of guys back in Los Robles who could use a shot of that.

"Look at the Who, as long as we're in classic-rock mode," I said. "You didn't see Roger Daltrey bitching that Pete Townshend wrote all the tunes. They each played to their strengths, and I guess you could say it worked out fairly well."

"Amen, brother . . ."

"So?"

"So . . . what do you think of the 'bait'?"

I realized I'd put away quite a bit of sushi while we'd been talking, and I found myself wishing there was more. "It's good," I admitted. "You'll have to tell me what we just ate so I can order it again."

"Grab a to-go menu on the way out, and you can make notes."

"Good idea. But about your songs . . ."

"Look, I understand where you're coming from, and I appreciate what you're saying. But for now we're doing what we're doing." He paused. "Okay?"

What else could I say? "Okay." But I still didn't get why he was hanging in a cover-band situation, with those chops and those tunes.

Come to think of it, there were a lot of things I didn't get.

17

"Hey Jealousy"

From: Kimberly Milhouse [kimmilhouse@cencast.net]
Sent: Saturday, June 26 7:27 AM
To: Zach Ryan [ZR99@westnet.net]
Subject: RE: Road life

Hey, Zach,

Sounds like you're having such a wild time out there you can't even remember what day it is. (As of today you've been on the road for five days. Trust me.) And thanks for the schedule—that helps.

So you're a Musketeer now, huh? I suppose that's a good thing—hard to tell from here. (In other words: photos, please!) Summer school is exactly as you'd imagine it to be, so I'm not going to waste any time on *that*.

Yeah, the whole thing with you and Kyle is just sad. He won't talk about it, but I know he misses having you in the band. He really needs someone he can bounce ideas off of, someone who'll speak the truth. What they've got now is a bunch of yes-men, and I can tell he's not happy. And apparently Josh is not exactly cutting it in the studio—his dad is having to "Pro Tool" the heck out of his tracks to make them work, whatever *that* means. The other guys seem fine with it, but Kyle is worried . . . it might sound okay for the record, but he's not sure they can make that work live. (The band has started their standing gig @ LoL. I went last night and I think he's right to be worried.)

Sorry about being such a downer at your last gig before you left town. Kyle isn't the only one who wishes you were here. I miss having a rent-a-boyfriend around to keep the jerks away! You know where I can hire one?

And speaking of Kevin Flanders, no, I haven't heard a peep from him. But someone else asked me out—Toby. Can you believe it? The band is playing at the town picnic in the park on the 4th of July, and he asked me to go.

GTG. You'll have to tell me the story of little sister! ☺
Later,
Kimber

✳ ✳ ✳

I snugged up the headphones so they wouldn't slip when I drummed, then I reached across to my laptop and clicked *record.* That killer guitar riff of Glenn's started. I let it play once by itself as I nodded my head in time. On the second time around I started building up a series of pounding eighth notes on the snare. By the third repeat I was playing the full groove, using the syncopated part that had popped into my head the very first time I'd heard the riff. After four times through I stripped it down to a sparse, driving beat, making room for the vocals. Glenn's recorded voice came in. *You go north and I go south every day . . .*

I was working with the basic guitar/vocal demo Glenn had given me, trying to whip it into a finished production. It also needed bass guitar and backing vocals, but one thing at a time. . . .

I finished the take and played it back over the phones. It was almost there, but I'd gotten off a little during the final repeat chorus. I wasn't sure if I was pushing or Glenn's track had been pulling, but it didn't really matter. I spent about ten seconds considering the merits of trying to fix it in the mix later, then decided to just do it again—there were a few small things I could have done better, and whole takes are usually better than bits and pieces edited together.

After a couple more takes I was pretty happy. Maybe it wasn't mathematically perfect, but it sounded about as locked together as it could be, and more important, the *feel* was there . . . it actually rocked pretty damn hard.

I looked at my watch. *Whoa* . . . the other guys would be here pretty soon. I put the mics back to their original positions onstage, then saved and shut down the session before I fired off a quick email.

From: Zach Ryan [ZR99@westnet.net]
Sent: Saturday, June 26 9:46 AM
To: Kimberly Milhouse [kimmilhouse@cencast.net]
Subject: RE: Road life

Got your reply. I've decided not to bore you with the little sister stuff now. I'll tell you in person next time I see you, if you care. Or not.

Personally, I don't get it, but have fun at the picnic.
Later.

∗ ∗ ∗

"Hey, baby brother/den mother, what's shakin'?" That would be Brad, walking up onto the stage with Jamie. He seemed to be in a good mood, and I guess I could understand why. The last two nights had gone a lot smoother than the first, and our woodshedding was paying off—we were just about ready for the stupid classic-rock thing that evening.

A few minutes later Danny and Amber showed up. Amber was carrying a hot pot and Danny had a tray full of cups and spoons. They set it all up on a small table at the side of the stage. Amber poured a cup and brought it up to me. "Here you go, Zach. No jokes, no kidding, no frog-at-the-bottom. Just coffee." She grinned. "And no receipt—we raided the kitchen."

"Thanks."

Jamie looked around. "Anyone seen GT?"

The way things were going, I was half expecting him to walk in with Jackie-the-waitress or something, probably carrying a basket of blueberry muffins.

"Uh, he was still asleep when I left the room," I said, neglecting to mention that was like two hours ago. "You want me to go get him?"

"Naw, he's a big boy. He doesn't need a den mother," Brad said. "Besides, he's never late—he's a *professional.*"

That pretty much guaranteed his late arrival, didn't it? And he was. Almost. Right at ten he showed up in a hurry and headed for the stage to get his gear ready. As he walked by, I raised both eyebrows.

"Working on a song," he said, shaking his head. "Sorry." He

looked up at the stage, where Jamie was talking with Brad. "But when the muse strikes . . ." He paused. "Hey, through the floor I thought I heard you working on something down here. Anything interesting?"

"Not sure yet," I said, which wasn't complete fiction, because you never really know how something's going to come out until the final mix is done. "Maybe later." I nodded toward the others, getting ready to play. "Right now I think we have a date with some oldies but goodies."

He pulled a face. "Don't remind me. Yeah, let's do it."

It actually went pretty well. We didn't have time to play through everything one more time—that would have taken at least four hours. But we had a complete set list, based on the stuff I'd taken from my computer, and we went down the list, stopping at any song where someone had a question. Sometimes we'd play an intro and a verse, and once in a while we'd play the entire song, but usually we'd all go "Got it," and we'd move on to the next one. I kept a copy of the set list at my drums, and whenever I wasn't that familiar with something, I'd jot a word or two next to the song title, just as a reminder. Like "fast shuffle" or "6/8 ballad" or whatever.

By the time they opened their doors for lunch, we were done with the list and feeling pretty good about it. As I zipped up my stick bag, my phone buzzed—someone was texting me. Kimber.

Hey, Zach—what's wrong?

I put it away and went to join the others.

"You know," Brad said, "this is sounding *done*. I say we take the afternoon off."

I looked out the window—it was a totally killer day, and I

felt the sudden urge to get the hell out of there for a while. "Hey, does anybody feel like going for a bike ride or something?"

"You mean we rent some Harleys and go for a putt? Hell yeah!" Danny said.

"Uh . . . I was actually thinking bicycles."

He shrugged. "Okay, that works, too." He looked at Amber. "You in?"

"You up for a tandem, big guy?"

"I guess there's a first time for everything."

"I'll take that as a yes," I said, then looked at the others. "You guys up for it?"

Jamie looked at Brad. She didn't say anything, but I had the impression she was giving him her version of the look.

"Naw, I think I'll just stay here and chill," he said.

Wow. He'd totally missed it. Or maybe he didn't care . . . ?

Jamie just sat there, staring at him. Finally, she turned to me. "Count me in."

"Great," I said. "Glenn . . . ?"

He avoided looking at either Brad or Jamie. After a minute he shrugged. "Okay."

Just then Jake came up to us. "Hey, guys, how we doing?"

We all nodded and said hi and stuff.

"I just wanted to say I've noticed you guys bustin' your butts, learning songs for tonight. I appreciate that. It'll be a great night, you'll see."

"Thanks," Brad said. "I hope so."

"Oh, it will. Trust me." He smiled. "But if you guys really want to put the cherry on the ice cream, you need to look the part, too." He called over to the bar. "Rachel, can you bring over the magic duffel?"

Rachel brought over a big blue duffel bag and set it down in front of us. "Don't worry, they're all laundered," she said.

The girls immediately started digging through it as Jake went on. "Look, guys. I'm not going to make you wear this stuff if you don't want to, but it's a theme night and it really helps set the tone. Trust me—this ain't my first rodeo."

Brad buried his face in his hands and shook his head. *"Oh, man . . ."* And I hate to say it, but I was feeling the same way.

It was the girls that won us over. "C'mon," Jamie said, holding up a pair of lime-green stretch pants and a black-and-white-striped top. "You'll all look great in this stuff. It'll be a blast."

"Yeah," Amber said. "It'll be like a giant costume party."

"Then you've gotta do it, too," said Danny.

"Bring it on," she shot back.

Personally, I think it all comes down to the fact that girls like to dress up, but at least Danny got something for us out of the potential humiliation.

"Okay," he said to Jake. "Here's the deal. We'll wear this stuff and put on a rockin' retro show for you . . ."

"But . . . ?"

"Do you think you can scare up five bicycles for us this afternoon so we can see your beautiful community in style?" Amber cleared her throat and Danny caught her look. "Uh, make that three and a tandem," he added.

Jake didn't even blink. "Done." He grinned. "And here I

thought you were going to ask for something hard. Tell you what: go up the street a block and turn left, you'll see Mountain Sports around the corner. Talk to Andy—I'll call and set it up."

"That's nice of you," Glenn said, with a sideways glance at Danny. "But we don't want to cost you a bunch of money."

"Don't sweat it. Us locals look out for each other. Andy won't charge me, and I'll buy the beer for him and his crew when they show up tonight. Win-win."

✳ ✳ ✳

Amber and Danny seemed to have a great time on the tandem bike. Apparently, Amber had some experience at this, because she just laid down a few rules for Danny and away they went. As Glenn, Jamie, and I got to the crest of a particularly long hill a few miles out of town, Amber and Danny were waiting at the top for us, looking at the little map Andy had given us. "Looks like there's a park on the right maybe ten miles up the road," Amber said. "How about we all meet there?"

We agreed and they took off, with the three of us following. I cruised along, enjoying the view, and Glenn and Jamie talked away behind me. It's not like I was eavesdropping, but I couldn't help overhearing bits and pieces. They were talking about the gig at first, then they played a little musical *Celebrity Death-match,* and then they went on about music in general.

What surprised me was Jamie. She almost seemed like a different person. I mean, she was super-nice, but I hadn't thought of her as a deep thinker.

Well, I was clearly out to lunch on that one. She and Glenn were bouncing concepts back and forth like a Ping-Pong ball, and she was definitely holding her own, kinda like an older version of Kimber in full-on professor mode.

They rode along side by side, totally oblivious to everything else, which made me feel like I was intruding on something private. So I slowly pulled ahead, and pretty soon I was by myself. With several miles to go. Which gave me time to think. Too much time, actually. Because something was bugging me, and I was going to have a hard time avoiding it, out here all by my lonesome.

God, it was so lame. What was bugging me was a stupid little email. That's all. No, what was *really* bugging me was my *reaction* to a stupid little email. I mean, it's a free country, right? What the hell do I care if my ex–bass player's sister goes to a picnic with some jerk?

Don't answer that. . . .

18

"I Bet You Look Good on the Dancefloor"

Spandex sucks.

And that's not even considering fashion issues. Have you ever tried actually *working* in the stuff? I mean, who wants to put on tight-fitting drastic/plastic/spastic/elastic clothing and go *exercise* in it? Under hot lights? In a crowded room? With limited air circulation? Yuck!

"Uh, anything else available?" I asked Amber, our self-designated wardrobe girl. "Like maybe something with a little, you know, *cotton* in it?"

"Aw, you look hot in that, Z-man."

I didn't really care—I needed to be able to move and breathe. Plus, she was almost certainly just working me. "Thanks. It might work for Jamie and Brad, but I'd melt like the Wicked Witch of the West before we finished the first set."

She was already nodding and digging through the magic duffel, throwing stuff left and right. "Here you go—made for the aerobically active percussionist, and you'll look even hotter in this. Give you a chance to show off those drummer-boy arms."

God, was she *ever* serious? What she'd come up with was a pair of puffy black parachute pants and a tiger-striped muscle shirt. But hey—at least they were cotton.

But as she held the outfit up, she said, "Hmm, it's kind of the wrong era. . . ."

"That's okay—I'll take it. Thanks for the help." I grabbed it and bailed out of there quick before she found something more "era-appropriate."

I went back to my room and started an email to Kimber. I wrote half a page, then decided it didn't say what I wanted to say . . . or maybe I just didn't know *what* I wanted to say. So I deleted the whole thing and went downstairs to join the others for dinner.

Things were pretty quiet around the ol' D&P dining table. I mean, I wasn't exactly in a talkative mood, and Brad seemed downright sullen. When I arrived, he was just sitting there, with a beer going and an empty on the table. And this time Glenn wasn't saying anything about it. In fact, he wasn't saying much of anything at all, and neither was Jamie. Which was quite a change from this afternoon. And in contrast to all of the above—and making it even more obvious—was the fact that Danny and Amber were completely unaware of the silence around them, just talking and laughing and having a good old time.

I had to get out of there. I'd barely touched my food, but I'd had enough weirdness in my day already, so I made some lame excuse and left. I suppose I could have gone back to the room and taken a last look at tonight's set list or something, but I went for a walk instead.

It was almost eight and I was on my way back to get ready when I ran into Glenn on the street.

"Hey, man, how's it going?" I asked.

"I'm good," he said. "How about you?"

"Fine."

He nodded, but as he watched me, his nod morphed from up and down into side to side. "I don't think so," he said. "What's up?"

I almost said, *Well, ya see, there's this girl* . . . as sort of a joke, but I didn't really want to go there. "I don't know . . . things are a little weird."

"Do you mean here, or back home? Is it us? The music?"

"How about E: all of the above?"

He laughed. "I hear ya."

"I mean, sometimes this seems a little like one of those behind-the-scenes TV shows or something. And even a newbie like me can tell I'm only seeing the tip of the iceberg."

"And you're sitting there wondering when the whole thing's going to come apart at speed . . . ?"

Man, he'd nailed it. "Yeah, and leave bodies strewn all over the road."

"If I do my job right, it won't."

"Why is that your job?"

He shrugged. "Things work best if you let everyone play to their strengths." He changed the subject. "And about the music thing, I don't love doing some of that stuff any more than you do, but that's part of being a pro—making the customer happy."

I snorted. "Assuming you can even figure out what they want. I mean, this place is *way* different than clubs back home."

"Yeah, and the venue next week might be different than this. That's another part of the job—sussing out what the people want."

"Maybe, but the way I see it, *another* part of our job is getting past the human-jukebox level to where we can do what *we* want."

He cocked his head. "Touché, brother."

✱ ✱ ✱

I clicked my sticks in tempo. "One ... two ... one, two, three ..." *Slam!*

As we launched into "Can't Get Enough," I looked around and took in the whole scene. Whoa. It was too bad Kimber wasn't here—she would have appreciated the surrealism of the moment. It was freakin' wildish.

After the dinner crowd had left, Jake and his crew had opened the movable wall between the club and the dining area, effectively doubling the size of the gig. I thought that was pretty optimistic, as there was almost no one in the room at the time, but I kept my newbie yap shut. Good move. . . .

It turned out the place was empty because the club doors were kept closed by design, which was actually a pretty shrewd idea. I mean, having people lined up around the block is better advertising than a dozen billboards, and it's free. Right before nine, one of the bouncers opened the doors and the place filled up in a hurry—there were like five hundred throwback rockers packed into a club made for half that many. I swear, I thought the fire marshal was going to show up and shut us down, except that apparently half the Bozeman fire crew was out there sucking down dollar beers and free tacos along with the rest of the locals.

And there was an actual soundman doing the mix and a guy on lights—including a follow spot, if you can believe that—so we looked and sounded totally pro and we didn't have to worry about anything but the music. Well, the music and the *wardrobe* . . .

I was wearing those goofy balloon pants and the tiger tank top, and I was probably the most conservatively dressed one in the band. Brad was in full-on spandex, while Glenn had on a black-and-red jumpsuit and a kamikaze headband in this weird sort of Hendrix-meets-Def Leppard thing. Danny was Spinal Tapping it to the max with faux leather from head to toe, more eyeliner than all the members of My Chem put together, and a big, scruffy black wig that made him look like Slash on Rogaine.

Amber and Jamie were both done up like an unholy cross between a biker-chick-from-hell and a sixties go-go dancer . . . tall black boots, tiny-ass miniskirts, leather push-up bras, and hair and makeup all over the place. Totally over the top, but I had to admit they looked pretty freakin' hot. And Amber wasn't just sitting out in the crowd, either. Sometimes she was strutting it on the floor with no one in particular, but she spent most of her time up onstage with us, dancing, playing tambourine, or just swaying to the beat and having fun.

When I saw her pick up the tambourine the first time, I cringed and thought, *Thank God she's hanging on Danny's side of the stage,* because Danny doesn't sing, so there's no microphone near him. You get a tambourine anywhere near an open mic and the whole world can hear it, which can be pretty bad if you only *think* you can play tambourine, like everyone does until they actually try it. But guess what? She was actually not bad. She wasn't doing anything fancy, mostly just whacking it on the backbeat, but everything she played was in the pocket.

As we came offstage during the first break, I fell in next to her. "So, where'd you learn to play tambourine like that?"

She winked at me. "Church."

"Wow. *My* church sure didn't do music like this. No drums, no guitars . . ." I cleared my throat. "And certainly no badass percussionist–dancer-girl at stage left."

Instead of laughing like I'd expected, she shot me a worried look. "That wasn't planned, believe me. I wasn't sure what to do, but Danny said, 'Hey, it's just a giant costume party. Come hang with us and add to the vibe.' Was I stupid up there?"

I thought it was funny that Amber, of all people, would worry about what I might think of her dancing or playing tambourine onstage during a gig. "You were great," I said. "You didn't even drop a beat. Seriously, it's totally cool with me."

Just then one of the customers—who'd evidently gotten a head start on the festivities—came up to her. "Hey, brown sugar, that's some hot dancin'," he shouted, talking way too loud, like the band was still playing. Then he reached over and grabbed her ass. "Do you do private parties?"

I didn't even stop to think. I just stepped between them, shouldering him out of the way. "She's with the band. Keep your freakin' hands off her, man."

He looked me over like, *Who the hell are you?* Oh crap, it

was going to be that whole Kevin Flanders thing all over again. Then out of the corner of my eye I saw Danny approaching, fast. I had no doubt—there was gonna be a fight.

But instead of laying into this asshole, Danny put his arm around him like he was a long-lost friend. "Hey, buddy, how's it going?" he said cheerfully. "You having a good time tonight?"

"Well, I *was*, until—"

"Good!" he interrupted. He nodded toward me and Amber. "These are my friends Zach and Zelda. My name's Danny." He steered the guy away from us. "You like our music?"

The guy nodded. "Uh, yeah."

"Cool! I can tell you're a fun guy. Is there anything special you'd like to hear . . . ?"

By then they were out of earshot, heading over toward the restaurant side of the club.

Amber turned to me and let out a big breath. "Thanks." She shook her head. "I don't know why guys think that being a total jerk could ever work."

"Because sometimes it does," I mumbled.

She just looked at me for a moment. "Are we talking about anybody in particular?"

"Nobody you know." I went to go get a coke and a bottle of water for the next set. As I made my way back to the stage, Danny came up to me.

"Hey, bro, thanks for watching out for Amber. That dude was *hammered*."

"No problem. Man, you did a stellar job of turning him around."

"Drunks are mimics—they pick up your attitude and adopt

it, like a chameleon. Half the time, the only difference between a friendly drunk and a mean one is the mood of the guys around him."

I looked around at the raucous crowd. "Well, then we'd better get up there and keep all these guys happy."

And by all accounts that's exactly what we did for the rest of the evening, although I got a little lesson in mob psychology on the way.

We'd blazed through most of the third set by midnight, and the place was in total party mode when suddenly I noticed some sort of commotion back by the bar. I could barely see the area from my little perch up on the stage, so I craned my neck for a better view. At first I wasn't sure what was going on. If it had been happening in front of the stage instead of in the back of the room—and if we'd been playing more Anti-Flag and less Aerosmith—I would have sworn it was a mosh pit. But I was willing to bet most of this crowd had never moshed in their lives. Nope, I was seeing my first classic bar brawl.

I couldn't make out the details, but it spread quickly as people kinda backed away in a circle and others tried to crowd in for a better look. Meanwhile, the floor was still packed with people dancing, but I could see things getting out of control. I wasn't sure what to do but I figured I should do something, so I stopped playing. The other guys, however, tried to keep going. Didn't they know what was happening?

Glenn came back to me and shouted over the noise, "Keep playing, man!"

I jumped back into it and believe it or not, people kept on dancing, oblivious to what was happening. I looked back at the fight, and two of Jake's guys had waded into the mess and dragged someone out by the arms. As quick as it had flared up, it was over.

By the time we ended the song, they were marching the guy to the door, and they didn't seem too worried about hurting his feelings, either. I got a good look as they tossed him out. He was beat up, bloody, and belligerent. And guess what else? He was the same drunk who'd been such a butthead to Amber.

But I didn't have a lot of time to think about it, because we lit a fuse under "My Generation" and kept the party blazin'. . . .

SON: "WHEN I GROW UP, I WANT TO BE A DRUMMER."

MOM: "MAKE UP YOUR MIND—YOU CAN'T DO BOTH."

"That was a great Saturday night," Jake said, "even by our standards. I've said since the beginning of the week that you guys sounded great, but with the classic tunes and those clothes and all . . . Well, it was just about perfect—they ate it up. You can bet I'll be giving Corey an outstanding report on you."

We were hanging in the bar well after the last set was done. It was long past last call, and by law the place was supposed to be closed down by now. Hell, by law I wasn't supposed to be there at all once the gig was over. But there we were, along with a dozen customers and the staff, just kinda basking in the afterglow.

"Hey," Danny said, raising his glass, "we appreciate it." He was sitting at the bar with Amber. I was at a table near them, talking with a couple of locals about bike trails, and Brad and Jamie were at the table next to me.

Somebody sent up a cheer. "Here's to Big Habit!" Everyone raised their drinks and toasted. I couldn't resist. I raised my glass and joined in, louder than anyone. "Yeah, to Big Habit . . . whoever they are!"

Brad corrected them. "It's Bad Habit. *Bad* Habit."

"Okay, here's to Fat Habit!" someone else said. They were drunk, but not that drunk. It was like an inside joke or something.

"It's *Bad* . . . ," Brad insisted.

"All right, three cheers for Big Fat Habit!"

"Bad . . ."

"Sorry. Hooray for Big Bad Fat Habit!" And on it went, with bigger and better messed-up versions of our name. . . .

Finally, after a few minutes of this, some guy stands up on a table. "Okay, everyone—I've got it! *Big-Fat-Badass-Funky-Monkey-Hobbit-Habit!*" Everyone cheered and he took a bow and sat down. And that, apparently, was our new official name.

Where was Glenn? He was missing all the fun. I looked around and spotted him at a table across the room. With Jackie-the-waitress on his lap.

I would have expected him to look a little happier, considering. But he was just sitting there, not saying much. She put her mouth to his ear while her hands went elsewhere. He looked at her, then finally shook his head. She leaned forward and kissed him—long and slow—then stood up and left.

The scene reminded me of the last time I'd seen Kimber. Uh, except for the kiss . . .

Shit. I had to get back to her.

From: Zach Ryan [ZR99@westnet.net]
Sent: Sunday, June 27 3:04 AM
To: Kimberly Milhouse [kimmilhouse@cencast.net]
Subject: RE: Road life

Yo, Kimber—

Got your text. Nothing's wrong—we're good. (Well . . . you could do *so* much better than Toby. Trust me. But whatever.)

Other than that, things are going good here. We finished the week knowing maybe forty more songs than when we started (necessity being a mother, etc.). Per Your Majesty's request, attached is a pic Amber took of us before tonight's gig. Yes, that's really me in the middle, and no, it's not 1980. (I know . . . major throwback time. Although I'd pay some serious money to see you in the outfits Jamie and Amber wore tonight. Ha!)

It's been a little weird, the whole group dynamic of this band. Not that there are knock-down, drag-out fights onstage or anything. (Well, there *was* one of those tonight, but not onstage.)

But it was a pretty good week overall. The place was nice, the people at the club treated us great, and the locals were friendly.

Well, I'm toast and I'd better get some sleep—tomorrow's a travel day. We pack everything up and head to Billings, then Helena, then Butte, then . . . (Okay, I'm not going to lie to you—it's going to be a long summer.)

Take care of yourself, okay . . . ?
Talk soon,
Z

PART III
RASH

19

"Shot Down in Flames"

"What's the name of the club again?" Jamie asked from the passenger seat as we were coming down I-15 from Helena into Butte. After three weeks on the road, the venues were starting to run together in our heads.

"Hang on," Brad said, scrolling through his phone. "Uh, it's called the Four Leaf Clover."

"Okay, everybody," she announced. "Keep an eye out—we're looking for some good luck."

Less than thirty seconds later Glenn drawled from the driver's seat, "Well, if that's the club up there on the corner, we sure could use some."

As we approached it, the big green blob painted on the side of the building resolved into a faded clover. Except one of the leaves had halfway flaked away, so it was more like a three-and-a-half-leaf clover. And it got better from there. . . .

The front of the building was all windows, but the faded blue curtains were pulled so the light of day wouldn't scare away the roaches. Some of the windows had been broken and were boarded up with plywood. Above one of the boarded-up windows was the universal symbol for a classy joint: a neon sign—also broken—depicting a martini glass. And if there was any remaining question, this was resolved by another sign that simply said LIQUOR. But hey—this one actually flickered a little.

There was a marquee above the door, but instead of announcing the band playing, it just said LIVE MUSIC. Brilliant—that way you didn't have to change it every week.

We parked and got out, looking at the place. "This can't really be it, can it?" Jamie asked.

I was thinking the same thing, but when we got to the front door, we saw a sign taped up inside one of the windows, like someone had taken a piece of paper and scrawled a quick note on it. . . .

BAD HABIT ~ TUE-SAT

***

The last couple of weeks had flown by, almost in a blur. The bookings at Billings and Helena were fine. Not as nice as Bozeman—I was starting to realize we were spoiled there—but the clubs were decent and the people were nice. And the gigs themselves went okay—the crowds seemed to like us and people danced a lot (once we decoded the vibe of each particular venue, that is). But nothing really memorable like that classic gig at the Dog & Pony. Okay, one thing that sticks out was an email from Kimber, which I got the evening after I'd written her.

From: Kimberly Milhouse [kimmilhouse@cencast.net]
Sent: Sunday, June 27 8:18 PM
To: Zach Ryan [ZR99@westnet.net]
Subject: Goofy boy!

Dear Zach,

Thanks for the email. Sounds like you're having a great time out there without me . . . ha ha!

About the Toby thing, all I can say is—you're goofy! I just mentioned that he'd asked me—I never even hinted that I'd actually go with him. I'm not sure whether to be insulted that you thought I might consider it or flattered that you care. ☺

Thanks for the pic of you! Yeah, the clothes are a scream, but I'm seriously liking that goatee. Is that what you meant by the Musketeer comment? If so, just call me Constance, *mon bel ami.*

In other news, Kyle's got his hands full trying to deal with the Sock Monkeys, and between you and me, he's not loving it. I heard some of the tracks coming out of their sessions. I guess they're not terrible, but that's about the best I can say. (He probably won't tell you this, but I can tell he really misses you—as a drummer and as a friend.)

GTG—I have some homework to finish for tomorrow morning. Some of us have to further our education—we can't all be traveling around the country without a care!

L,

K

For some reason I was in a better mood after that. And that lasted all the way up to when I finally finished that track I'd been working on.

It needed a bass part. I could have asked Danny to play it—he would have nailed it, first take. But that would have meant telling him I was working on one of Glenn's original tunes, and I hadn't even told Glenn yet. . . .

So on a day when the rest of the band was going to take a sightseeing trip around Billings, I asked Glenn if I could borrow a guitar.

"Aren't you going with us? You're the unofficial cruise director, man."

"Thanks, but I'll pass. I'm just going to stay here and hang, maybe work on a few things."

"Okay." He nodded at the acoustic leaning against a chair. "Help yourself."

"Um, it sort of needs to be an electric. . . ."

He considered this for a moment. "All right." He looked at the case next to the bed. "But please put it back in the case as soon as you're done with it."

I realized he thought I meant his main Strat. Wow. "Thanks. Really. But there's no way I'm touching Blackie. I just want to use your backup or something." He kept a new MIM tuned and ready to go behind his amp onstage. It looked like Blackie, minus all the road rash, but its financial value was only ten percent as much. And its emotional value was more like *one* percent.

"Oh—no problem," he said. "Knock yourself out."

Once they'd left, I fired up my computer and got to work.

I'm not going to lie—I'm not much of a guitar player. I've been goofing around with it for a couple of years, mostly so I could get some song ideas out of my head and into the hands of a *real* guitarist. But there's an advantage to being a drummer—you already have the "rhythm" part of the instrument down. For basic rhythm playing—which is all I can really do—the main challenge was learning how to fret the fundamental chords. Once I got my left hand to do that, the strumming part with the right hand was pretty easy, and I could fake my way through some simple stuff.

My plan was to play a very basic bass part, using the lower strings of the guitar. I'd already figured out the chord changes for the song, and as it played in my headphones, I laid down a driving bass line. I wasn't nearly good enough to play all over the neck, but by making myself stick to root/fifth stuff, I could get through it okay.

It sounded weird when I listened to it playing back, because I had this lame guitar part along with Glenn's killer stuff. But then I pitch-shifted my entire part down an octave, and that did it. Instead of hearing two guitar parts, there was just the one hot guitar part, supported by a bass part underneath it.

Doing it this way really made me miss Kyle. He was great at this sort of thing—he would have come up with something way better that would have added more sophistication to the track. But the part I played worked well enough to drive the tune along and beef up the bottom end without getting in the way, and that's what mattered right now.

Next up was backing vocals. Compared to patching together a bass part, this was easy money. I set up a mic in the room and ran it in flat and dry—I could always process it later if I needed to.

The first thing I did was double the parts Glenn sang on the choruses. I tried to clone his phrasing and sing as much like him as possible, in unison. Once I did that, I put down an actual backing track. I'd started to think of the tune as "Every Day," because that was the hook line. So I went back and hit all those *every day* parts, singing a fifth above Glenn. And I didn't try to be real smooth about it this time—I sang those with a little more rasp in my voice to help give it an edge.

All this took a couple of hours, so I saved the session and shut down my computer before the others came back. I didn't get a chance to work on it again until Helena, but that was the part I was really looking forward to—the final mix.

There are a hundred different approaches you can take to mixing a song, but for a high-energy tune like this I usually start with the drums. My feeling is that they're the bedrock—if the drums aren't happening, *nothing's* happening.

I only had four tracks of drums—kick, snare, and two overheads—so I had them dialed in pretty quickly. I went for a simple but hard-hitting sound. But I wanted them to have some punch, so I compressed the kick and snare, giving them more impact without totally drowning out the other stuff.

Then I brought up both of Glenn's tracks—the guitar and lead vocals—which were the heart of this song. But guitar and vocals occupy the same space, frequency-wise, so you have to be careful or they'll start competing. I had the guitar pretty hot in the mix to showcase that killer riff at the top, but then I pulled it back when his voice came in. Things are funny that way. Once the listener gets used to a certain part, you can pull it way down (or even off) and they'll still hear it in their head. Weird, huh?

So once I had a balance between the vocal and guitar, I brought in the bass to warm it up and fill in some gaps. Then I brought up the doubled vocal, which made the mix sound bigger and . . . I don't know . . . more *urgent,* if that makes any sense. Then I cranked in the backing vocals on the hook lines, and that brought the energy level even higher.

After that, it was just a matter of playing with the balance, going with my gut until it did that same hair-up-on-the-back-of-your-neck thing that it did the first time I'd heard Glenn sing it. I was pretty happy with it at that point, so I burned a copy on disc, then saved and shut down. But I wasn't quite finished yet. I'd done all this on headphones and my little computer speakers, and while I'm pretty familiar with how things should sound on them, you never really know until you listen on something a little more . . . substantial.

So I took it over to the club.

It was early afternoon and the club was empty, so I fired up the PA system and played the mix through it, cranking it up pretty freakin' loud. Then I sat in the middle of the room and listened with my gut. I was trying *not* to think *Does the kick have enough compression?* or *Should I boost the mids on the guitar a little?* I was just letting it pump out of those big fat speakers at me.

I ended up with a big-ass grin on my face. It may not have been perfect, but that thing *slammed.* I got an unsolicited second opinion, too. There was a scruffy kid cleaning glasses behind the bar, and after I'd listened to the song a couple of times and shut down the PA, he called over.

"Hey, is that you guys?"

"Uh, yeah," I admitted. Close enough, anyway.

He nodded three or four times slowly. "That song kicks *ass,* dude."

That made up my mind. . . .

＊＊＊

He took out his earbuds and shook his head. "No way."

"Huh?" I guess I really *am* stupid, expecting Brad to have an open mind about one of Glenn's original songs.

"Doesn't do anything for me at *all.* Plus, no one's ever heard it, so it ain't gonna fly at a club."

"But if we started playing it, and maybe some other originals, then people *would* hear it. You can only get so far covering other people's stuff. . . ."

"So you're not happy with 'how far you've gotten' in the last couple of months? Last I remember, you were tossed out of some little high school band that wasn't so hot to begin with. If GT hadn't convinced us you were the second coming of Travis Barker, you'd still be back in Los Robles shoveling manure or whatever."

Whoa. "Okay, I was just asking if—"

"Yeah," he interrupted. "And I was just answering."

And that was the end of that.

I guess I'd had some dumb vision of Brad and Danny and Jamie loving the song and wanting to learn it and of us surprising Glenn with it or something. I knew Brad would be the hardest to convince so I'd tried him first. And last, apparently. There wasn't any point in showing it to Glenn. I tossed it in a nearby wastebasket. All that work for nothing . . .

Then I stopped. *Okay,* I thought, *so the score's one to one.* That didn't mean it was game over. So far it was No-Name-scruffy-dishwasher-dude versus Mr. Semipro-Rock-God. (My vote sure didn't count.) I took the disc back out of the trash. What I needed was a third-party opinion. From someone who had half a clue but who didn't have their ego involved.

And I knew just where to get it. . . .

20

"Welcome to Paradise"

Dear Mom, Dad & Alicia-the-monkey-girl... ☺

So far, this has been a great trip. Butte's our last stop
up here before we head toward Yellowstone for the next
leg. It's totally cool—an old mining town with a ton of
history. The downtown area is kind of like the courthouse
square in LR, only bigger and older.

   The club here is different than the others—I guess
you'd say it's got a real "vintage" vibe to it...

Cheers!

Zach

The Four Leaf Clover was actually better on the inside than it
looked from the outside—the decades-old stench in the place
was 60/40 beer to urine, as opposed to the other way around.

The first thing we did was check in with the guy behind the
bar. Well, we *tried*—he was a surly dude who wouldn't make

eye contact and didn't say more than five words to us. We got a grunt and a nod, "No," and "Alex is in back." Okay, the last was accompanied by a thumb jerked over his shoulder to indicate the supposed location of the supposed owner, so maybe I should give him credit for six words. Eight, if you include the *FU* phrase tattooed across his throat right below his Adam's apple. Nice . . .

Of course there was no house system involved, so we had to haul in and set up our own PA. Same deal with stage lights. We didn't carry much lighting, but the situation was so poor that our six little LED PAR 64 cans would probably double the onstage brightness, so we dug them out and set them up.

After we got our gear loaded in, we went through a quick sound check. Everything sounded fine, but the response from the few people working there was a little underwhelming. As in, absolutely *nada*. Not *Hey, you guys sound pretty good*, or even, *Man, that guitar was loud.* (Hell, I would have been happy with *You suck!*—at least that would have indicated they'd actually noticed that a live band was playing in the same room.) But it was like they'd seen it all before and just couldn't be bothered.

After sound check Alex, the owner, finally appeared behind the bar and waved us over—apparently, it was too much effort to actually come to the stage and welcome his new band for the week.

"Here's the deal," he grunted by way of greeting. No handshake, no *How was the trip?* or *Can I get you anything?* and certainly no time for introductions. We were obviously expected to know who *he* was, while he obviously didn't give a shit who *we* were. "Start at nine o'clock, fifteen-minute break at ten-thirty and midnight."

"Wait—we're going until one-thirty, aren't we?" asked Brad.

He looked at Brad like he was an idiot. "Yup" was all he said.

Four sets was the usual minimum. Heck, a lot of clubs set it up where you're on for forty-five and off for fifteen, every hour, giving you five shorter sets. Better for the band, and anyone with half a clue will tell you that the time when customers buy the most drinks is during a break. But apparently this guy only had a quarter of a clue, and he was going to wring every last minute of music out of us.

"I'll start a tab for you," he continued, totally ignoring the implied question about what happened to our third break, "and it'll come out of your paycheck at the end of the week."

"Okay," Brad said. "What's the policy on meals?"

Alex gave him that I-don't-have-time-for-idiots look again and said, "Like I said, you run a tab and everything comes out of your pay." In other words, they weren't comping us for *anything*.

He slid three keys across the counter. Each one was wired to a grimy length of cut off broomstick, like when you ask to use the restroom at some funky gas station. "Rooms are upstairs." He turned to leave, then thought better of it and turned back. I don't know, maybe his higher math skills finally kicked in and he realized there were two guys for every girl in our little entourage. "We ain't runnin' a free flophouse for locals here, either," he grumbled. "You get a bunch of sluts who wanna party with the band, you're either gonna pay extra or you get a room at the Super 8 across the street."

And with that, our official welcome to the Four Leaf Clover was brought to a close.

✱ ✱ ✱

"Holy crap!"

"Welcome to the other side of the road," Glenn said.

We'd just walked into our room above the club. The funk was so bad that it felt like a movie set from one of Mr. Langley's films on the Depression.

There was a pair of saggy twin beds separated by a beat-up old dresser in a small room with a high ceiling. Dangling from the cracked, yellowed plaster over our heads was a single bare bulb on a cord, with a pull chain. Across from the beds was a thrashed sofa that literally had a spring sticking out of it—I honestly thought they only had those in cartoons. On the floor was this rug that looked like they'd taken some old rope that'd been lying in a barn for a hundred years and coiled it into a big oval. If you kicked it, little clouds of dust arose.

But hey—bonus! Our window looked down on the gravel lot behind the bar, giving us a bird's-eye view of the pukefest that almost certainly occurred there every Saturday night after closing time.

The idea that anyone would actually bring a girl back to a place like this was just sad. I had half a mind to go get a room at the Super 8 myself, just to make sure I wasn't carried off by roaches in the middle of the night.

"You know," Glenn said, "suddenly I have this urge to go somewhere. As in, *anywhere*."

"Ditto," I said, dropping my duffel on one of the beds.

"So let's go get some coffee or something."

"Okay, just a sec . . ." I held up my phone. "I've gotta get some pics of this place, or no one will believe it." I took some quick shots of the room and the view. "Okay, I'm good to go."

We ended up walking uphill, toward what looked like the original downtown.

"This okay with you?"

We were going by a coffeehouse a few blocks from the club. Bert's Best Brew. Kind of a funky, organic version of Starbucks. It smelled *great* from the doorway. "Sure, looks perfect," I said.

Glenn ordered a coffee and a sandwich from the deli case. Good idea—I don't think I'd want to eat at the ol' Four Leaf Clover even if it *didn't* go on our tab.

So it's my turn to order and I'm looking at the sandwiches, too, kinda distracted, when out of my mouth comes, "Venti half-caf three-pump white mocha . . . nonfat, no whip, extra-hot . . ."

The guy behind the counter just looks at me like I'm from Jupiter or something. Glenn finally elbows me and says, "Man, we're not at Starbucks."

"Huh?" I look up. Oops.

"Yeah, *dude*," the guy says in this completely over-the-top LA surfer talk. "Like, totally."

"Dude! I am, like, *so* totally sorry. Just flew in from the Coast and I am, like, *so* majorly jet-lagged it's, like, unbelievable. . . ." I dropped it. "Cup of house, and that turkey sandwich. Thanks."

We got our stuff and sat down. What was so weird about it wasn't just that I tried to give the guy a Starbucks order—it was the order itself. That was *Kimber's* drink, exactly the way she liked it.

Glenn looked at me. "You okay?"

"Well, there's this girl . . ." Seems like my mouth was totally off the leash and there was no getting it back.

He just laughed. "Yeah, that's kind of a given." He blew on his coffee and took a sip. "Anything you want to talk about?"

I shook my head. "I'm not withholding—I'm just not sure what's up with her yet. Her brother was in my old band, and he and I were really tight. *Were . . .*"

"Man, that sucks. What happened?"

So I told him the whole semi–sob story about being replaced by Justin's cousin and how it turned out that Josh's dad had a studio and was all connected and stuff.

". . . and the pisser is, I know I'm as solid as he is. I mean, I don't think I'm God's gift to music or anything, but—"

He held up his hand, palm out. "Stop. Man, you are head and shoulders above him. End of story."

"You've heard him play?"

"Yeah, I caught them at Land of Lights before we left. I only stayed for half a set, but it was enough. They were fools to let you go."

"Thanks. But they ended up with free access to a pro studio and a guy with connections."

"Yeah, but *I* ended up with a very musical drummer, so I win. Connections and studios are great, but in the end it's all about the songs and the performance."

"Maybe, but what if you have all that but no real contacts?"

He grinned. "That's pretty much our situation right now, isn't it? And they're sitting in the opposite bus. So if you had to choose, which one would you rather be driving?"

He had a point there. If only things were that simple . . .

* * *

After a while Glenn headed back to the FLC. I decided I'd stay and send the pics. When I checked my email, there were a couple of messages. One of them was from an address I knew as well as my own. Well, I *used* to know it that well. . . .

From: Ky [EADG@cencast.net]
Sent: Monday, July 12 11:21 PM
To: Zach Ryan [ZR99@westnet.net]
Subject: [none]

Hey, just wanted to give you a quick heads-up that Kim's b-day is next week, in case you weren't aware. No big.
Later,
Kyle

Whoa . . . That was, like, totally unexpected. Even though I *did* know when her birthday was. I'd been thinking I might call her. *Hmm . . . maybe I should send her a card, too.*

I recognized the address of the second email, too. And to tell the truth, I didn't really want to open it. It felt like when my phone said that Glenn Taylor had called after the audition. I was pretty sure what the email said, but if I actually read it, then any shred of hope would be gone.

Not that I really had high expectations anyway. I'd just been looking for a second opinion.

Yeah, right . . .

From: Dandy Don Davis [DDD@W107.com]
Sent: Tuesday, July 13 12:26 PM
To: Zach Ryan [ZR99@westnet.net]
Subject: RE: Song Entry

Hey Zach!
Thanks for submitting the song "Every Day," by your band, Killer Jones. I just heard it this morning, and that track totally kicked my butt!

The deadline for submissions is the day after tomorrow, but I can save myself an email and tell you right now that this song will definitely be on our upcoming *Best in the Rockin' West* compilation CD. It's the strongest entry we've gotten so far, and unless something unexpected comes in under the wire, we're going to make it the opening track on the record.

The CD goes to replication this week and hits the street by the end of the month. We'll start playing cuts from it on the air before it comes out. I'll get you your five free copies as soon as they're available.
Hope this news rocks your day!!!
Don

I just sat there for a minute, basking in this weird mix of elation . . . and fear.

21

"Original Prankster"

From: Zach Ryan [ZR99@westnet.net]
Sent: Tuesday, July 13 3:14 PM
To: Kimberly Milhouse [kimmilhouse@cencast.net]
Subject: News

Mi Hermana Pequeña...

(Oh yeah, I wasn't going to call you that anymore, was I? Sorry...)

It was the best of tunes, it was the worst of rooms... Take a look at the attached pics. This is the room they gave me and Glenn at the Four Leaf Clover. (I know I told you the last few places weren't fancy, but they should rename *this* place the Grapes of Wrath—seriously!) But you know, it doesn't matter, because...

And then I was going to give her the good news. Tell her all about the song I'd produced . . . how Brad had totally shot it down . . . how I'd sent it to Wild 107 on a whim and just gotten this email that changed everything. What a relief it was to finally get a little validation.

But none of that was really the point, was it?

... because I'm out here to play music and become a better musician and see the country and all of that good stuff. And if sleeping in a total dive once in a while is part of that experience, then so be it.

I've had my confidence shaken during the past few months, but you were always there, telling me I was worthy. Well, you know what? I finally got some news that supports your hypothesis, my dear professor.

More later, when I'm sure. But for now—thanks.
L,
Z

She really *was* the only one that had given me any support when things weren't going so well—she deserved more than a phone call and a card for her birthday.

I had a few hours, so I headed to the older section of town and browsed the store windows, but I couldn't seem to find anything. Part of the problem was, I wasn't sure what I was looking for. I mean, was I looking for something like music or books? *Booorrring . . .* Or maybe for clothes, like a sweater or whatever? Get real—I was totally clueless when it came to that stuff. I spent most of my time hoping I'd get inspired by something, but I was striking out, big-time.

Finally, I found myself walking through what must have been a little gallery district, because every other shop was selling paintings or knickknacks or ceramics or whatever. There was a handcrafted-jewelry shop that had some cool-looking stuff in the window, but no *way* was I getting her jewelry.

Then I spotted them. I couldn't believe it—a pair of silver

earrings shaped like pi signs. You know: π. Perfect. Plus, the novelty of the mathematical symbol would take away from the scary jewelry-ness of the whole thing.

I went in and asked the woman behind the counter if I could see them. Actually, what I really wanted to see was the price tag. I mean, why do they have to write the price of jewelry on this little microsized tag and then turn it around so you can't see it?

Anyway, they were a hundred bucks. She must have seen my face.

"Who are they for?" she asked.

"A friend. Uh, a girl."

She smiled. "I see. I'll tell you what—those happen to be on sale for seventy-nine dollars, but just for today."

That was still a lot of money, but Kimber *had* been real nice to me. And I'd saved a little of my gig money after expenses, and there was no getting around it—they were perfect for her.

"Thanks. I'll take them. Can you wrap them for me?"

"Certainly."

Then I bought a card next door and I got directions to a place where I could get it shipped off to her. When I got there, I filled out the card.

Don't ever let anyone tell you that πr^2.
Because believe me, baby, pie are round...
Have a great 16th!

L,

Z

***

You know, for being such a dive, the FLC actually drew a pretty good-sized crowd. Not that they gave us standing ovations or anything, but at least they were more responsive than the staff. Which might have had something to do with the fact that they were also the hardest-drinking crowd we'd seen. At some clubs the people are there for the music, and the food and drinks are kind of a bonus. Other places are all about the social scene—the dancing, flirting, who's-going-home-with-who thing. (And each of these places required some fine-tuning of our set list, believe me—we kept applying the hard-earned lesson we'd been taught back at the Dog & Pony. . . .)

But at the FLC the name of the main game was alcohol. Okay . . . judging by some of the people leaving and then coming back in, maybe other chemicals were involved, too. But for such a hard-drinking crowd they were reasonably behaved. At least for the first part of the week . . .

Friday night was packed, and the place seemed a little tense. A few fights broke out, but here the staff just let them run their course. Usually the fights ended up going outside, where you could hear shouting with lots of f-bombs being thrown back and forth. During the second set there was the sound of breaking glass, and a few minutes later I could make out the flashing red lights of a police car through the grimy windows.

At the next break Glenn came up to me. "Hey, can you live without your eighteen-inch crash?"

"I guess so."

"Good. I just want to be ready if something breaks. If you

take the stand apart, we'll have some pretty good lengths of pipe up here onstage."

And not thirty minutes later I damn near used one of them. We were in the middle of a song when this total assbite decided he'd get up onstage. Maybe he just had the urge to sing along—who knows? Glenn said something to him, probably asking him to get down, and the guy ignored him. When Glenn said something again, the guy pushed him away and started heading toward Jamie. I was about to stop and help, but before I could budge, Glenn unslung his guitar—Blackie!—and swung it like a bat.

He tagged the guy in the shoulder, which spun him around, and then Glenn gave him a hard shove in the hip with his boot, and *crash* . . . the guy went flailing over the front of the stage. The whole thing took maybe ten seconds, and Glenn had his guitar back on and was back in the song. The guy lay there for a minute, then staggered to his feet. He made like he was going to try to climb back up onstage, and I decided that if he did, I was going after him with a piece of that stand in my hand for insurance. But his friends grabbed him and dragged him out the door instead. Holy wow . . .

Thankfully, we got through the rest of the night without anything else breaking—that was one gig I was glad to see end.

I didn't hang around afterward to unwind—I was toast. I fell asleep wondering if this is what they meant by "paying your dues."

***

Someone was shaking me. "Zach! Zach, get up, man—someone's messing with our motor home!"

"Huh . . ." I opened my eyes. It was Glenn. "What's going on?"

"I need some backup. Someone's down in the parking lot, breaking into the Bad-Mobile. Let's go!"

WTF . . . ? I rolled out of bed and pulled my jeans and shoes on. It was still dark out. I looked around, wishing my cymbal stand or something were nearby, but I couldn't see anything worthwhile. I would have given anything for at least a flashlight.

He must have seen me look at the pull chain for the bulb. "Don't turn the light on—they'll see it."

Crap. "Okay, let's roll."

As we flew down the hallway, I said, "So why don't we call the cops?"

"Take too long . . . all our stuff'll be gone by then."

By the time we got down to the parking lot, the door to the Bad-Mobile was wide open. There was no one in sight—whoever they were, they must have been inside.

I looked at Glenn. *"Now what?"* I was trying to whisper but it was difficult because I was panting so hard. "How many guys did you see?"

He shrugged, but I wasn't exactly sure which question he was answering. It didn't really matter, because just then he picked up a beer bottle off the gravel and flung it at the motor home, where it hit the side with a loud *thunk*. *"Hey!"* he yelled, his voice surprisingly loud and deep. "Get the hell out of there!"

At first there was no response. Then there was some commotion inside, and after a minute someone stuck his face out for half a second. The face disappeared, then a few seconds later three guys came out. One of them might have been the butthead who'd climbed onstage, but at that moment I was more concerned by the fact that there were three of them, they weren't exactly little, and one of them had a bass guitar in his hands while the other two were each carrying some of our spare electronic equipment.

We stood there for a second, maybe fifty feet apart, looking at each other in the dim blue light of a distant streetlamp. Then Glenn spoke up. "The cops are on their way—they'll be here any second. If they catch you with that stuff, it'll be B&E plus grand larceny and you're going to prison. All for some crap that ain't worth a hundred bucks in a pawnshop. So if you're smart, you'll put it back and get the hell out of here."

One of them said something to the others that I couldn't catch, then turned back to us. "You didn't call no cops," he shouted hoarsely. "Screw you!" He started to move away from the Bad-Mobile with the bass in his hands.

"No," came a voice from beside us. "Screw *you*."

I whipped around. It was Danny, holding a gun in his hands. And he looked like he knew how to handle it, too. All of a sudden I could feel my heart pounding in my chest like a freakin' bass drum.

"All right, guys," Glenn said. "Game over. Put the stuff down and clear out."

The two guys who hadn't said anything set their stuff down and backed away with their hands up, then turned and ran off. The other one hesitated.

Danny pointed the pistol right at him, holding it up with both hands as he looked at the guy over the sights and squinted one eye. "Bro," he said slowly, "that's my 1965 Fender Precision bass you're holding there, and there's no way I'm gonna stand here and watch you walk away with it. *Comprende?*"

Even though the guy was probably drunk or high or whatever, that seemed to get through. He put it down and half ran, half staggered away.

"And don't come back!" I yelled for some stupid reason, probably because I hadn't said anything yet.

I took a deep breath . . . I could feel it kinda shake as I let it out. I turned to Danny. "Wow . . . I didn't know you'd brought a gun on the road with you."

He bristled. "You got a problem with that?"

"No, I just—" Then I stopped stone-cold—he was pointing it at *me*. "Are you crazy?" I said. "What the hell are you doing?"

He put his finger on the trigger.

I took a step back. "Hey!"

He pulled the trigger.

Squirt . . .

I looked down at the drops of water on my bare chest, then I looked back up at him. He tried to keep a straight face, but he busted up, and pretty soon so did Glenn.

I was pissed. "You son of a . . ." But it was hard to stay mad, and that kind of laughter is totally contagious. Pretty soon all three of us were standing in the parking lot at four in the morning, laughing so hard we had tears coming out of our eyes.

22

"Whiskey in the Morning"

We spent the next hour or so unloading anything of value from the Bad-Mobile and putting it up in our room—we figured there was no guarantee they *wouldn't* come back, in spite of my parting words. And whenever the conversation wound down, either Danny or Glenn would hold up a finger and shake it like a strict teacher and say, *"And don't come back!"* and then they'd be doubled up all over again, laughing so hard they could barely breathe.

By the time we were done, the sun was up, and we were so wired from the excitement and the exercise that there was no way we were going back to sleep.

"Anyone up for breakfast?" Danny asked. "I found the perfect local joint. It's like the total *funk de funk,* man."

So he led us downtown, past the coffeehouse Glenn and I had been to earlier. We turned the corner onto Main Street and followed him into this place with a big vintage sign out front that said B&W BAR & CAFÉ.

"This is it, guys. What do you think?"

"I think . . . ," Glenn said dryly, "that the name is certainly accurate."

He wasn't kidding. You walked in the double doors—NEVER LOCKED!, the sign said—and running down the right side of the long room was a lunch counter. Or breakfast counter, as the case may be. Complete with vinyl-topped chrome stools bolted to the white linoleum tile. Right out of some old movie. And there were actors on the set, in the form of locals sitting on those stools drinking coffee and eating from plates piled high with home fries and ham steaks and hotcakes. And a guy behind the counter with one of those tall, round paper chef's hats, cooking up a storm on a huge griddle. And a waitress with a uniform, complete with name tag which—I swear to God—said MARGE. And yeah, she was a little large. And she was *definitely* in charge.

But going down the *left* side of the room was a bar. With metal stools, too, only not bolted to the floor. Of course. How could you have a bar fight with the stools bolted to the floor? And the floor was also linoleum, but it was more a blotchy black, not cheery white. The different types of flooring met down the middle of the room, like the borders of two totally different countries. And yeah, the bar side of the movie set had its own characters, too. There was this skinny dude behind the bar, pouring shots. He was so pale he looked like he'd never left the place. (At least while the sun was up. I looked for pointy canines, but I couldn't tell. . . .) And there were rough-looking old guys lined up at the bar, pounding down whiskey. At six in the morning. (I guess that's kinda the definition of "rough old guy," isn't it?)

It was surreal, the two opposite sides of the room, each with its own group of people at their own counters, back to back maybe ten feet away from each other . . . but worlds apart.

There was no chirpy little hostess waiting to seat us, either. You just walked in, chose your poison—coronaries on the right, cirrhosis on the left—and took your stool accordingly. We just stood there for a minute, taking it in. I think we were all pretty loopy from the whole parking-lot adventure and the lack of sleep that followed.

"I'm liking it," I finally said.

"Me too," Glenn agreed. "It's real."

Danny looked around the room. "If I lived around here," he announced, "this would be my regular hang." He paused. "The girls would absolutely hate it."

Glenn nodded. "Maybe that's part of the attraction?"

We looked at each other and slowly grinned. Like I said, it was a goofy morning.

We found some stools at the breakfast counter and had a seat. After a few minutes Marge-the-waitress came by—with a pen jammed behind her ear and a cigarette dangling from her mouth—and took our order. I swear, she was the one that Jackie, back in Bozeman, must have used as her role model.

"Back in a few," Glenn said after we'd ordered, and he took off in search of the restroom.

Maybe it was the loopiness of the morning—I don't know—but out of the blue I turned to Danny. "Hey, you wanna listen to this tune I found? I think we could cover it."

"Sure, let's hear it."

So I dialed up "Every Day" on my phone, handed him the earbuds, and pressed *play*. After a few seconds he was nodding in time and tapping his foot. And then he was smiling as he was nodding and tapping.

When it was over, he took out the buds. "That was pretty awesome." He looked at the phone. "KJ? Never heard of them. Where'd you find it?"

"I think they're an indie band out of California. The tune's getting a little airplay." Close enough . . . just a matter of tense, right? "Anyway, I heard it and liked it, so I downloaded it."

"I could totally see us doing that. It rocks."

I just nodded casually, but inside I was thinking, *Yesss!*

When Glenn came back, Danny was all like, "GT, you've gotta hear this cool song Zach found. It'd be a killer tune for us to cover."

Note to self: *You have got to learn to think these things through. . . .*

I waved it off. "Remind me later," I said to Glenn. "Actually, I've got a few different things I want you to hear." I put my phone away, then looked over at Danny and changed the subject. "Was that really your P Bass that that guy had?"

He shook his head. "You think I'd leave that alone in the Bad-Mobile overnight? But I thought it was better than saying it was my cheap backup that I could replace at any Guitar Center." He grinned. "Worked, didn't it?"

Just then the food showed up. And as we ate, we rehashed our heroic foiling of the robbery of the faithful Bad-Mobile. When we were about done with breakfast, I brought up something that had popped into my mind earlier. "So, you heard us go down the hall, and then you heard us in the parking lot below?" I asked Danny.

"Yeah, my window was cracked open. And you guys weren't too quiet down there." He imitated Glenn in the parking lot. *"Hey,"* he called in a deep dumb-guy voice that sounded like Patrick on *SpongeBob. "Get the hell out of there . . . !"*

"Well, I'm glad we were so noisy. So, how come Brad didn't come down with you?"

He paused, just for half a second. "Ya know, I guess he's a heavier sleeper than me. Maybe he had a couple of beers after the gig?" He shrugged. "But you had those dudes handled. . . ." He held up that finger again, and he and Glenn chimed in with, *"And don't come back!"*

As they were cracking up all over again, Danny put some money on the counter and spun around on his stool. *"Woo-hoo.* This was fun, but I've gotta get back to . . . um, I'm gonna try and get some sleep. See you guys back at the club."

After he left, Glenn and I got some coffee and just watched the customers. I used my phone to take a quick video of the place, slowly panning to show the total funkiness of the whole room.

"Hey," I said, "do you suppose there's a rule that once you pick a side, you can't cross over?"

He considered it. "I'm thinking you can," he decided, "but not on the same visit. You have to pay your bill, leave, and then you can come back later. But did ya know, there's also gambling in the back?"

"No way! Next you'll be saying there's a whorehouse up-stairs."

"Used to be," he said matter-of-factly, "at least according to the sign over there. But seriously, there's a card table back by the head. And it's going full-on, right now. Literally, liquor in the front and poker in the rear."

We laughed at the absurdity of it. Then for some reason I thought about that email from Don Davis. Well, it had already gone to press, so what the heck. . . .

I pulled it up and handed my phone to Glenn without a word.

He took it, and I watched his reaction as he read it. It started with a little smile, but by the end it was a total BFG. He stuck out his hand. "Congratulations, man," he said. "That's awesome. I'd thought about submitting to that before, but I could never seem to get one of my tunes all tracked in time. So who's in this band? Some sort of side project you had back in LR?"

Man, I'd been sweating this moment ever since I'd gotten the reply from Don. I'd come close to telling Glenn a couple of times, but each time I had second thoughts, unsure how he'd take it. I swear, I almost made up some bullshit story right there in the diner to avoid it again.

But instead I shook my head slowly as I called up the tune and handed him the earbuds. "I *told* you it was good," I said as he put in the earbuds. "You've gotta learn to trust my judgment."

He looked confused, but I just pressed *play* and leaned back, folding my arms and watching. I wasn't sure what to expect.

For about two seconds the confused look remained, like he was trying to figure out how this familiar guitar line had made it into someone's song. Then he got it and looked at me like, *WTF . . . ?*

I held my finger to my lips, then pointed to my ears like, *Just be quiet and listen.* And he did. All the way to the end. Then he took the buds out and just stared at me, not saying a word.

I could tell something wasn't right. He looked . . . mad.

He stood up and pointed at the stool I was sitting on. "Stay right there." Then he walked out the doors that were never locked. Taking my phone with him.

Q: WHAT'S THE DIFFERENCE BETWEEN A DRUMMER AND A SAVINGS BOND?

A: ONE WILL MATURE AND MAKE MONEY SOMEDAY.

He was gone for two more cups of coffee. And a side of sourdough toast. With peanut butter. I was worried—it was dawning on me that I'd finished his song . . . without him. Or his permission. *Shit.*

He finally came back.

"I've got a few questions," he said. "Like, when did you do it? Where did you do it? How did you do it? But what I really want to know is, *why* did you do it?"

So I told him the whole story. It took me quite a while, especially explaining the why, and when I was done, he sat there for a long time, looking up at the ceiling. Finally, he looked at me.

"Okay. When I first heard it, yeah, I was pissed. That song was personal, man. You should have asked before you messed with it." I started to say something but he held up his hand. "Good intentions or not, that was my tune. And you absolutely need permission before you do something crazy like submit it for a CD. Right?"

He was staring at me and I finally realized it wasn't a rhetorical question. "Uh, yeah . . . right. Of course."

He nodded. "Good. Just making sure. But what really matters is the intent. If you were just doing this to score a track on a CD to impress your buddies back in LR or something, well . . . we'd have a problem."

I swallowed, and it was my turn to nod. I don't know why, but I'd rather have just about anyone else but Glenn mad at me.

"So, where'd you go?" I finally asked.

"Just walking around, thinking about it. And listening to it." He smiled for the first time. "If you'd butchered that tune, man, I'd hammer you. But you gave it just what it needed. I like it. And now . . ." He paused. "And now it's going to be on the Wild 107 CD. And it's going to get some airplay."

"Uh . . . that's a good thing, right?" I asked, still a little worried.

"That's a *great* thing. Seriously." Then he reached over and gave me a hug. "So thanks."

I swear, for the second time in a week I was about to cry in public.

23
"Out of Line"

From: Kimberly Milhouse [kimmilhouse@cencast.net]
Sent: Saturday, July 17 10:55 AM
To: Zach Ryan [ZR99@westnet.net]
Subject: RE: News

Dear Zach,

Like I said, I understood about the "rooms," but still not sure about the "tunes."
Am I being dense here, or . . . ?

So I've been cogitating . . . if I'm not your *hermana pequeña* , then what am I?
Inquiring minds want to know!

Wow! Sorry about the rooms they gave you. They look bad, even by Langley
standards. I guess this is a practical application of that old what-doesn't-kill-
you-makes-you-stronger idea, huh? In the meantime, please don't get carried
off by those roaches . . . !

Thanks again for the kind words. And guess what? I *am* right—you *are* worthy.
(And I'm dying to hear what happened to make you finally believe it. ☺)

GTG—talk soon.

L,

K

I'd just put my phone away when Danny came up to me.

"Hey, Zach, can you send me that tune? The one by KJ? I want to check it out again." I was in the club, getting ready to do a little maintenance on my drums.

I hesitated. "Uh, okay." I took out my phone and sent it. "Done. But don't . . ."

Too late—he was up and moving. "Gotta go . . . thanks, bro!" And he was gone.

I mentally shrugged. Oh well, you can't go around walking on eggshells and treating the world with kid gloves . . . or whatever that whole goat/egg metaphor is supposed to be. Right?

Whatever. I went to the stage to swap out my snare head— nothing makes a drumset sound new like a minty, freshly tuned head on the snare. I finally got it to that magical place where it had a sharp crack on top but wasn't so tight that you lose that big fat meaty tone underneath. Then I touched up the tuning on the toms. It's funny—most people think drums are just round shells with heads on either side and you just whack the crap out of 'em and that's it. But you can make even a budget drumset sound pretty damn good if you make the effort. (Which was a good thing in my case, believe me.)

I'd started playing in school during fifth grade. I never really had any formal lessons—I just screwed around in the band room during lunch until I learned how to keep a basic beat. The music teacher heard me one day and I guess he was desperate, because before you knew it I was drafted into the school band. So at first I played the school's drumset, but that didn't work when I wanted to play outside of school. My dad made me a deal—he'd pay for half of my first set if I saved up for the rest. I ended up getting a secondhand beginner's kit from a kid down the block who'd gotten it for Christmas but had never really learned how to play. That was good for a year or so, but in junior high I got in a garage band and we actually played a few parties, so I needed something better. I took all my gig money and found my current kit on Craigslist.

At first I wasn't too happy with the sound. I took it to the local drum shop and Howard—the owner—took pity on me, even though I hadn't purchased it there. I bought new heads from him and he helped me install them and gave me a lesson in drum tuning. When he was done, he held up a tom and smacked it. Instead of the dead little *thud* it had been making, now it had that big fat *doooouum* sound. Wow. Ever since, I've made sure to keep those puppies in tune.

Anyway, after I got done tweaking my set I headed back to my room. When I got upstairs, I heard loud voices coming from the girls' room. The door was open and when I walked by I could see the whole gang in there, so I popped in. Brad was raving away about something, but when he saw me he stopped cold.

"Well, well . . . there he is now. So, what part of *no* doesn't your little brain understand?"

Huh . . . ? "What are you talking about?"

"You know damn well what I'm talking about. 'If Dad says no, go ask Mom,' right? Well, that kind of behind-the-back crap doesn't work with me, man!" He was totally pissed, but I still didn't have a clue.

"One more time—what the hell are you talking about?"

"Don't give me that shit! I turn down your precious little demo, so you try to get the others to gang up on me. Well, let me tell you something." He looked around the room. "Hell, let me tell you *all* something. You think you can dump all over me and get away with it just because there's more of you? Well, guess what—this ain't a goddamn democracy. And you know why?" He was full-on raging now. "Huh? Do any of you even have a *clue?*" He whipped his head around, glaring at each of us. "Because you aren't worth shit without me, that's why!"

I've never seen anyone actually "storm out of a room" before, but that's exactly what he did, knocking over his chair in the process and slamming the door behind him.

Dead freakin' silence . . .

"*So* . . . ," I finally said. "Anyone want to fill me in?"

"Well," Danny said, "I listened to that song again, and then I ran into Jamie. I played it for her, and she liked it, too. So we played it for Brad, and he just came unglued. Big-time. That's all I know."

"What song?" Glenn asked.

"That tune Zach found, 'Every Day.'"

Glenn just looked at me and raised his eyebrows. *Shit.*

I turned to the others. "Here's the deal. I'll try to make it short, but it's kinda convoluted, so hang with me." I took a deep breath and told them the story of how and why I'd tracked the song and what Brad must have thought when Danny showed up with it, wanting to cover it.

When I was done, they were quiet for a minute. Then Danny said, "You're right, that's one convoluted story, bro. So you tracked that cut?"

"I started with Glenn's guitar and vocal demo. I just added some stuff to flesh it out."

"Well, it sounds great."

"Danny's right," Amber added. "It rocks. I loved it." She tried to stifle a big yawn.

"Yeah, I can tell how excited you are," I said.

She looked embarrassed. "I'm sorry . . . long night."

Jamie looked over at Glenn. "You wrote that." It was more a statement than a question. He just nodded. "That's a wonderful song," she said.

As long as I was in full-confession mode, I decided to spill the rest. I held up my hand like a kid in class. "Um . . . there's more." They looked at me like, *Holy shit, what else?* "I was totally pissed about the way Brad treated me and the song. So I sent it to Don Davis, back in Los Robles."

"The DJ?"

"Yeah, they were taking submissions for their annual *Best in the Rockin' West* CD, so I figured what the hell. And, well . . . they picked it. It's going to be the opening track on this year's CD—drops in a couple of weeks."

"Bro, that's awesome!" Danny said. "For both of you."

Jamie gave Glenn a hug. "I'm so happy for you." She looked at me. "And I'm sure that Brad'll come around sooner or later. He always does—sometimes it just takes a while. . . ."

I wasn't at all sure about that one, but I didn't want to be negative. "Uh . . . Brad doesn't know about the Wild 107 CD thing, so maybe we shouldn't say anything. At least for now?"

They all nodded—we were definitely on the same page, but I was still feeling uneasy about the whole thing. Brad had been *flaming* when he'd left.

I went back to my room and sat on that funk-o-matic sofa, avoiding the spring at all costs. And thought. Mostly what went through my head was *This is the weirdest day ever.*

As it turns out, it wasn't over yet. Not even.

24
"The Letter"

I couldn't take sitting around that toilet of a room any longer, so I went out in search of coffee and a bite . . . and maybe a clue as to what to do next.

From: Zach Ryan [ZR99@westnet.net]
Sent: Saturday, July 17 3:57 PM
To: Kimberly Milhouse [kimmilhouse@cencast.net]
Subject: Wild West Show, etc. . . .

Yo, Kimbo—

It's been the weirdest day *ever* (among some pretty weird ones). Some goofballs woke us at oh-four-hundred by breaking into the royal motor home. We went down there and drove them off at squirt-gun-point. For reals. And all this after some idiot tried to climb onstage last night to either sing with the band or molest Jamie. Either idea was a bad one, and he ended up getting booted offstage . . . literally.

And then to come down from that O.K. Corral thing, us Musketeers went to this place all the locals call the Black & White Club for breakfast. It was the most Twilight Zone-ish joint I've ever seen. (See attached flick, and yeah, those old guys across from me are pounding shots—at six in the a.m. I sure as hell ain't in Kansas anymore, baby.)

Anyway, to get back to your email:

Hmm, rooms & tunes ... Let's see ... I did some production work on a song, and it came out pretty good. Uh, maybe *too* good. Right now Brad is flamingly pissed at yours truly because ... well, it's a long story, but some people get very territorial. 'Nuff said.

So, what are you, with your inquiring little mind? I guess that's the question of the day. To quote my favorite professor, I'll have to cogitate on that one ...

In the meantime, I've got to run—stuff is totally messed up, and I want to un-messify it before tonight's gig.
Talk later,
Z

When I got back from eating, I figured I'd swing by Brad's room and see if I could patch things up. Brad wasn't there, so I went next door to the girls' room. Nope. But Jamie and Glenn were there.

"Anyone seen Brad?" I asked.

"No, that was going to be my question," Jamie said.

"Can I come in?"

"Sure."

I didn't know where to start. "I feel pretty stupid about this whole thing. . . ." They shut me down.

"It's not your fault," they said together at exactly the same time.

"Hey, that was pretty cool," I said. "Could you try it again, in harmony?" That got a smile out of them. "We can talk about blame later. But if either of you sees Brad, could you tell him I'd like to talk to him . . . I need to try and clear things up."

"Thanks," said Jamie quietly. "I'll tell him."

Glenn looked sideways at her, then back at me. "Dude, sometimes I think you're the oldest guy in this band, instead of the other way around." He paused. "But then you'll come out with something like *'And don't come back!'* and remind us that you're still our lovable little brother."

They were both laughing when I left. As I went out the door, Jamie called out, "Zach?"

"Yeah . . ."

"We're not laughing *at* you, we're laughing *with* you. Right?"

"Yeah . . ."

✳ ✳ ✳

Okay, so if Brad wasn't going to come to me, then I guess it was my job to go to him. I figured I'd go look in the nearby bars—he was on foot, so that shouldn't be too hard, right? Maybe not, if you weren't in Butte, Montana . . . where bars apparently grow on every corner like weeds after a rainstorm. Somewhere in the middle of making the rounds—with no luck—I got an email.

From: Kimberly Milhouse [kimmilhouse@cencast.net]
Sent: Saturday, July 17 5:07 PM
To: Zach Ryan [ZR99@westnet.net]
Subject: Kevin

Zach—

God, I'm so upset I don't know where to start.

I don't really feel like talking to you, but I should at least let you know why. I just learned the truth about what happened between you and Kevin.

I'd been hearing a rumor that it had something to do with me. And really, I would have just asked you, but you've already told me your story, which was something totally different than the rumors I've been hearing.

Then I met Kevin at the mall today. And he wasn't a jerk, he was actually nice. He didn't want to tell me what had happened—I had to pull it out of him, and even then he skipped the gory details to save my feelings. He basically told me that you were making crude comments about me after that night at LoL, and he asked you to stop (he even admitted he had a crush on me, which is why he came to my defense), and then one thing led to another, and it ended up with you punching him.

I didn't want to believe him, but a *bunch* of people have told me they'd heard the same thing . . . including Ginger. And why would you make up that story about him slamming the Sock Monkeys unless you had something to hide? Why would you care about them anyway? I can't believe I actually *bought* that lame excuse.

So, I don't really know what to do at this point. Everything is completely upside down for me right now. I mean, I was thinking you were one thing, and now it's like you're suddenly the opposite. I'm *so* angry. Mostly at myself.

But the worst part is, I miss you. Not the *you* you, but the you that I *thought* was you. And that's worse than missing a real person, because there's no way to get the old you back, because you never really were.

Don't bother replying. I just need to be alone.
K

I called her. Nothing. I texted her. Nothing. I was bouncing around town like I was stuck in some out-of-control pinball game, trying to figure out what the hell to do. Finally, I sat my ass down on the curb and wrote her back.

From: Zach Ryan [ZR99@westnet.net]
Sent: Saturday, July 17 6:46 PM
To: Kimberly Milhouse [kimmilhouse@cencast.net]
Subject: RE: Kevin

Hey, there's no way I can let this go . . .

You've got your facts wrong. Way wrong. If you'd answer your damn phone, I could explain it to you. Yes, I told you some minor fiction about what happened, but it's nothing compared to the crap that slimy loser's been spreading around. I can't believe you're even listening to him . . . if you are, then there's no point trying to explain myself.

But I will say this one more time: You're wrong about this. One hundred percent, one hundred eighty degrees, completely, absolutely . . . *wrong.*

You let me know when you want to hear the real truth, and we'll talk.
Z

God, was I pissed . . . I had all kinds of stupid thoughts. Like driving back home right then and making Kimber listen to me. Like finding Kevin Flanders and finishing the job I'd started at the 7-Eleven. Like doing the same thing to that suck-butt Toby, who was part of the reason I was stuck out here a zillion miles away from home in the first place.

I called Kimber again. Her phone was turned off, which it *never* was. I thought about calling Kyle, but he probably wouldn't have a lot to say to me, either. I mean, I'd lied to him about the whole Kevin thing, too. And now he thought I'd been going around making rude comments about his little sister, so he probably wouldn't be the most receptive person in the world, either. I even thought about calling Kimber's friend Ginger, which shows just how stupid I was. First of all, the only one I knew with her number was Kimber, but beyond that, who was she going to believe?

Finally, I took a deep breath and told myself to chill. . . . If she wanted to buy that bullshit, there was nothing I could do about it, right? If she was going to take that loser's word over mine, that was her choice, right? If she was going to be that way, he could freakin' have her.

Right?

* * *

I got back to the club with an hour to go. I was really hoping to get some time with Brad—to clear at least *one* thing up before the gig—but I couldn't find him anywhere. And the other guys were gone, too.

I went back to my room and tried to read . . . tried to

sleep . . . tried to not feel trapped in this roach-infested shit hole. All with zero success. I gave up and went downstairs at a quarter till, but I still didn't see the others, so I just went up onstage and fiddled with my drums, making sure everything was right.

In a packed club that relies more on open doors than air-conditioning (can you say the Four Leaf Clover?), I like to have a water bottle and a hand towel nearby and, if possible, a little clip-on fan clamped to a cymbal stand blowing air at me. Looking at the crowd that was already packing the place, I knew it was gonna be warm. I checked my set list taped to the floor—this would be a bad night to screw up, but it was going to be hard to keep my head in the game.

I shouldn't have even bothered. . . . With about five minutes to go Glenn, Jamie, Danny, and Amber hustled into the room.

"Where's Brad?" I asked.

They looked at each other and their faces fell. Not good.

"Uh, we were out looking for him, and we were really hoping he'd be here when we got back," Danny said.

"And you called him? Left a message?" They were nodding as I spoke. "Then maybe *I* should text him, saying it's my bad, I'm sorry, I'm an idiot, and now won't he please come home and save us?" As I eyed the rowdy-ass crowd, I realized I was only half kidding about that last part. They'd freakin' *kill* us if we didn't play.

Apparently, I wasn't the only one thinking that. Mr. Friendly there, behind the bar, yelled "Hey!" at us and pointed to the clock angrily.

"Wouldn't help," Glenn replied to me as he waved back at

the bartender, "and we don't have time. We've got to get playing. Now."

"Uh, so we're going to just jam for a while, waiting for Brad to show?" Danny asked.

"No, we're going to get up there and play songs." He turned to Jamie and me. "Look, I know a bunch of tunes, and you each know some, too. We'll just do those for as long as we can. It'll have to do."

That was going to be a challenge, since if it was a song the band already did, then Brad was likely the only one who'd ever sung it. So they'd mostly be songs we hadn't all played together before.

"Man, we'll have to totally be on our toes for that," I said.

"No kidding," Danny said.

"Yeah, we'll try to keep it simple," Glenn said. "Let's go."

And that was our cheerful preflight.

As I got up onstage and got ready, I found myself getting majorly pissed all over again. Unless he'd been hit by a truck or something, Brad had some serious explaining to do. No matter what, you didn't leave your bandmates hanging out to dry like this.

Suddenly I knew exactly what I wanted to sing. "Hey, I can at least make the first one easy," I said. "Let's start with our usual opener—I know it."

"You sure?" Glenn asked. "That ain't no halfhearted song."

"If I can't cover it now, I'll never be ready for it."

"Okay—you got it." He hit the lights, and without any introduction he went blazing into the opening riff of "So Far," by Buckcherry. I really liked that song because it was about why musicians—at least the ninety-nine percent of us that aren't rich and famous rock stars—do what we do. It had a few f-bombs in it, and some venues weren't cool with that.

But I was pissed, and the FLC wasn't exactly a class joint anyway. I just spat out the words, and after the first time, Glenn got with it and jumped in on backing vocals. I may not be the best singer in the world, but I made up for it in attitude. At least, no one complained, and we actually got a few hoots and hollers afterward.

"Hey, B-Bro, that wasn't half bad," Danny said, with a big grin on his face.

"Yeah," Glenn agreed. "Pretty damn solid. I think this might work."

"Thanks, but it's mostly gonna have to be you from here on out, because I only know a few tunes from our set list." If Glenn knew how to play and sing a song, he could show the chord changes to Danny and Jamie and tell me the basic groove, and we could probably get through it alive.

"Okay . . ."

So on we went. We stuck with standards and classic blues tunes, and Glenn sang most of them. It was actually pretty amazing, all the stuff he kept pulling out of his ass. I'm fairly sure that things looked pretty normal from the crowd's point of view, but to us it was anything but.

Once we got over the initial nervousness and realized we weren't going to get stoned to death by an angry mob, we relaxed. A little. But it was still definitely not your usual gig. We were focused on each other more than we were on the audience, as opposed to the other way around. It was weird, like we were in the flow so much that the crowd didn't even exist. Anyway, by the time we got into the middle of the second set, the song choices got kind of, um . . . interesting.

Glenn looked over at me. "You know 'Take Me to the River'?"

"Sure. Al Green or Talking Heads?"

He grinned at that and I knew I'd shed my little-brother identity again, at least for the moment. "A little of both. Four-on-the-floor, about like this . . ." He tapped his guitar in tempo with his pick.

So we go into it, only he lets the intro build for a *long* time, until it's like being at a church revival or something. I'm talking like a couple of minutes nonstop, just vamping, and the room is absolutely pounding. Then suddenly he stops playing and tucks his guitar behind his back, so it's just me and Danny playing the groove. I automatically strip it way down, so I'm just playing the kick and a little hi-hat. I mean, it's still a solid-ass pulse, but it's way sparse. That's how you put a spotlight on something—get so simple that it grabs people's attention and makes them focus on what's coming next.

Then Glenn strides up to the mic and grabs the stand like he's gonna preach to the congregation, but he's looking side-ways, over toward the keyboards.

> *I don't know why I love you like I do*
> *After all these changes you put me through . . .*

It was like Glenn's intensity fed my anger, which found its way into my drumming, which fed his intensity even more. I guess what I'm saying is, that song *killed*.

It suddenly hit me that what I really wanted was for someone to be recording the gig, because it was clearly something special. But even a recording is nothing like being there, in the eye of it all. You play your part, it goes out into the universe, then it's gone. Forever. All you can hope to do is experience it as it happens and remember it the best you can. Believe me, I tried.

We were all over the map that night, song-selection-wise. We followed that with "Can't Stand Losing You," "Girlshaped-lovedrug," and "Want You Bad." All with Glenn singing.

Then Jamie says something to Glenn and he nods, then he comes back to me.

"You know 'Right Hand Man'?"

I shook my head. "Sorry. What's the groove?"

"Well, that's the thing—Danny and I'll be playing in 7/4, but you just stay in 4/4 the whole time, no matter what. It'll feel weird at first, but trust me on this."

I nodded. "Got it."

Danny started this riff on the bass, and it seemed like it dropped a beat at the end of every other bar. But I did like Glenn said and played it straight instead of trying to follow him, and sure enough, it wrapped back around and things lined up. I thought it was pretty cool, but that was just the beginning, because then Jamie started singing. Holy freakin' wow. She normally had a nice, smooth voice, but this was just plain *nasty*.

Let me use your toothbrush. Have you got a clean shirt?
My panties in a wad at the bottom of my purse . . .

Whoa. She was in full-on skank mode, but she made you buy it. Big-time.

After the song was over, Glenn looked at me with his eyes open wide like, *Yeah . . . that was hot.* Then he glanced at the clock. "We've gotta stretch this one out before we break," he said. "Let's do 'The Sky Is Crying.'" He looked at Jamie. "Hey, JD-girl . . . can you get an old Hammond sound, like a B-3 or something?"

"Sure." She hit a few buttons on her keyboard, then played a note.

"Perfect!" Glenn said. "It's a blues, in C." He turned to me and Danny. "You guys know it?"

"Stevie Ray version?" I asked.

"Yeah, slow 6/8 thing."

Danny and I had a wordless exchange, then I nodded. "We're all over it."

Glenn stood at the microphone, but the crowd was noisy, not paying much attention. "Hey, *listen up!*" he belted into the mic. It sounded like a football coach addressing a team. Everyone got quiet all of a sudden and looked up to see what the heck was going on. "*Shhhh . . . ,*" he said softly. "Listen close. Can you hear it?" Then he started singing.

The sky is crying . . .

On the word *crying* I came in hard and slow, trying to lay down that big fat slammin' blues thing. Danny was right there in the pocket, totally locked in on the kick drum. After the first verse Glenn took a little solo, fast and furious. Then after the next verse he nodded to Jamie and she took twelve bars, playing a really tasty solo of her own. He sang another verse, then he walked over and stood in front of his amp, with his back to the crowd. He reached over and threw that sucker wide open and freakin' cut loose. I don't mean he played a bunch of busy, show-offy crap. I mean it was one of those tell-a-story-with-your-ax moments, and it totally translated. Long, slow, bending notes. In the middle of it he threw his Strat up behind his neck and just wailed.

Funny thing . . . it was like the opposite of the time Justin had tried it. *That* had been all about the look, the pose, the chicks-dig-it factor. In this case, I think if you'd asked Glenn afterward, he wouldn't have even been aware he'd done it. Danny and I were hammering out the groove while Glenn shredded, and in the middle of it all Danny came over to me with a big grin on his face and yelled over the music, "Double frickin' Trouble, bro!"

After he'd gotten out whatever he had to say, Glenn took it back down by bringing it around to a verse, then in classic blues fashion we came to a crashing halt just before the very last line, which Glenn sang by himself.

Can't you see the tears roll down my nose?

We got some serious applause after that, and someone yelled out, "*That's* how you do it!"

We took a break, and as we were sitting at a table off to the side of the stage trying to figure out what the hell to play next, a guy came up to us who didn't really fit in with the decor. He was kind of short, with a long leather coat, black dress shoes, and a spiky hundred-dollar haircut. And he was carrying a *briefcase*.

He just walked over and sat down, without asking or saying a word.

"Hey, guys, how's it hangin'?" he said after he'd seated himself. "I'm Corey Lankenship."

We looked at him blankly for a second. I guess we were tired.

"Uh, you know, your agent . . . ?"

25

"Why Does Love Got to Be So Sad?"

He was younger than I would have expected. Maybe Glenn's age. But he was trying hard to be a whole lot older, like a kid dressing up in his dad's suit or something.

"Sure, I remember," Glenn said, putting out his hand. "I'm Glenn Taylor. We spoke a few times on the phone." Glenn introduced the rest of us, then said, "So what brings you out here? You guys are based out of Spokane, right?"

"Sure are. But I swing out this way every few weeks to check in with our clients. I was over in Missoula today, so I figured I'd do a drive-by to see how things are going. It's only a couple of hours."

"Do you know the Dog and Pony in Bozeman?" Danny asked.

"They're only one of our best accounts. I saw Jake last week. He told me you guys were awesome—he can't wait to have you back."

"Cool," Danny said. "We liked them, too. But there's something new going on there that you might want to know about.

On Saturdays they've started this old-school classic-rock night. I figured you might want to tell your other bands so they don't get, like . . . caught unexpectedly?" He cleared his throat. "Just looking out for you, bro."

"Umm, thanks. Yeah, it's not usually my job. Uh . . . Brooke— back in Spokane—is usually the band liaison . . . yeah . . . but I'll pass the word to her. Hey, sorry if you were taken by surprise."

"*Hey*, no problem," Danny replied. It wasn't a full-on mock and I doubt if Corey even caught it, but I was having a hard time not busting up.

Corey looked like he'd just remembered something. "I thought you guys were a five-piece." He turned to Amber. "You're not in the band, right? I thought there was only one girl. . . ."

"One of our guys isn't feeling so good, so he's taking the night off," Glenn said. That was it—no apology, no detailed explanation . . . and no lie. Technically speaking.

To be honest, I was expecting to catch some grief over it. Of all the nights for our agent to drop in on us . . .

But he said, "Okay, I guess I can understand that. And hey, don't sweat it. You guys totally rock." He took out his wallet and started handing out his business card, giving one to each of us, including Amber. "Seriously, you're good. Next time we have you come out, we'll get you into some of our bigger venues." He looked at his watch. "Which reminds me—I've gotta get rolling. My Beemer's parked out front and this place can be a war zone after midnight. Say hi to Alex for me." He got up. "Hey, check you later." And he was gone.

We just looked at each other, doing that shake-your-head-

and-chuckle thing. Finally, Danny said, "Somewhere there's a sales office at a car dealership with his name on it."

Q: WHY ARE SET BREAKS LIMITED TO TWENTY MINUTES?
A: SO THEY DON'T HAVE TO RETRAIN THE DRUMMER.

"Hey, guys, here's a little story from K's Choice," Jamie was saying to the crowd. Glenn and Danny were still tuning and plugging in, and she was just tap-dancing for a minute until they were ready. "It's about being in a band on the road. And take it from me, this is no exaggeration."

She had a piano sound going and she played a few chords that sounded familiar, then she sang softly:

When your pubic hair's on fire . . .

Without thinking, I joined in on backing vocals with the tagline: *Something's wrong.*

She looked over at me and smiled before the next line.

When you think you're the Messiah . . .

And again:

Something's wrong.

By the time she got to the next verse, the other guys were good to go and they'd started singing the *something's wrong* parts along with me and Jamie. Danny waved Amber up, too, and all three of them were standing around Glenn's mic, singing.

Danny and Amber don't really sing, but you get enough people together and—as long as some of them can carry a tune—it'll work, at least in a sing-along fashion. And on some level I guess it did, because the crowd really seemed to enjoy it.

Glenn had his Strat on after this, so I called him and Danny over and said, "Let's do the original. 'Every Day.'"

Glenn was hesitant, but Danny leaned on him. "C'mon, GT. It's a killer tune, and I've heard it enough to get through it. What is it, A to E to D on the verse?"

"Yeah, with a G at the top of the chorus. Got that, JD?" Jamie nodded back.

"Cool," Danny went on. "Let's fire it up and see what happens. Who's gonna care, tonight?"

Glenn shrugged, but that was good enough for me. I said into my mic, "This is one of our original tunes, written by our guitar player, Glenn 'GT' Taylor. Hope you enjoy it as much as we do."

Glenn turned to me and kind of made a face, but I just pulled an Alicia and stuck out my tongue. Then I started clicking my sticks in time and counted it off. He had no choice—he started playing.

It's funny. I'd heard that thing a million times during the production process, but this was the first time I'd actually played it with a band. Hell, this was the first time the song had ever really been *played*, period. And it felt even better than the recording. Way better.

The intro drove hard, with me pounding the kick and snare and Danny doing a much better job with the bass line than I ever could have. Then we pulled way back for the vocals.

You go north
and I go south . . .
every day.
You hear words
that don't come from my mouth . . .
every day.

And hearing him sing it—the raw emotion in his voice—I got chills. Seriously.

I sang the *every day* parts, like I had on the recording, and Jamie joined in with me in unison, strengthening the line.

By the time we got to the solo, we were burning. I heard something that made me look up, and I had to smile. Amber was standing next to Danny, whacking the crap out of the tambourine on the backbeats and making my snare sound even stronger.

I kept the energy level up through the repeat chorus and all the way to the end, never letting up until we got to the big crash ending. And the crowd loved it. One guy even yelled out, "That was bitchin', man! You got any more originals like that?"

"Not yet," Glenn admitted. "But here's one you'll like." We ended up doing "Bad Luck"—which I thought was pretty appropriate for me tonight—then followed it up with a bunch of other strong tunes.

Near the end of the set—as we finished up "Naive," by the Kooks—Glenn broke a string. He started to go for his backup guitar, which is what you'd normally do at a gig until your next break, but this wasn't a normal gig and there weren't any more breaks—we were close to being done. Plus, I knew he'd way rather be playing Blackie. So I stopped him.

"Just change your string, we'll cover." I was thinking that Danny, Jamie, and I would jam for a minute, but then I remembered how much the audience had liked "Something's Wrong." It only had a few simple chords, and I knew them.

I strapped on Glenn's acoustic and stepped up to his microphone. Damn, it felt like I was naked. I'd never sung onstage without the comfort of being behind my drumset, but this was the perfect night for it. "We're going to do a little sing-along," I said into the mic. There were a few grumbles, so I said, "This is so easy you can do it if you're hammered. In fact, it'll probably sound *better* if you're hammered!" That brought a few laughs. "It goes like this—we sing a line, then you sing *something's wrong*. Easy money, honey." Then I strummed the opening chord and jumped into one of the verses.

> *When you like music more than life,*
> *Something's wrong.*
> *When you start sleeping as you drive,*
> *Something's wrong.*

Every time I got to *something's wrong*, I pointed to the crowd and they sang it. Okay, they more like drunkenly shouted it, but at least they went along with it. I looked over my shoulder—Glenn wasn't quite done yet. So I went to the front of the stage and held the mic out and let people make up their own first lines, then everyone would join in on the refrain. Some of them were lame, of course, but some were pretty damn funny. One girl obviously needed a change in her relationship status:

When your boyfriend is a monkey,
  Something's wrong.
When his socks are smelling funky,
  Something's wrong.

And then this came from the grizzled old guy next to her, who sang back at her:

So you need a new banana
  Something's wrong.
But you're stuck in Butte, Montana!
  Something's wrong.

I don't know if he was a popular local dude or what, but the crowd totally cracked up at him. Either way, I figured I should quit while I was ahead, so I wrapped it up.

By then Glenn was good to go. "Thanks, man," he said to me. "That was some first-rate tap-dancing."

Then Jamie sang the hell out of "Can't Getcha Out of My Mind," by Deep Dark Robot, her voice almost cracking on the line *I'm feelin' like a junkie that's jonesin' for a broken heart....* When that was over, we realized we were just about done. We were debating what to do for our last song when someone shouted out, "Clapton!" Then other people started joining in. "Yeah, play some Clapton!" Man, these guys loved their oldies....

I figured we'd do "Crossroads," like last time, or one of the old barroom standards, like "Cocaine" or maybe even "Bell

Bottom Blues." I looked over at Glenn for some direction, but he was messing with his amp. Then he walked to the front of the stage and just stood there, looking down. I couldn't be sure from where I was sitting, but I had the impression his eyes were closed. Then he looked up toward the ceiling and, without checking with us or anything, whipped out the signature riff from "Layla."

That's all he played at first, just those half dozen opening notes, and he let the last one sustain. The crowd recognized it immediately and went crazy. Glenn milked that one note until it built into a howl of feedback from his cranked-up Marshall combo, then he did one of those dive-bomb-down-the-guitar-neck things and went into the main groove of the song.

I caught Danny's attention and held one finger to my lips and twirled my other finger in the air—*Wait and let it build a little.* I let Glenn go through that part four times—instead of twice, like it usually goes—before I came in on full drumset, and during the third and fourth times Danny and I built up pounding eighth notes all the way through, starting from nothing and slowly adding tension, so that when we finally exploded and joined Glenn in the groove, it was this massive release.

I kinda channeled Steve Gadd's take on it and played just a hair behind the beat. It's hard to explain, but it makes it sound more . . . profound or something. And I definitely got my money's worth—I sat there and took it all in, even as I played. And what a show it was. . . .

Glenn absolutely nailed the song, guitar *and* vocals, and that's not an easy thing to do with that tune—usually one guy plays the soaring guitar melody while someone else sings. And halfway through it I realized I wasn't hearing any keys. I glanced over at Jamie but she was just sitting there, not moving, watching Glenn. He came out of the first chorus and went into the next verse.

I tried to give you consolation
When your old man had let you down.
Like a fool, I fell in love with you,
Turned my whole world upside down . . .

I couldn't blame her—this was a perfect example of what I was always trying to tell the guys in the Sock Monkeys about emotion overriding perfection. Yeah, I'm sure Brad could have sung it technically better, and yeah, it would have been nice to have another guitar playing, but none of that mattered—this had that real-deal thing going on that made everything else trivial.

Anyway, we made it to the end of the rock part of the song and I figured we'd probably wrap things up right there, but as my cymbal swells were starting to fade away and the applause started, Jamie began playing the slow piano coda that builds into the instrumental second movement of the whole thing. Man, that's got to be one of the prettiest pieces of music ever written.

I let her get through it by herself once, then I came in with a simple ride-cymbal accompaniment and Danny started playing that real smooth bass line. Glenn did this thing where he'd back off his volume pedal, pick the string silently, then step on the pedal and let the note swell. It totally changed the attack of the note, making it sound more like a violin than a guitar. If Kimber were here, she would have called it "ethereal."

We went through that cycle several times, each time getting a little bigger and a little fuller until we were freakin' *soaring*. My strongest memory of the evening is gazing out over the crowd and seeing all these faces looking up at us, just listening and swaying in time to the music. As far as I was concerned, it could have gone on forever. . . .

26

"Midnight Confessions"

We didn't have to be anywhere until Tuesday, when we started at West Yellowstone, so we were going to meet at noon on Sunday and strike everything and load up our gear like usual. But I ended up staying to tear down and pack up all my gear after the other guys disappeared. It wasn't my incredible work ethic—I just had way too many things swirling through my head to go to sleep. But when I was halfway done taking my set apart, I saw Jamie walk up to the bar and get a cup of coffee. All of a sudden coffee sounded good.

The place had just about emptied out as I sat on the stool next to her. "How's it going?"

She shrugged. "Okay, I guess." She was way subdued, nothing at all like she'd been onstage just a little while ago. "How about you?"

I didn't *even* want to get into the Kimber thing. "I'm fine." The woman behind the bar came by and I asked her for a cup of coffee. She seemed a lot nicer than Mr. Friendly and I briefly wondered if it was going to show up on our tab. I turned back to Jamie and held my hands up. "So? Any word on Brad?"

"Yeah. He's up in the room, crashed out."

I almost asked, *Whose room?* but I didn't. "Any, uh, explanation on where he was?"

"Not really . . ." She glanced over at me, then looked down at her coffee. "He wasn't in any condition to explain anything," she added, "but wherever he was, they were serving green beer."

"Huh?"

"I saw it. Coming back up."

Whoa—TMI. But I just nodded, as if seeing people puke up green beer was something that happened every day.

"He'll be fine tomorrow," she said. She shook her head slowly. "And I'm sure he'll explain and apologize. He always does."

"He's done this before?"

She sighed. "Well, not exactly like this, but he can be, um . . . impulsive." She thought about it. "He's like the yang to GT's yin."

"Yeah, I can see that. But Glenn wasn't exactly Mr. Passionless tonight, was he?"

I meant it as a joke. Mostly. But she took it seriously. "No," she said, shaking her head slowly as she considered it. "No, he certainly was not."

The hell with it. It was 2:30 a.m. after a bizarre gig after a bizarre day following a *really* bizarre morning—was there ever going to be a better time? "It's none of my business . . ." *Other than the fact that I'm a thousand miles away from home with you guys, stuck inside some sort of weird reality show.* "But what's the deal with you and Glenn? I mean, I don't know much of the band history or anything, but I'm not blind. . . ."

She took a deep breath and let out a big shaky sigh. I was thinking of a way to backpedal when I realized there were tears in her eyes.

"Oh, hey," I said. "I'm really sorry. I didn't mean to—"

She held up her hand. "No, it's fine . . . I actually appreciate you asking." She took a sip of her coffee, then called over to the bartender, who was nearby. "I know it's after last call, but is there any way I could get a shot of Baileys in here?"

The woman looked around, then took Jamie's cup, dumped it, and poured in fresh coffee followed by a good slug of Irish cream. "It's on the house, honey."

"Oh, thanks. I never do that, but it's been a rough day."

"I can tell." She winked. "Just don't tell Alex."

Jamie smiled. "Cross my heart."

She sat back, took a sip, and kinda went *aah* . . . I swear, I almost asked her what it tasted like, but I caught myself in time.

She looked over at me. "GT's nice. Super-nice. And he's smart, and he's really talented. And I'll kill you if you tell him I said this, but he's sexy as hell, too."

And I'm sitting there thinking, *And the problem with all this is . . . ?*

I guess I was thinking a little too loud. "But the problem is," she said, "he's married to his music. Or at least seriously engaged. You ever see that old movie *That Thing You Do?*"

I shook my head. "Sorry."

"Watch it sometime—you'd love it. The main character is a

drummer who joins this band at the last minute and has a big influence on them, changing their destiny."

"Huh."

"I know, right? But my point is, there's a girl in the film who's in love with the bandleader, only all he cares about is his music—he's the main writer and singer. He's also a butthead who treats her badly, and that's where the analogy is kind of backward, because GT isn't like that at all—in some ways he's actually more like the drummer, who's a smart but positive guy. But he does share that trait about putting the music first. Trust me."

"Have you ever talked to him about that? I mean, specifically?"

"No. He is who he is, and that's not a bad thing at all."

"You know, you sound just like him—he said almost the exact same thing to me once."

She snorted. "Well, *that's* just great."

I laughed. "Hey, I call 'em like I see 'em. But you never know—it might be worth a try."

"Look, Zach, I know you like GT. You've got a little of that same attitude in you yourself. It's sweet of you to put in a good word for him, and maybe you're looking out for me, too. But I think it's too little, too late." She paused. "I've been in a band with Brad for four or five years now, and we've always gotten along really well. But for most of that time he's had one girl-friend or another."

"And now?" I had a sinking feeling I already knew the answer.

"And now he's single, been that way for a while, since shortly after GT joined. He's fun. He's a regular guy. Sure, he's a great singer, but he doesn't just live for music. That's the difference."

I was throwing my opinion around right and left tonight, so why stop now? "I don't think that Glenn only lives for his music. I think he's someone who follows his passion, regardless, and I think that would hold true whether it was music"—I looked at her—"or you."

She didn't say anything for a long time. "You know, you're actually quite a bit like him," she finally said. "And I mean that as a compliment. Mostly. You're going to make some girl very happy someday." She took a drink of her coffee and laughed. "Or miserable."

"God, you're psychic tonight," I mumbled. I nodded toward her cup. "So, how is that?"

She slid it over and I took a sip. "Wow, that's good!" I took another, bigger swig.

She pulled it back in mock horror. "In that case, stay away— you're a mere child!" She got serious. "Really, Zach, thanks for caring . . . you've given me something to think about. Not that that makes it any easier." She smiled, but it was the saddest smile I've ever seen. "I'd better get going now."

"Yeah, me too. Hey—one question. The girl? In that movie?"

"Yeah . . . ?"

"Who'd she end up with?"

She stopped and thought about it. "Hmm. I guess you'd say she followed her passion."

Q: WHAT DO YOU CALL A DRUMMER WHO BREAKS UP WITH HIS GIRLFRIEND?

A: HOMELESS.

I woke up before nine o'clock and couldn't get back to sleep. I lay there for a while thinking about Kimber's email, but *that* got old really quick, so I rolled out of bed, got dressed quietly, and went down to the club.

I had the rest of my stuff packed up and was starting in on coiling up the PA cables when Glenn showed up.

"Hey, you don't have to do that all by yourself," he said. "The others'll be down in a while and we'll all tear down."

"Couldn't sleep, so I thought I'd make myself useful."

"Same here. I'm thinking about getting paid, actually."

"Uh . . . we didn't get paid last night?" Usually the managers paid us on Saturday night. Sometimes they'd even pay you before you went on, so they didn't have to deal with it afterward on a late night.

"Nope, couldn't find him anywhere. So I'm going looking. Want to join me?"

"Sure."

Glenn went over to some guy cleaning up behind the bar. He was like Mr. Friendly's brother or something, but more grumpy than downright mean.

"How's it going?" Glenn said.

Mr. Happy kinda nodded, but not even a microscopic hint of a smile.

"We're looking for Alex. Is he around?"

"Who wants to know?"

"We're the band. We'll be pulling out in a few hours, and we need to get paid."

"Ain't seen 'im. He don't always come in on Sundays."

Glenn thought about this. "Okay, thanks. Would you do us a favor? If you see him, mention that we'd like to settle up today, because we weren't planning on staying over tonight."

Mr. Happy just nodded, then went back to wiping down the scarred-up bar.

As we walked away, I said quietly to Glenn, "So what do we do now—wait around all day in case His Majesty shows up?"

"Not if we can help it."

We went back toward the stage, but Glenn kept going until we were outside. He looked up a number in his phone, then punched *send* and turned the speaker on.

"Yeah?" That would be one Mr. Happy, best receptionist in the West.

"Hey, howzit goin', this is Mike," Glenn said quickly in a low, gruff voice. "Need ta talk ta Alex."

"Hang on a sec, he's in the back." There was a click, then someone picked up the line.

"This is Alex."

Glenn hung up.

"Come on, let's go," he said.

"Go where?"

"To get paid."

"Maybe I should bring my cymbal stand?" I was joking.

"Probably not a bad idea." I had to look twice to see that he was kidding. I think.

We went back inside and worked onstage, pulling cables and coiling them up, killing a few minutes before Glenn said, "Follow me."

We headed over near the bar, but we went past it and through the door to the back. There was a sign on it that said EMPLOY- EES ONLY, but we went through it like we worked there.

Mr. Happy said "Hey!" in his cheerful way, but Glenn just said "Alex is waiting for us," and kept on going.

The FLC was in a hundred-year-old brick building, like most of the places in that part of town, and there were lots of little rooms off the winding, narrow hallway. We poked around un- til we finally came to a ratty little office, where Alex and Mr. Friendly were talking. They both stopped and looked up when we came in.

"Who let you back here?" Alex asked.

"It's Sunday," Glenn said, ignoring his question. "We're down the road in a couple of hours, soon as we're packed. So we came to settle up."

"Yeah, I was gonna talk to you about that." Uh-oh. "Looks like you boys didn't fulfill your end of the contract."

"What are you talking about?"

He dug through a pile of papers on the messy desk in front of him, then held up a one-page printout. "It's a copy of your contract." He handed it to Glenn. "How many pieces does it say the band Bad Habit has?"

Glenn didn't even look at it. "Five."

"Well, there you go. Now, if you boys'll excuse me . . ."

"Wait a minute. What does that mean?" Glenn said.

"That means you didn't live up to your end of the contract, plain and simple."

"So you're saying the *one* guy who missed *one* night doesn't get paid for that night, then? Fine by me."

Alex shook his head. "Not quite that simple. You violated the contract, so I don't have any legal obligation to pay you anything."

"You want to stiff us for the whole week because one guy was out sick one time? After we played here five nights?" Glenn was calm on the outside but I could tell he was righteously pissed.

This was complete bullshit. "Time for the cymbal stand?" I asked under my breath.

He never looked away from Alex. "Not yet."

"Look, guys," Alex said. "Don't get too upset. I'll contact Corey and I'm sure we'll come to some kind of agreement."

"That's kind of funny, because Corey was here last night and he didn't have any problem with the fact that there were only four of us. In fact, he said we were great. And I noticed your customers didn't seem to mind, either. What was your bar take for last night?"

It was Alex's turn to ignore the question. "I never said I wasn't going to pay you. I just said I'll have to negotiate with the agency first."

"Maybe so. But then again, maybe not. It's impossible for a band to collect once they're out of state, and there's no way we can afford to stick around and take you to court and all that. And you know it."

Alex didn't say anything. Finally, he shrugged. "That's the way you want to see it, fine. I'll talk to Corey, and he'll be in touch with you. Now, I've got work to do. . . ."

When we didn't move, Mr. Friendly finally spoke. "Boss, you want I should get these guys outta here?"

"Not so fast," Glenn said. "There's a little something he

might want to know first." He sat on the corner of Alex's desk, right in front of him, and leaned in and talked quietly. "A couple of hours after Friday's gig, some guys broke into our motor home out back."

"I'm sorry to hear that."

"I'll bet. But the interesting part is, they were your patrons. And they were pretty bold about the whole thing, too. We had to stick a gun in their faces to drive them off, and even then we came this close"—he held up his fingers half an inch apart— "to dropping the hammer on one of them, because he was just too drunk to get it. But they eventually put our stuff down and left. And like I said, we can't stick around and we didn't want to make a big stink, so we let it go at that. But I'm thinking maybe we need to do our civic duty and contact the police after all. They might be interested to know *your* customers go around robbing citizens right outside *your* club, especially after *you've* been serving them way beyond the point where you should cut them off. Hell, the local paper and TV news might be interested in that, too."

"You lying son of a bitch, you're bluffing."

"I might be a son of a bitch, but I'm not lying and I'm sure as hell not bluffing—that really happened. I'm only asking for what we earned."

Alex thought for a minute. "Okay, I'll pay you for Tuesday through Friday." He folded his arms. "And that's it. Take it or leave it."

I'd had enough. As they were yakking away, I reached across the desk, picked up the phone, and dialed 911.

"Silver Bow County Sheriff's Office. Is this an emergency?"

"Not at the moment. I want to know if I can still file a report on a robbery that happened early yesterday morning."

"Why, yes you can. What's your location? We can have a patrol car come by and take a report."

I held the phone against my chest and said loudly, interrupting the conversation, "Excuse me! What's the address here? The police dispatcher wants to know so she can send an officer by to take our report."

All of a sudden everyone got quiet.

Alex looked at me. I just stared back at him, the phone still in my hand. Finally, he spoke. "Okay . . ."

27
"All Apologies"

We played it cool until we got out of the office, but once we'd escaped with the money, we were slapping hands like a Little League team that'd just won the World Series.

"Man, that was classic," Glenn said, and I couldn't argue with him.

We went back into the club and started tearing down sound and lights. After a while the other guys began trickling in— Danny, then Amber, then finally Brad and Jamie.

When Brad showed up, Glenn said, "How's it going?"

Actually, I was expecting maybe an apology or something, if not to me, then at least to the band for leaving them high and dry. But all he said was "I'm good." That was it.

"Well, *I'm* not." Whoa. I was stunned to hear that come from *my* mouth. "I get why you're pissed at me, because of that whole stupid song thing . . . which I'm sorry about, by the way. But there's no way you should have screwed the whole band and bailed on the gig last night."

Brad gave me that same look I'd seen yesterday and started

to open his mouth as I braced for him to go off on me. And then . . .

"He's completely right."

Jamie had spoken very quietly, but it shut Brad down like a bucket of cold water. I looked at her like, *Thanks*.

"Hey, it was only one night," Brad finally said, "and it's not like this dive matters to anyone. Apparently, you guys covered okay."

"Right," Glenn said. "No big deal . . . especially if you don't care about getting paid."

"Huh?"

"Yeah, *huh*. We're in violation of our contract because of you, and our buddy Alex basically said *Screw you, I ain't paying you. You wanna stick around Montana for six months and sue me, go right ahead*." Glenn let that sink in for a moment. "And if not for some quick thinking by our not-so-baby brother here, we'd be walking out empty-handed right now." He caught Brad's eye. "So you owe him a few thousand dollars' worth of thanks."

"C'mon, Alex was just yanking your chain—"

Glenn cut him off. "It's also not a big deal, *if* you don't care about having a band anymore."

Brad squinted. "What the hell is that supposed to mean?"

"It means if you ever pull something like that again, I'm out of here."

"Where do you get off with that shit? Lemme tell you something. This band was up and running long before I hired you, and we'll be playing long after you're gone. You think we couldn't do our gigs without you?"

"Yeah, you probably could," I piped in. "But good luck doing them without a drummer." Boy, my mouth was really enjoying running the show today, wasn't it?

He glared at me. "Oh, so now you're leaving, too? After we picked you up off the shit pile?"

"I don't *want* to, but I also don't want to worry you're gonna bail every time we have a disagreement." I just shook my head.

Danny spoke up. "He's right, man—that wasn't cool."

Brad looked at all of us. The room was dead quiet. Finally, he nodded. "Okay, you guys are right. I was totally pissed, but still, I shouldn't have let that push me into doing something stupid." He let that hang in the air a minute. "So, we good?"

To be honest, I wasn't. But I would have been a total jerk to say *No, your little half-assed non-apology didn't really do it for me.* So I said yeah, like everyone else, and we all bumped fists and had a group hug.

Then we packed everything up and got the hell out of there.

Q: WHAT DO YOU CALL A DRUMMER WITH HALF A BRAIN?
A: GIFTED.

As we headed east on I-90 on our way toward Yellowstone, I thought about the whole deal with Brad. I don't really know why I was wasting time worrying about it—*he* owed *me* an apology and not the other way around.

Right?

But something was nagging at me. It took me a while, but somewhere between Butte and what Kimber would have described as the ironically named town of Manhattan, Montana, I figured out what it was. . . .

Apologies aren't really for when you're absolutely certain you're a hundred percent at fault. I mean, by then the whole world knows it anyway, and even a totally self-centered jerk pretty much has to cough it up.

Right?

* * *

We stopped at a Subway in Belgrade to eat. And when we were about done, just sitting around, it was quieter than normal. Like something was still hanging there, invisible.

"Uh, I'd like to say something," I announced. I wasn't exactly sure *what* I was going to say, but I hated the vibe that was in the air and I had to do something.

"If it's about what I did, just drop it," Brad said.

"No, it's about what *I* did." I took a drink of water. "I just want to apologize for this whole thing. I own a big piece of this because . . . well, because I wove this whole tangled web in the first place. It would have been a lot better if I'd just played the song for everyone at the same time and been honest about what it was. So if nothing else, I've learned I should say what I think."

I took a deep breath. "So . . . here's what I think." I looked at Brad. "I think you're a great singer, just like Jamie and Glenn and Danny are great at what they do."

"Hey, hey! I think you're leaving someone out here," Amber threw in.

I laughed. "Sorry. You're an outstanding outlaw-tambourine-dancer-girl-type creature. Definitely."

"That's better!"

I turned back to Brad. "But besides being a great singer, you're also a freakin' great front man, which is a whole different thing. Well, besides being a great guitarist, part of what Glenn does is write awesome songs. And the only way to make it to the next level is to have some good original material. It doesn't mean Glenn has to write everything by himself—it can be him, or him and you, or the whole band jamming together." I paused. "But I think that's the next step. In case anyone's interested." I stopped then, before I wore out my soapbox.

The table went graveyard for a minute, then Jamie said, "That makes a lot of sense—we should be spending more time working on original material. And besides being a great drummer, Zach's really good at arranging and tracking music." She looked at Brad. "Don't you think?"

Brad nodded. "Like I said, he's our baby brother/den mother."

I let it go. If it made him feel better to put me in that little box, well, whatever.

✱✱✱

"We weren't expecting you guys until Tuesday," the lady said. "But let's see what we've got." She hit a few keys on her computer, then picked up the phone. "Hey, Scotty," she said. "The band's here . . . yeah, I guess they couldn't wait. So, are 207, 208, and 209 open . . . ? Well, what do we have . . . ?" She waited a minute. "Hmm. Okay, let's do that. Can you call Chuck and get right back to me? Thanks, babe."

She hung up. "I'm sorry, guys, but we're full up—we're smack in the middle of the high season. We'll definitely have rooms for you tomorrow. Meanwhile, we'll try to find you something nearby."

We were in the club at the Western Star Inn in West Yellowstone. Usually we'd take a day or two to get to the next gig, sightseeing along the way and either staying at cheap motels or crashing in the Bad-Mobile to save money. But we'd all wanted to get here and see the area and it wasn't that far from Butte, so we'd just driven straight down.

"Would it be all right if we unloaded our gear in the meantime?" Glenn asked.

"Sure, go right ahead."

So we unloaded our stuff onto the stage. Well, all except the PA and lights—this place had a nice house system and a dozen cans up in the overhead. When we were done, the lady waved us over to her desk.

She introduced herself—she was Donna, and she and her husband, Scott, ran the place—then she gave us the semi-good news. "Chuck over at the Lodge has a few rooms left, and we got him to give you the courtesy rate. You'll like it there—they have a pretty nice club, too. Not as nice as ours, of course, but not bad. He'll try to steal you from us, but don't you let him." She winked. "We serve complimentary breakfast from six to ten, so if you get here by then, we'll be happy to feed you, then we'll scare up some rooms for you as soon as they open up."

We got directions and headed over to the Lodge. Since we weren't staying long, I didn't really unpack. I just dragged in my duffel and took up residence in a chair with my laptop.

"Hey, we're gonna go find some food," Danny said, poking his head into the room. "You coming?"

"Naw," I said. "I'll catch you guys later."

As they left, I checked my email. I hadn't gotten anything since that flaming email from Kimber, which I guess was to be expected. Still, I had something I needed to say. . . .

From: Zach Ryan [ZR99@westnet.net]
Sent: Sunday, July 18 7:32 PM
To: Kimberly Milhouse [kimmilhouse@cencast.net]
Cc: Ky [EADG@cencast.net]
Subject: Sorry

Dear Kimberly—
I'm writing to apologize. Not for hitting your buddy Kevin. He deserved that and more. (It's like I told Alicia: he's lucky *Kyle* wasn't there!)

No, I'm writing to apologize for lying to you in the first place. What I should have done was either tell you what really happened or just said "I'd rather not go into it right now" and left it at that.

So, I'm sorry. It was wrong, and I won't do it again.

And now for the hard part. I mean, why should you apologize to someone for some minor deal when they've done worse and *they* haven't really apologized? But the more I thought about it, the more I realized that the answer was in the question. So I had to say it, even if it was more than he deserved. And then maybe I could forget about it and get on with my life.

Yo, Kyle—I'm copying you because I want to apologize to you too, for the same thing. Not that it matters at this point, but no more fiction, man. (Well, the part about Kevin reminding me of Toby wasn't fiction. And the part about it feeling great to deck him was *definitely* true. Those facts may be connected . . .)

Thanks for listening. I won't bug you guys anymore.
Zach

28
"Lit Up"

Dear Mom, Dad & Ali...

Butte was interesting and educational—Glenn and I attended a business meeting just this morning that was a real eye-opener. But now we're at Yellowstone! Okay, technically we're about five blocks outside the park boundary, but still, it's totally cool. Hey, Ali-Boo-Boo... I'll keep my eye out for Yogi! ☺

Cheers!
Zach

After I finished the postcard, I checked my email again. Nothing. Of course. I put my phone away and realized I was hungry. I couldn't find the other guys anywhere, so I walked down the street and got a bite at this place called the Grizzly Grubstake. It was a total tourist joint, but I had to admit it was kind of fun. The waiters were dressed like cowboys or gold miners or something, and the waitresses were like saloon girls. All the drinks were in these widemouthed jars, you ate off tin plates, and the piped-in music was pure corn pie—I expected dancing bears to take the stage any minute.

After I ate, I wandered around a little, looking at the town. And I came to the conclusion that the Grizzly Grubstake actually fit right in here. The entire town was like a set from a western, complete with wooden sidewalks and hitching posts out front of the general store. You half expected the sheriff and his posse to ride up at any moment, and I really did see a couple of guys on horses on one of the side streets.

When I got back to the hotel, I could hear music coming from the lounge and I remembered seeing something about a Sunday evening show, but I passed on it and went up to my room. And yeah, I checked my email again. *Nada*.

I dug out a recent issue of *Mix* magazine and tried to get through another article on how everything's over-compressed these days. I finally put it aside and started working on this song I'd been messing with. It was an idea that had come to me as we'd driven through the Mojave Desert between Barstow and Baker on our way out of California, using the barren landscape as a metaphor for a dry spell in someone's love life. I called it "Pray for Rain." It had a hypnotic chorus that I almost liked, but I thought the verses were lame so I was trying to rework them.

I spent a lot of time on it without much progress. I don't know . . . maybe the song hit a little *too* close to home. But I was also distracted because I could hear music from the club through the floor. Not much, but enough to make it hard to work on a song.

So I gave up and was just lying there, zoning out, when I

gradually realized that the singer in the club sounded a little like Brad. And the more I listened, the *more* it sounded like him.

I headed down. Sure enough, Brad was onstage singing "Burn This City," by Cartel. The band—two guitars, bass, and drums—seemed pretty competent, but Brad was nailing that tune with so much energy and stage presence that the other guys just disappeared. He was prowling back and forth like he was in front of twenty thousand people, and every eye in the club was on him.

The rest of the Bad Habit crew was sitting off to the side, so I pulled up a chair. When the song was over, I said, "Wow. It's been a while since I've seen him from out front—pretty impressive."

"You're not kidding," Glenn said. "He's amazing."

We kinda nodded in unison. I was thinking, *Yup, and with some great original material to work with, we could really go somewhere.* And I had a hunch Glenn was thinking something similar.

Brad stepped off the stage as the band started into some Neverland song. As I sat there listening, I felt someone lean up against me. "You wanna dance?"

Before I even turned, I could smell perfume. And booze. It was this drunk lady, in her thirties or forties, and she was majorly pressing herself up against me. "Uh, no thanks." I almost added *ma'am,* but I didn't want to get bitch-slapped in public. "I'm just here for the music."

She frowned and stumbled off, looking for some other poor bastard.

"Hey, it could've been your lucky night," Amber said with a grin.

"Yeah, and she could've been my mom."

"So?" She ruffled my hair, then made cat claws at me. "*Rowrrr*... Cougar bait!"

"Very freakin' funny ..."

Q: WHAT DO YOU CALL A BEAUTIFUL GIRL ON A DRUMMER'S ARM?

A: A TATTOO.

"So where ya'll from?"

"We're from Los Robles," Brad said. "West Coast, between L.A. and San Francisco."

"Whoa, dudes ... California! We've always wanted to play Cali."

"Cool. We've always wanted to play Monti and Wyo," Danny said with a straight face.

We were talking with the other band after they'd finished playing. They called themselves Bowl Patrol, and they were from Oklahoma. And as it turned out, they used the same booking agency we did. Corey wasn't their specific agent, but this was their third tour with the agency and they knew all about him, so we sat around and swapped Corey stories for a few minutes until a group of guys and girls came along and swept the band away with them. "Hey, we're up in three-twelve!" the drummer yelled back over his shoulder as they left. "Swing by!"

"*Hey*, check you later," Danny said in a perfect Corey imitation. They didn't get it.

We hung for a while, until Brad got up and said, "I'm going to go visit our esteemed colleagues. With a name like Bowl Patrol, I'm sure they know how to throw an after."

Right, I was thinking, *but are they sparking up a bowl or puking into one?* Either way, we all followed along.

Turns out Brad was right—by the time we got there, the after-party was in full swing. Instead of getting a few smaller rooms, these guys had opted for one large suite . . . basically a couple of bedrooms off a big, open living room and kitchen area. Perfect for four dudes. But at the moment the place was occupied by more like *forty*, which was probably double the fire-code limit.

The drummer—I think his name was Lars or Larson or something—was by the door as we walked in. "Yo, Cali dudes! Drinks in the kitchen, smoke in the shitter only, okay?"

We just nodded our thanks and looked around. It was like a scene out of a movie . . . a bunch of wannabe-rock-star-looking people standing and lounging all over the place—and all over each other—music blasting, and beer cans everywhere. We made our way to the kitchen, where I looked for a coke among all the booze. No luck. I shrugged and grabbed a Coors. As we stood there, taking it all in, the bathroom door opened and three or four guys spilled out, coughing and laughing.

After a few minutes of this Jamie said, "Amber and I are out of here—see you guys tomorrow," and they took off. I was thinking similar thoughts when one of the guitar players came up to us and bumped fists with Brad. Well, he *tried* to bump fists. He missed. But hey, a fist is a small target—I'm sure people miss all the time.

"Dude! You were awesome!" he said. "You frickin' *rocked*, man. You ever get tired of these guys, you give us a shout and we'll make a place for you. Totally, man!"

Brad was lapping it up. "Thanks, bro. You guys sounded pretty hot yourselves. Give me your email before you head out, okay?"

"No problem, man." He nodded toward the bathroom. "Hey, you wanna catch a smoke?"

Brad looked back at us and raised his eyebrows in question. I shook my head and Glenn did likewise. I looked around but I couldn't see Danny anywhere.

What I did see—among other things—was a girl over in the far corner, where she was, uh . . . *servicing* these two guys. A small crowd had gathered, and someone was getting it all on video.

"Hey, look, a star is born," Glenn commented as Brad wandered off toward the bathroom. "I think I'm gonna head back to the room, maybe get some stuff done."

"Sounds good," I said. He held his hand toward the door like, *After you.* As we were working our way through the crowd, a couple of girls came up to us.

"Hey, aren't you guys in the band?" the taller one said, talking loudly to be heard over the music.

Glenn shook his head. "Nope."

She looked us over. "Okay, maybe not the one playing here tonight, but you two are in a band, aren't you?"

Her partner nodded. "Yeah, Lacey, look at them. Totally." She turned to me and smiled. "So, what do you play?" She looked me up and down. "Drums, right?"

I was amazed she got it right, and to be honest, she *was* kinda cute. But before I could open my mouth, she took the beer out of my hand and killed it with one long swallow, then tossed the empty back over her shoulder without looking.

She wiped her mouth with the back of her hand and smiled, then she beckoned me closer with her finger. "C'mere. I wanna ask you something."

As I leaned in to hear her over the noise, she put her hand behind my neck and kissed me. Okay, it wasn't my idea, but I didn't exactly fight it, either. I mean, it was this totally beer-and-cigarette-drenched, spontaneous, nasty-ass, rock-and-freakin'-roll *kiss*. What's a boy to do . . . ?

When I finally came up for air, I saw that the other girl was evidently trying the same tactic on Glenn. "Sorry," he was saying, "not interested. And the only thing I know how to play is the radio. Thanks anyway."

She was clearly annoyed, and more than a little drunk. "What are you—gay?"

He just laughed at her. "I guess that'll be a mystery to you forever, won't it?" He turned to me. "You coming, or should I send out a search party in the morning?"

The girl was still hanging on me. I glanced at her. Man, she was ready. And willing. And I was certainly single. Big sigh. "Thanks for sharing," I finally told her, "but I've gotta go."

She stepped away, more confused than angry. "Whatever . . ."

She and her friend headed off the way they'd come, and Glenn and I eventually made it out the door. Once we were in the hallway, where it was quieter, he said, "Man, you're smarter than I thought."

"You know, smart is the *last* thing I feel right now."

"Don't I know. But you'll feel it tomorrow."

I was beginning to wonder if he'd snuck into that bathroom after all, but I let it go. "So, why the big secret about playing music? I mean, it's not like we *don't* want people to know who we are, and maybe even show up at our gigs. . . ."

He looked over at me. "Women who are only interested in you because you're in a band are the worst kind of trouble."

He didn't elaborate. And I didn't ask.

29

"No Woman No Cry"

"We're going to take the Bad-Mobile and go cruise the park," Danny said. "You want to go?" It was a little before ten and I was in the breakfast area, polishing off a plate of pancakes.

We'd gotten up and dragged ourselves back over to the Western Star half an hour before, and just like she'd said, Donna had given us three rooms that had opened up. I'd dropped off my stuff and headed down to find some food when Danny, Brad, Jamie, and Amber had shown up, ready for a little day trip.

My first instinct was to say *Hell yeah, let's go!* But then I took another look at them. And I didn't see four of my bandmates. I saw Danny-and-Amber and Brad-and-Jamie. Heck, Danny and Amber were holding hands, and Brad and Jamie might as well have been. Talk about awkward . . .

"I don't know," I replied. "What's Glenn up to?"

"We asked him to go," Danny said, "but I think he's gonna stay and work on some music."

"I think I'll do the same." I grinned. "Maybe I can keep him from writing something too corny. But thanks for asking. You kids have fun."

"Bye, Mom!" Brad called from the doorway. They all laughed, and then they were gone, just like that.

My phone went off. Kyle. I stared at it through all eight bars of "Can't Stop," but I didn't *even* want to deal with him now, so I let it roll over.

I went back up to the room and found Glenn just lying on his bed with his hands folded behind his head, staring at the ceiling. God, he looked whipped.

"You eaten yet?" I asked.

He didn't even look over. "Nope."

"They stop serving any minute now."

He just shrugged.

Wow. "I'll be back in a few. Don't go away." Not even a smile . . .

* * *

When I returned, he was exactly where I'd left him.

I dug in his dresser and threw some shorts and a T-shirt at him. "Get changed. We're going."

"Going where?"

I held up my new basketball. "Out."

"No thanks—I'm pretty lousy company today."

"Yeah, no kidding. Which is why we're going. Get your ass dressed."

When he finally got up, we went over to the park they'd told me about at the sporting-goods shop.

I passed him the ball. "There's this girl . . ."

He nodded as he dribbled. "Yeah, I think I recall. Your old bass player's sister, right?"

He'd actually listened. "Yup. You'd said it was a given. Did you mean it was a given for guys on the road, or it was just a given, period?"

He took a shot. "Both." *Swish* . . . "The road just makes it worse."

"Man, you got that right." I gave him the CliffsNotes version of the deal with Kimber and Kevin Flanders.

"But what *really* pisses me off," I continued as I tried a three-pointer, "is that this smooth bastard's feeding her a line of crap that *I* can smell all the way up here, but *she's* giving him the benefit of the doubt." I missed.

He laughed. "You've just described the entire male-female dynamic in one sentence."

"I could straighten it out in five minutes if I could just talk to her in person."

He passed me the ball. "Maybe. If you've got enough cred that she'll buy your story over his."

Ouch. "Okay, that's an issue. I'm trying to work on it. With her, with the band, with everything." Jumper . . . good for two.

"Cool." We just shot without saying anything for a minute. "You know," he finally said, "Jamie told me about you lobbying for me."

Oops. "Sorry. Sometimes my mouth has a life of its own."

"Don't apologize, man. I appreciate the effort."

"Well, I just think you guys would be good together, that's

all. So I tried to point out that the things that she might see as negatives, like your passion for music or whatever—"

"She calls it an obsession," he piped in, going for a layup.

"Whatever. My point is, that same sort of dedicated, stubborn, stick-to-it quality is a good thing in a relationship." As soon as the words came out of my mouth, I felt like an idiot. I mean, I couldn't even keep a stupid email relationship going for more than a month. "In all my vast experience, that is," I said with a laugh.

"No, what you said makes sense, and I'm sure you'll apply it someday."

I just stared at him for a second, then shot him a chest pass. Hard. "God, Jamie said the same damn thing to me the other day. And that wasn't the first time I've caught you guys spouting the same thoughts. You two seem so in sync."

"Yeah, well . . . not about everything." He lined up for a free throw. "It's sort of like that thing with your bud's sister— sometimes there's just no accounting for taste." Air ball. "I think Jamie feels like she's invested a lot into something, and she wants to hang in there for the payoff."

"Even if it's a bad deal?"

He didn't say anything, and I felt stupid for prying. The whole idea was to relieve some stress, not add to it.

"Okay," I suddenly said, "*Celebrity Deathmatch, Portlandia* edition! The Shins versus the Decemberists. Who wins . . . ?"

"Hmm . . ."

And on we went. As we talked, we played Around the World and H-O-R-S-E and a little one-on-one. We didn't even really keep score—we just played until we were both soaked in sweat, then we started back.

The day was warm and sunny, and it just felt great to be outside. Like some of our troubles had come out of our pores along with our sweat and evaporated on the breeze. Magic . . .

✳ ✳ ✳

"Here, check it out. . . ." I clicked *play* on my computer, and my rough demo of "Pray for Rain" came over my little speakers. I let it run for a minute, then stopped it. "See what I mean? I'm okay with the chorus, but the verses just aren't happening."

"They're not bad . . . ," he began.

"Time-out. You've gotta be honest, or this ain't gonna work. If you've got a better way, I want to hear it."

"Okay, here's what I think . . . I think you have a great concept, with a killer groove. Really strong chorus—I love the way it drones along. And I happen to think the verses aren't bad." He held up his hand to stop me. "*But* I'd like to hear those lyrics sung over a different section. The changes under the verse vocals are a little generic."

"Yeah, I hear ya. You got some chord ideas?"

"No, but you do. Can you take the chorus groove and loop it? Nothing fancy."

"Sure, gimme a second." I grabbed four bars and looped them, making a quick track a couple of minutes long . . . just bass, drums, scratch guitar, and the line *pray for rain,* over and over.

"Cool. Now pull the original chorus vocals way down, and try this—let it run four times, then sing the verse over that."

I wasn't sure I understood. "Sing the verse over the chorus?"

"Yeah, except it won't actually be the chorus during that part. It's just backing vocals under the verse, and we'll differentiate it with another guitar part."

"All right, let me try it." I played the chorus loop and tried to sing the verse over it. I had to change the melody slightly and it took me a few times to get it right, but I had to admit it worked pretty well.

"You know, I think it's got potential."

He grinned. "Like this young smart-ass once told me, you've gotta learn to trust my judgment. Now let me put down a guitar part over that."

I nodded. "Okay, it'll take a minute to rig up a mic."

"Cool. I'll grab my gear."

So I set up a microphone while he got his Strat and his little Fender practice amp. He dialed up the perfect tone—dark, dirty-sweet, drenched in spring reverb, with a little tremolo added, set to pulse in time with the eighth notes. He played a simple riff on the lower strings that said *desert . . . hot . . . dry . . .* Like the soundtrack to some dusty old western.

He had me start recording the overdub from the top. He came in with full chords during the actual chorus riff at the top, then he dropped back to that pulsing single-string thing during what would become the verse. Then he hammered it back up again after eight bars of verse to make the chorus pop out. Hearing this gave me a better idea of what he'd had in mind.

"That sounds great," I said. "Let me try a verse over it."

I put on headphones so the instrumentals wouldn't bleed into the vocals, then I routed the mic to a new track and hit *record.* I let the loop go for four bars, then I sang the first verse over the chorus groove. . . .

> *You want her with you*
> *But she's miles away,*
> *Don't know if she's coming back.*
> *You reach the station*
> *And you're out of breath,*
> *But the train's already down the track.*

Then I went into the actual chorus.

> *Pray for rain . . .*
> *Pray for rain . . .*

That sounded good, so I shrugged and kept going into the second verse. . . .

> *You're just prayin' for rain*
> *On a hot dry day,*
> *Without a cloud in the sky.*
> *Fall to your knees*
> *In an ocean of sand,*
> *The water fills your eyes.*

Then back to the chorus . . .

> *(You'd better) pray for rain . . .*

"Let me try some backing vocals on that," Glenn said.

I handed him the phones and moved so he could stand in front of the mic, then I started recording. On the verses he doubled the phrases *if she's coming back* and *already down the track,* then on the chorus he harmonized on the *pray for rain* parts.

We listened back as I did a rough on-the-fly mix. Very cool, in my opinion. Very, very cool.

"Man, that sounds great," I said. "Thanks."

"It was all there. Do me a favor and send me a mix so I can learn the whole song."

"Sure."

"You got anything else?"

"Yeah . . ." I scrolled through my files. "Here's one I'd like to hear finished." I double-clicked on it and played his original demo of the minor-key acoustic thing he'd played for me back on that first day in Bozeman. "I'd love to hear this with a full band arrangement. I can totally see it as a slow, grinding, half-time-type thing."

He thought about it for a while. Finally, he nodded, then he pulled some pages out of his case and cleared a spot on the bed.

"Okay," he said, "let's see what we can come up with. . . ."

30

"Self Esteem"

The Bad-Mobile was still gone when I crashed, but I didn't worry about it—why was *I* the designated den mother?

Besides, I was stoked from the progress Glenn and I had made. Yeah, it's cool to write something by yourself, but there's nothing like bouncing ideas back and forth with someone else and getting something way better than either of you could have come up with on your own. When it works, it's magic.

After we'd worked in the room on my tune and his ballad, he brought out three or four other things he'd been working on, in various stages of completion. Some were just rough sketches, but I thought two of them were almost good to go. So we went to the club to try them out—Donna said it was okay for an hour or so, until they opened for the evening.

While Glenn got the PA up and running, I put up a couple of mics out in front and hooked them up to my little laptop studio setup to make a basic live recording. Then we ran through each of the tunes a couple of times, and they actually sounded pretty good. I mean, they weren't complete by any means, but it was enough to give you the feeling that they could fly.

"Man, that wasn't a bad day," Glenn said when we were finished. "We've got half a dozen originals whipped into semi-decent shape."

I nodded. "Yeah, I can't wait to hear how they sound with the whole band playing them, and Brad singing—" I stopped. "Hey, is that okay? I mean, if Brad sings them? After all, most of them are *your* tunes, and—"

He held up a hand. "Not a problem. I'm the one who always says play to your strengths, and that guy can sing. I'm with you—they're going to kick ass."

* * *

Hey, Zach, I got your message yesterday. I don't know what's goin' on with Kimber, but she's pretty upset. Something about that dickhead Kevin . . . I couldn't help it—I laughed. *But you don't have to apologize to me, man. I don't care why you decked him . . . I'm sure you had a good reason. Hell, him lookin' like Toby is good enough for me. . . .* There was a long silence.

But you don't need to apologize, man. That's all I wanted to say. Beeeeep . . .

* * *

When I woke up, the Bad-Mobile was in the parking lot, safe and sound.

I wanted to listen to the stuff we'd done but Glenn was still asleep, so I got dressed and grabbed my computer and headed out to the breakfast room. There were people around when I arrived, so I set the music aside and read a little while I ate.

By the time I was finished, the place was empty, so I fired up my laptop to recheck yesterday's work. You wouldn't believe how many times something that seems great at the end of a long day turns out to be embarrassing the next morning. But what do you know . . . it still sounded pretty good. After that, I began working on some lyrics ideas I had.

Anyway, I was still sitting there when Danny and Brad showed up.

"Hey, guys," I said. "How was the park?"

"Man, it was amazing," Danny said. "How's about you—good day yesterday?"

"Yeah. Glenn and I got a few tunes hammered into shape."

"Cool. Care to share?"

Well, I was supposedly all about full disclosure now, right? "Um, sure, I guess so. They're still pretty rough, though."

"That's okay. Let's hear 'em."

I played the live mix of Glenn's ballad, followed by a little of the "Pray for Rain" remix. Then I stopped—I just wanted to give them a taste.

"That was awesome, bro. Seriously. I can't wait to try them."

"Thanks. They really need the whole band's help, but it's a good start."

Brad had been quiet the whole time. Not that there was a law that said he had to comment, but still . . . I raised my eyebrows a little, doing that well-what-do-*you*-think thing, in a low-key way.

"Uh, sorry, I'm not quite awake yet," he finally mumbled. "But yeah, it sounds cool."

"Thanks. They'll be much cooler with you singing and everyone playing on them." That reminded me . . . "Speaking of—are we gonna sound check sometime today?"

He yawned. "Sorry, it's still early for me. Uh, I'll think about it and let you know."

"Okay. Donna says we can play in there anytime before noon, and then maybe a little window somewhere between three and five. And that's it."

His eyes narrowed. "Like I said, I'll let you know." He grabbed a pastry and some coffee and left.

I looked at Danny like, *WTF?* but he just shrugged.

God, was I ever going to break the code on these guys?.

Q: WHAT DO YOU GET IF YOU CROSS A DRUMMER WITH A GORILLA?

A: A REALLY STUPID GORILLA . . . !

"Let's try it again—that intro sounded a little rushed." Brad turned and looked back at yours truly.

Rushed? It sure didn't feel that way to me. In fact, I thought it was right in the pocket. But whatever. "Okay," I said.

We'd done a quick sound check and were taking advantage of the stage time to work up a couple of new songs. Not the originals—no one had mentioned those and I sure wasn't going to push that button again. Instead, Brad had a Papa Roach tune he wanted to do, and something by the Killers.

We went through the tune again, and it felt great to me.

Danny dug it, too. I could tell because he had that in-the-groove posture going on and a big grin on his face.

"That was better," Brad said after we'd finished. "But it still seemed a little uneven in parts." He looked at me. "Hmm. Have you ever played to a click before?"

Where was he going with this? "Uh, yeah," I said. "We used one in the Sock Monkeys once in a while when we recorded. Why . . . ?"

"Just wondering." He turned and spoke to everyone. "Okay, that's probably as good as it's going to get for now. See you guys at preflight."

After sound check I checked my email. Okay, I guess I was still hoping for some response from Kimber, but no luck there. Maybe I'd have to get used to the fact that she was done with me.

Shit.

Anyway, there was something for me. . . .

From: Dandy Don Davis [DDD@W107.com]
Sent: Tuesday, July 20 11:17 AM
To: Wild 107 "Best in West" Artists
Subject: CD Airing

Hey, guys!

Just a quick heads-up to all of you that the Best in the Rockin' West CD drops next week. (As if you didn't know, since we've been hyping it all summer!) To build some advance promo for it, we'll be playing it on the air beginning this Thursday night. We'll play the whole thing at 9:00 PM, then again at midnight, and one more time the next day during Candy's Lunch Box Special show. After that, we'll put select cuts into regular rotation, depending on listener response.

So pass the word. Get all your friends to listen to your song on the air, and keep those listener requests coming!

Congrats again to all of you,

Don

Except for Alicia and my parents, I couldn't really think of anyone who'd give a damn. How freakin' sad is that?

The gig that night was weird, too. Well, not the gig itself . . . the venue was real nice—a big room with good sound and lights. And there was a great crowd, maybe the best we'd seen on a Tuesday all summer. Donna was sure right about it being the high season.

But something was messed up. Twice during the evening Brad turned around in the middle of a song and said, "You're rushing!" And during one of the breaks he commented, "Hey, Zach, your timing's drifting tonight. You tired or something?"

But I wasn't tired, and as far as I could tell, my playing was fine. Or at least, up till then I'd *thought* it was fine. The rest of the night I just did my best to make sure everything was in the pocket.

Q: HOW CAN YOU TELL A DRUMMER'S AT THE DOOR?
A: THE KNOCKING SPEEDS UP.

The next night, before preflight, Brad held some papers out to me.

"What's up?" I said, taking them. They looked like a set list, only with some numbers after each song.

"I guess I was channeling our baby brother and becoming a den mother," he said with a grin. "Anyway, here are the BPMs for all our songs. So before we start each tune, you can check the tempo with this"—he held up a little electronic metronome—"and we'll be right where we need to be." He handed it over. "Just trying to help," he added.

I wanted to tell him to go to hell, but could I really guarantee that I was always perfect? Not hardly. So I sucked it up and smiled as I took the metronome.

"Thanks, man," I said. "I'll give it a shot."

"Cool."

Actually, it was anything *but* cool. The more I thought about holding down the tempo, the more it seemed to slip away. I'd dial up the correct beats per minute, watch the flashing light for a few seconds, then count off the song. And a few bars in, it would feel too slow or too fast. Then the question becomes, do I try to hold the line no matter how much the band is pulling or pushing, or do I go with what feels right and deviate from the "correct" tempo?

I made it through the night, but it wasn't like playing music. It was more like being back at the yard-supply place, loading trucks in a hot warehouse. And I *love* drumming.

God, how did something that was so much fun turn into such a drag?

31

"You're Gonna Go Far, Kid"

If anything, Thursday's gig started out even worse. First of all, it was Kimber's birthday. She had to have gotten my present by now, but of course I didn't hear anything. And I sure wasn't going to call her, after she'd made it so clear that she wasn't interested. So I tried to forget about it and get on with my day. (Yeah, *right*. I wandered around town—a gorgeous place—but I couldn't tell you a single thing I saw.) By the time the gig rolled around, I wasn't exactly a bundle of joy.

Usually a gig will pick me up if I've had a crappy day, but I sure wasn't looking forward to another show like last night's.

Okay, whatever. I tried to quit feeling sorry for myself and spent the first set just concentrating on looking at the little blinking light and trying to keep things on the money. And it worked about as well as it had the night before. In other words, *not*.

What really bugged me was that—at least up until this week—things had been going great, music-wise. And now supposedly I didn't really know how to play in time anymore? What the hell?

During the first break I pulled Glenn aside. "Look," I said, "this metronome crap isn't working. I mean, I gave it a fair shot, but . . ." I stopped and looked him in the eye. "Okay, straight up—do I suck? Have I lost it or something?"

He shook his head. "What sucks is that you even have to ask."

"Well, something must be off if Brad's so concerned about it."

He just looked at me for a second. "Go get your set list and the metronome."

I ran and grabbed them, and he looked at the list and said, "Okay, start tapping out the tempo for 'Charlotte.'"

So I did. He listened to me for a second, kinda looking up into the corner of his eye and bopping his head along, then he nodded. "That's perfect." He checked it with the metronome. "About one-fifty." Then he checked the list. It said 142. We quickly went through a bunch of other songs. Some of them were close to what the list said, but at least half of them varied, by up to a dozen BPM in some cases. God, no wonder it felt like the band kept wanting to push or pull. . . .

"So . . . ?" I asked when we were done.

"Did you ever ask him where he got his starting tempos for this list?"

I shook my head.

"Well," he said, "I'd guess he either took them from the original songs, or he just sat down and went with whatever felt good to him at the moment. But neither of those is necessarily the way we play them onstage."

"So how does *that* help me?" I was more frustrated than ever.

"I mean, forget the theory—I've got to get up there and *play* in a few minutes, and I'm dreading it."

"Man, I'm really sorry about this bullshit . . . I guess I haven't been paying much attention lately. My bad. But this actually told us everything we need to know."

"Which is . . . ?"

"Which is that you and I agree about the correct tempo in every case. And if you called Danny over here, I promise he'd agree, too. In other words, you're fine. Hell, you're way beyond fine—you always were. Just trust yourself."

"Yeah, well . . . thanks. But none of that solves *this*." I held up the metronome.

He took it from me. "Oh, that's just a simple adjustment." He set it on the ground. "We just need to tweak this control right here"—he put the heel of his boot on it and applied pressure—"until we get the right setting"—something went *crack*—"and voilà, it's perfect!" He handed it back and checked his watch, then gave me a poker face. "What do you know—time's up."

We went back onstage and I tried to play without worrying so much. And for the first time all week I actually had a good time onstage. The other guys seemed to be feeling it, too—Danny had his happy face on again, and the floor was full most of the night with people dancing and getting into it.

Once or twice Brad tried to question the tempo. The first time he suggested I was off, I just shrugged and said, "It seemed okay to me."

Then later on during the third set he turned and looked back at me after we'd finished "Holographic Train," by Refuge.

"Hey, man, are you positive that was where it was supposed to be? I sure thought it dragged. . . ."

Oh God, not again. "Nope, it was fine."

"Did you check tempo?"

"I think I know how the song goes."

"Hey, I told you I wanted you to check each song! And now you're telling me—"

I stood up and threw him the metronome. "I'm telling you that song was right on the freakin' money, dude!"

He caught it and looked at it. "What happened to—"

Glenn walked over to him. "I turned it off. . . ."

"What the hell?"

Glenn moved closer to him, and even though he kept his voice low, I could still hear. He was seriously angry, big-time. "What's *your* problem, man? His playing is fine."

"Of course you're gonna say that," Brad shot back. "He was your choice. I think he's getting lazy and sloppy, and he needs to pay more attention. Nate never played like that."

"You're right—Nate was never this solid."

"You're full of shit. This kid's all over the map, time-wise. . . ."

I'd had enough. I looked over at Danny, who'd missed this little exchange because he'd been getting a water bottle from the side of the stage. *"Hey, Danny!"* I yelled. The other guys stopped their argument and looked over.

Danny turned. "Yo, what's up?"

"How'd that last song feel to you?"

He looked around, clearly surprised by the question, and shrugged. "It felt good."

"How was *my* playing? You know . . . tempo, volume, timing, whatever . . . ?"

"Perfect, bro—you're nailing it big-time." He grinned. "I've had a big ol' groove-woody all night."

I turned back to Brad and held my hands out wide like, *Pretty hard to argue with that.* Then I just stared at him for a minute. Not full-on mad-dogging it, but I'm sure he caught my vibe. I noticed people in the crowd looking at us, too.

"Let's play. . . ." I sat back down.

The rest of the gig I just ignored Brad and locked in with Danny and Glenn and Jamie and grooved as hard as I could, slammin' away but keeping things in the pocket.

Brad took off right after we were done, so I tried to get some answers from Glenn. "What the hell's going on?" I asked. "Everything seemed fine for the past month, and now he isn't happy with my playing?"

"I'm pretty sure—" He stopped himself. I waited. *Nada.*

"Finish your thought, man."

"I'm pretty sure this has nothing to do with your playing."

Q: WHY IS A DRUM MACHINE BETTER THAN A DRUMMER?

A: BECAUSE IT KEEPS GOOD TIME AND WON'T SLEEP WITH YOUR GIRLFRIEND.

"Can I get an honest answer about something?" I asked.

"I don't know," she said. "Those are mighty hard to come by around here these days."

Hmm . . .

We were hanging in the club after the gig. It was sort of

like after the final gig in Butte, but there were still people in the place, there was music playing, and we were drinking cokes instead of coffee . . . laced or otherwise.

"I'm just trying to figure out what's up with Brad," I said. "He's getting more and more critical of my playing."

"Have you asked him?"

I almost laughed, but I stopped myself. "Yeah, I tried. But he just gives me some story about trying to help me be a better musician."

"Is there any chance that maybe that's it?"

"Well, you tell me—*is* there something wrong with my playing?"

She held her hands up. "You know, I really don't want to get in the middle of all this. . . ."

"I think you pretty much already are."

She was quiet for a moment. "Brad hasn't told me anything other than what he's told you. Personally, I just think he has a lot going on. . . ." She took a drink from her coke. "He feels a lot of responsibility for the band . . . for keeping us booked up and working and so on. He takes it pretty seriously."

"And the rest of us don't?"

She sighed. "Like I said, I really don't want to get into this. I've got enough to deal with right now." She got up to go, then sat back down. "I'm sorry. Look, if it matters, I think your playing's fine. Okay?" She stood. "I have to go now. I'll talk to you later."

"Okay, thanks." Not exactly what I was looking for, if you know what I mean . . .

I got a refill on my coke and just sat there, lost in thought.

"Hey, man, you did a real good job up there tonight."

"Huh?" I glanced over at the guy a couple of stools down the bar. He looked like some old hippie. Receding hairline, graying hair, ponytail. There seemed to be a few of those types around here. I nodded at him. "Thanks."

He moved over to the empty stool next to me. "No, I mean it," he said. "You were really good."

Great. Some old guy wanted to yak at me. Probably drunk, too. "Hey, thanks," I said again, then kinda turned away, hoping he'd go bug someone else.

Instead, he got up and went behind the bar. The staff didn't say a word. "Hey, Scotty," he called out. "You mind if I play something for the youngster here?"

"No problem, Gare. Go for it."

He pulled down the background music playing over the bar system and dug a CD out of the stack next to the register. *How the West Was Won.* I'd heard of it but had never actually heard it—it was some long-lost Zeppelin live stuff that was found and remastered.

He turned to me. "Listen to this. Especially Bonzo." Then he pressed *play* and cranked it up. There was no mistaking the voice of Robert Plant wailing the opening lines of "Black Dog." No one else sounded like that.

>   *Hey hey mama said the way you move,*
>   *Gonna make you sweat, gonna make you groove . . .*

Then that famous off-kilter guitar part came in, with the band pumping behind it. The impressive thing was, the tune had extra beats added and removed throughout, but John

Bonham totally *ruled* that song, playing this syncopated stuff with reckless abandon. It was powerful, it was live—not some studio wizardry—and it was absolutely fearless.

When it was over, the guy pulled the CD and put the house music back on, then he walked over until he was standing behind the bar, directly in front of me, with his hands resting on the counter. His forearms were really ripped for a skinny old guy—like a long-haired version of Popeye.

"Did you get it?"

I wasn't exactly sure what he meant, but I'd certainly gotten *some*thing from it, so I nodded.

"I thought you would. That was at the Forum, in L.A. Seventy-three. I was there. Man, there was nothing like Bonzo in his heyday. Hammer of the gods and all that crap, right?" He paused and looked at me, and suddenly he didn't seem like such a drunk anymore. "You remind me of him. Not all the technique, but you'll learn that with time. But you got the important part . . . the part you can't fake." He leaned forward and tapped the side of my head. "The *intent*, man. Any fool can hit hard. It's about laying back and listening, then grabbing the wheel and driving that bus when you need to." He leaned back and folded his arms. "So keep your ears open. Keep listening. And keep on it."

Then he turned and walked away.

Wow. I looked at Scotty and shook my head in disbelief. "That old hippie dude seems to know something."

"Uh, yeah, I'd say he knows a little."

"Is he a drummer, or something?"

He looked at me like I was an idiot. "Yeah, you might say.

That 'old hippie dude' happens to be Gary Koenig, from Black-light."

"Huh?" I swear to God, my eyes must have bugged clean out of my head. "Hairy Gary? That's him? No way!" Heck, we'd kept a couple of their songs in our set list, left over from that classic-rock thing in Bozeman. They were two of my favorites.

"Yup, he's a semi-local. Got a nice place up by the lake, where he spends his downtime between tours." He chuckled. "He ain't quite as hairy anymore, but he's still all Gary, believe me."

But I wasn't sure I *did* believe him. I went to the front of the club, looking for him. *Nada.* I was headed back to the bar when I heard an outrageously loud roar from out front. I turned and ran back to look out the front window. He was pulling away from the curb on a totally tricked-out chopper with a dark purple custom paint job on the tank and flames shooting out the pipes. I got there just in time to catch a glimpse of the license plate: BL XPRSS.

32

"You! Me! Dancing!"

". . . and we'll get right back to today's locals-only edition of the Lunch Box Special after this from our sponsors." Then a commercial for the Trans-King transmission shop in Los Robles came on. It actually made me a little homesick, if you can believe that.

Danny walked in. "Hey, guys, what's going on?"

"I would think it's obvious," Amber replied. "We're listening to the radio."

He sat down next to her and snagged half of her sandwich, taking a big bite. "Thanks, babe," he said through a mouthful of turkey on sourdough. "I wasn't sure *what* that noise was." I swear, those two were made for each other. Well, plus the fact that no one else would put up with them. . . .

We were hanging in the club, having lunch. I'd asked Scotty if he'd let me hook up my laptop to the stereo system in the bar, and I was streaming the Wild 107 broadcast through it. Glenn and I had been kind of keeping it on the down-low, since that song had caused more grief per beat than any tune in recent history. But first Jamie showed up, and then Amber, and when they asked what we were listening to, well, what were we *supposed* to say . . . ?

The commercials ended. "Hey, everybody, Candy here with your Lunch Box Special coming at you from Wild 107. And like I promised, today we have something *extra*-special in store. We're going to do a replay of the new *Best in the Rockin' West* CD in its entirety, in case you missed its debut last night. First up is a band I don't really know much about, to be honest. Here's everything I've got on them: they're called Killer Jones, they're from Los Robles, and they're currently on the road out of state. But they'll be back in the area at the end of summer, which has got me all hot and bothered because I'm really looking forward to seeing them, and so will you after you hear this cut. They picked the right name, because their song 'Every Day' *is* killer. . . ."

"Here it is, here it is!" Jamie said. She was sitting next to Glenn and she grabbed his arm, all excited. I swear, I think she was more amped than we were.

And then that familiar guitar riff started. . . . In reality, the actual sound quality coming over the speakers probably wasn't all that hot—the audio streaming live over the internet wasn't exactly master quality. And of course I'd heard the song a bunch of times already.

But you know what? None of that mattered. They were playing it on the freakin' *radio,* and I gotta tell ya—it was absolute magic.

We just sat there listening, and it took me until halfway through the song to realize I had such a big-ass grin on my face that my cheeks hurt. Glenn looked pretty stoked, too. For that matter, so did Danny and the girls, especially Jamie.

The song ended and Candy came back on. "Whew! That was 'Every Day,' by Killer Jones, off the upcoming *Best in the Rockin' West* CD. That was smokin'—can't wait to hear more from those guys. Now we've got a cut from Messenger Bag, who home-base out of San Luis Beach . . ."

I turned it down. The other guys were still jazzed, just talking and congratulating us and stuff. And then I noticed Brad, standing near the back of the club. I don't know how long he'd been there . . . all I really saw was his back as he walked out.

***

In theory the gig that night should have been the most stressed-out show for me yet, after the whole deal between me and Brad, to say nothing of *Glenn* and Brad.

And yeah, it started out that way. Brad and Jamie didn't even show up for preflight. As I took my seat behind the drums, I didn't know *what* to expect. But once everyone was in place and good to go, they looked at me, I counted off the first song on the set list, and away we went.

The good part for me was that I played with a little confidence, and I honestly enjoyed myself up there for the first time all week. My stress over the whole timing issue was gone. Not that I didn't care about keeping things on the money, but I finally learned it's not one of those things you can improve by overthinking it.

The first set went pretty well, at least from a musical standpoint. Brad didn't say a lot to me, or anyone else. But I just drove forward, hoping he'd come around sooner rather than later.

So I was actually feeling pretty good as I came offstage for the first break. The place was filled to capacity with the Friday night crowd, mostly people on vacation, and the entire room had that happy-to-be-here vibe. We'd put on our set-break music, and "Brighter Than Sunshine," by Aqualung, started playing from the sound system as I walked up to the crowded bar to get a coke.

Someone behind me put a hand on my waist. "Care to dance?" a girl's voice said softly in my ear.

I turned to reply and stopped cold.

She was freakin' gorgeous.

I could have asked her a bunch of questions. And I probably should have. But I didn't. "Sure," I said. "Let's go."

We went out on the dance floor and slow-danced without speaking, and it felt so natural. It wasn't weird at all, which was extremely weird, if that makes any sense. Her head was buried in my neck and she had that whole soft-and-warm thing going on. God, she smelled great, too. It wasn't even fair.

The song swelled around us and then dropped way down, almost a cappella. . . .

> Love will remain a mystery
> But give me your hand and you will see
> Your heart is keeping time with me . . .

It was like a dream to be standing there, holding her, as the music played. You know how it feels when you're chilled to the bone and then you take a hot shower? It was like I'd been standing outside all winter, without even a coat to keep me warm, and now I was finally inside, just letting the warm water rain down on me. It felt so damn nice I didn't *ever* want to turn it off.

As the song faded, another slow tune came up. Which was strange, because we never had two slow ones in a row during break, but the last thing I was going to do was complain. She was giving me the look, but it was a totally unnecessary use of eye shadow—I would have danced like that with her all night. The song was "You Ain't Alone," by Alabama Shakes. Whoa . . .

Are you scared to tell somebody how you feel about somebody?
Are you scared what somebody's gonna think?

"Hi," I finally said, speaking quietly into her ear.

"Hi."

"How are you?"

She took in a deep breath and let it out real slow and hugged me tighter. "A lot better now," she said.

"Me too," I said. "I love"—I tilted her head back so I could see her—"your earrings."

She smiled. "Really?" She reached up and fingered them. "My boyfriend gave them to me."

"Is that so? Hmm, he's got good taste."

"If you say so."

"I do. So what brings you way out here?"

"I've just turned sixteen, and I've never been properly . . ." She stopped and looked up at me, and I made the fatal mistake of looking back. I swear, we just stared at each other without moving for God knows how long. She swallowed. "Been properly, um . . . shown around Yellowstone."

It was my turn to smile. "Really? I think I could help you out, if you don't mind."

"Not one bit. I'm in serious need of . . . some help." She put her hand on my face. "And I've got to say, I'm loving your whiskers."

We were still staring at each other. It was like we were two magnets—I couldn't look away, and my face kept getting closer and closer to hers. "You know," I said, "I have about a million questions for you."

She nodded. "I know."

"Here's the first one." Our lips were only a few inches apart. And closing. "What does this taste like . . . ?"

✱✱✱

We didn't talk much after that. A couple more songs played during the break, both slow, but they went by in a blur. And then suddenly the music stopped and it was time for the next set.

"I hate to tell you this," I said as we stood there in the silence, still kind of holding each other, "but I have to get up there and play now. . . ."

She smiled. "It's okay. We'll talk during your next break." She leaned forward and gave me a quick kiss. "See you soon."

As I got back up onstage, Jamie and Amber accosted me.

"So, young man!" Jamie said. "Exactly who was that you were swapping spit with in front of God and everybody?" She had her arms crossed and her foot tapping on the floor. "Do you even know her name? *Hmm . . . ?*"

"You got some splainin' to do, sonny," Amber added. "After all, not just anyone is fit for our baby brother. Whoever that shameless hussy is, you kids need to go get yourselves a room."

"Or maybe a fire hose . . . ," Danny offered.

Glenn walked over and joined in. "So that would be your former bass player's sister," he said. I nodded.

The girls perked up at that. "Do you know her?" Jamie asked.

"Nope," Glenn said. "But I know Zach, which means that pretty much has to be her."

He turned to me. "So is the drought over, or is this just a passing rain cloud?"

I shook my head. "You're asking an awful lot of me at the moment, considering." Then I looked at them real confused, like I'd never seen them before. "Hey! Do I know you guys? What's your name? Hell, what's *my* name?"

They all laughed. "If nothing else," Glenn said, "it says a lot that she's here. This isn't exactly a stroll down to the corner store."

"Yeah, you're not kidding. So, who was playing DJ during the break?" I figured it was some combination of Danny and/or Amber.

Jamie put her hand up, looking sheepish. "Guilty." Suddenly she looked across the stage and said, "Hey, we've got to get playing."

I glanced over. Brad was standing at his mic, looking over at us and tapping his watch.

"He can wait ten seconds." I gave her a hug and said quietly, "Thanks, Cupid—that was perfect. I knew you were a sucker for romance."

33
"Sorry"

"So, how'd you get here?"

We were at a table back near the dining area having cokes during the second break, and even though we were just sitting and talking instead of all that other, uh . . . *stuff,* it was still wonderful having her there.

"I flew here with Ginger. And Sarah."

"Whoa. So you got your sister to come with you?"

"Yeah, thank God, because there's no way my parents would've let me come alone. It took some serious plea bargaining to get to *this* arrangement, even with Sarah as my chaperone."

"So where are they now?"

She looked around. "They're here somewhere. Sarah came in with me to make sure the place was okay, then she and Ginger went next door to grab a bite."

"They can come and hang, if they want. As long as they stay back here away from the bar when we're playing, it'll be okay. The owners are totally cool."

"Okay, I'll call them as soon as your break's over."

I nodded, then I paused for a second. It seemed like a stupid question, but I needed some answers. "I'm really glad you're here." I laughed. "God, *that's* the understatement of the century. But the last thing I heard from you was that you didn't want to see me again. So . . . why are you here?"

"To apologize. Zach, I am *so* sorry I didn't listen to you. When I heard all that stuff, it just seemed so believable. . . ."

"Well, that was partly because I didn't tell you the truth myself. Did you get my message apologizing about that?"

"Yes. That's what made me go talk to Alicia, and—"

"Wait a minute. You talked to my monkey-girl sister?"

"She's actually really nice, and smart, too. And without her I wouldn't be here right now, so don't go making fun of her."

"I wasn't. I love her. Usually. Sometimes. But I don't understand how—"

"Let me back up to where I got sidetracked." She took a big breath. "*So* . . . When I heard the stuff that Kevin had been spreading around, it seemed to make sense. At least, *I* thought it did. And it took me a while to figure this out, but the reason I took it so hard is because you had become really important to me. And that's *my* understatement of the year. So here's the outline version: There's this guy, and I'm totally crazy about him, and then I find out he's not what I thought he was, and I'm devastated. And he insists I'm wrong, but I've got a dozen other people saying the opposite and he's already lied about it once. I need to know for sure, so I go digging, and that eventually leads me to his sister. She fills in some important missing details and

I realize I was an idiot for doubting him. Then I tell my parents that what I want for my sixteenth birthday more than anything is to take a trip to Yellowstone. They quickly figure out that I'm not going there to see Old Faithful, but they know this guy a little, and even though they're not thrilled that I want to go a thousand miles to see some rock drummer on tour, I bust out all my negotiating skills and"—she threw up her hands like, *Ta-da!*—"here I am!"

"Yup, no doubt about it—here you am. Wow . . . that's quite a story. So, you came all this way just to tell me you're sorry for misjudging me?"

She put down her drink, came around the table, and climbed in my lap. Talk about déjà vu . . .

"Mr. Ryan," she said in her professor voice, "I am here to offer my most sincere apologies for ever doubting the righteousness of your intentions." She dropped the act and whispered in my ear, "And to do this . . ."

Then she kissed me. For reals.

* * *

Sarah and Ginger sat with Kimber during the next set. When we broke, I grabbed a coke and joined them.

Sarah smiled. "Hi, Zach. Nice to see you."

"Good to see you, too." I turned to Ginger and grinned. "Hey, thanks for being the responsible adult and escorting these two children all the way out here."

"No problem," she said with a straight face. "That's why their parents paid me to come."

"*What?*" Kimber and Sarah both said.

She just laughed. Kinda reminded me of a junior Amber. "You guys sound great," she added.

"Thanks."

Ginger and Sarah left to get something to drink. Kimber turned to me and smiled. "I think my sister kind of likes your guitar player."

"That's only fair . . . I think his drummer kind of likes Sarah's sister." She laughed, and I said, "Speaking of music, how're the Sock Monkeys doing? Last I heard, they were in some pro studio making a record."

"Kyle didn't tell you?"

Oops. He might have tried, but I hadn't exactly been taking his calls. "Uh, he and I really aren't speaking too much these days."

"I know he bailed on you when you left the band, and I don't blame you for being upset about it. But"—she kinda sighed—"he feels really bad about it. You two guys are best buds, and—"

"*Used* to be," I corrected.

"Okay, but I think he's starting to realize what a butthead he's been."

"You know, I don't really want to talk about him right now—I'd much rather talk about you."

She reached over and shoved me. "*You* brought it up."

I held my hands up. "Guilty as charged."

She got serious. "The truth is, I don't know *how* they're doing, because Kyle's out."

"Of the band?"

She nodded. "Uh-huh."

Now *that* was news. "They fired him, too? God, those guys are bigger idiots than I thought." No matter what, Kyle was a rock-solid player.

"Actually, he quit."

"Quit? Those guys have a steady gig all summer and access to a studio and a producer who's helping them make a pro recording . . ."

"I guess none of that matters if you're miserable, right? Personally, I think he finally woke up. Let's see . . ." She looked up, like she was trying to remember something. "He said, 'Toby's a butthead, Justin's a pawn, and Josh is a spoiled brat who couldn't keep it in the pocket if there was a button, a zipper, and a frickin' Velcro flap holding that pocket closed.' At least, I think that's an accurate quote."

I had to smile. "Yeah, that sounds like Kyle. But I got news for you—Toby was always a butthead."

"No kidding." She paused. "Look . . . Kyle should have walked when they kicked you out. He's a little slow, but he's catching on. I think a lot of the reason that he left the Sock Monkeys was that it wasn't fun anymore without you."

I almost shot back a sarcastic reply, but I didn't feel it. I mean, I was still pretty resentful, but I just couldn't seem to work up a good case of the hates for Kyle after hearing all that.

Besides, having Kimber here made it hard to be unhappy about anything. . . .

34

"Good Times Bad Times"

Hey, guys . . .

So guess where I am right now? (Well, I suppose the pic of the geyser on the other side kind of gives it away, huh?) Kimber, Ginger, Sarah, and I are in Yellowstone Park and it's totally awesome. (Thanks for the help, Alicia— I owe you, big-time!) ☺

Zach

Saturday was a blur.

A wonderful blur, but a blur just the same. Bits and pieces stick out in my mind. . . . Having a picnic lunch in the middle of a steaming lunar landscape; eating blueberry-cheesecake ice cream inside a giant log-cabin lodge with the roof seven stories above our heads; walking around the Upper Geyser Basin with Kimber's hand in mine; watching a wayward herd of elk wander across the road next to Yellowstone Lake; and the four of us just cruising around the park in their rental car with the windows down—music blasting away—being amazed by everything we saw. But as hokey as it sounds, probably the best part was seeing Old Faithful. . . .

The four of us were sitting on the viewing benches with a few hundred of our closest friends, waiting for the eruption. Kimber was in the middle of telling me about the thrills of summer school when there was a noise from the crowd, like a chorus of oohs and aahs. I looked over at the geyser cone. Okay, there was some steam drifting from it now, and water was splashing up and out intermittently. Was that it? I didn't get what the big deal was. I mean, I guess it was kind of interesting, but I didn't really see why everyone was so—

And then it blew. Holy freakin' smoke. That thing went off like a freight train, pushing God knows how many thousands of gallons of steaming water two hundred feet straight up into the sky. And it wasn't just one burst, either. It went on and on. . . .

I turned to Kimber and said the most brilliant thing I could think of. "Wow . . ."

She smiled back at me. "Yeah. Wow." And then we kissed. It felt so natural I didn't even think about anybody else being there. But when we were done, both Sarah and Ginger were looking at us. It was semi-weird until Kimber announced, "You know, I really like this scruffy-drummer-dude-type guy. Plus, he smells faintly of Starbucks. So get used to it, you guys."

They both laughed, and that was that. Funny how quickly the weird can become the norm, huh?

***

All of that was absolutely wonderful.

What absolutely sucked, however, was saying goodbye.

They had to drive back to Bozeman that evening in order to catch their flight, so they couldn't go to the gig. We were just hanging out on the street back in West Yellowstone after dinner, and before you knew it, it was after eight. It's funny, but it seems like all of a sudden you cross that line from *This is so much fun it's never going to end* to *Oh crap, it's almost over.* And from the moment you first think that, it's *not* fun anymore. There was no getting around it—I had to get back to the club and they had to hit the road.

What I really wanted to do instead was hole up in an out-of-the-way coffeehouse with Kimber for the next several hours and just hang. And maybe have a listening party, where you take turns choosing and playing favorite songs for each other. (Okay, maybe with occasional breaks for something "less cerebral," as Kimber would say.) We'd known each other for a couple of years, but now there was this whole other . . . *thing*. It was like we'd just met, and we were absolutely dying to get to know each other better.

I stalled as long as I could, but it finally got to the point where if I left right now, I could just make preflight. "Thanks again for coming up here with them," I said to Sarah. "I think that was totally cool of you."

She smiled and nodded. "No problem—we had a great time."

I looked at Ginger. "You too—thanks for making the trip with Kimber. You're a good friend."

She grinned. "So are you, Zach. Enjoy the rest of your summer."

Then I turned to Kimber. She tried to smile, but there were tears forming in her eyes. "Hey, it's okay, birthday girl," I said. "We're halfway done—I'll be home in four or five weeks. And you can talk to me anytime you want. Because *I* leave my phone on . . . unlike a certain little brat that I could name."

She hugged me. "Five weeks is a long time," she said quietly. "And I'm going to miss you like hell."

"Even more than you missed me when you thought I wasn't me anymore?" I was just kidding with her, trying to lighten her load a little, but it didn't work.

"Worse. Because you are you, after all." She finally grinned a little. "And then some."

"Thanks. I think. And I'm going to miss you like hell, too." I thought of a hundred different things to say, but none of them really seemed to fit, so I just picked her up and held her. Finally, I set her down. "I have to go now."

She couldn't really talk. She just nodded.

I turned away and headed up the street. Pretty soon I was running.

✳✳✳

I was late. Not for the gig itself, thank God, but I'd missed pre-flight.

"Sorry," I said as I ran up onstage. "Uh, my friends are flying back and I was saying goodbye and . . ." Suddenly I felt like I was back in the Sock Monkeys, making excuses for myself all over again. God, I hated that. "Never mind, it doesn't matter. I'm just sorry."

Glenn and Danny were totally cool with it, and Brad acted

like, *Drummer? What drummer?* But Jamie came over and talked to me as I was getting my stuff together to play. "Hey, how're you doing?"

"I'm good. Thanks."

She just looked at me for a second. "You're a terrible liar. . . ."

Q: HOW MANY LEAD SINGERS DOES IT TAKE TO CHANGE A LIGHTBULB?

A: DUDE ... REALLY?

The gig sucked. Not because I played poorly. To be honest, I was on autopilot, but I played fine and I doubt anyone could tell I was less than a hundred percent engaged. I saw Billy Ward at a local drum clinic once and he basically said that the mark of a professional is that even on their worst night they're still at least acceptable.

No, for the most part the band sounded fairly good. But Brad was doing his patented pissed-at-the-world thing, acting like he didn't really give a damn about anyone or anything. Even though he's the supposed leader of the band, I'd say he was the one who most often let his mood affect his performance.

But tonight something was definitely up with Glenn, too. His playing was technically fine, like always, but he hardly said a word the whole night. He just did his job onstage without any interaction with the rest of us, and he sat off by himself during breaks. I tried joining him between sets, but he sent the message loud and clear that he didn't want company. And all I got from Jamie was a shake of the head.

Even Danny seemed a little subdued, which was pretty unusual. I don't think I heard a single joke out of him all night, and during breaks he just hung at a table with Amber.

Something had clearly happened during the day, but I didn't have a clue what it was. So I basically spent the evening with my head down and my arms up.

Near the end of the gig things finally heated up, but not in a good way. We'd just finished "Long Walk Home," by Neverland, when Brad walked over to Glenn's side of the stage.

"Hey, man," he said. Only he said it more like, *Hey, maaaaannnn!* "I know you're a frustrated lead singer, but that's no reason to noodle your guitar all over my vocals."

Glenn looked honestly surprised. "What are you talking about?"

"Don't give me that. You were just wailing away right through all my verses, way too frickin' loud. You got a problem with something, keep it off the stage . . . at least when *I'm* up here singing."

I thought it was funny the way he phrased it: *all* my *verses.* Like when he's singing, nothing else exists. But the weird part was, Glenn wasn't doing anything wrong. I mean, yeah, sometimes lead guitarists get all ego'd up and do that look-at-me thing. But Glenn was just laying down a solid foundation behind the vocals and then stepping out when he was supposed to.

But I guess Brad didn't see it that way. In fact, he was *still* going off on Glenn, who wasn't saying anything back. I couldn't help myself . . .

"Dude!" I finally said. "He's playing it just like he always does, and it sounds fine with your vocals."

Brad looked over at me like I was a fly he'd found in his beer.

"Oh. So now little miss I-don't-need-no-metronome is telling me about singing, too. Hey, you wanna give Danny some bass lessons while you're at it?"

"Knock it off!" Glenn said. "They're not paying us to stand up here and bitch. Play now, talk later." He looked at me. "Zach, count off the next song."

So I did. And those were the last words spoken onstage.

Q: WHAT'S THE DIFFERENCE BETWEEN A DRUM MACHINE AND A DRUMMER?

A: YOU ONLY HAVE TO PUNCH THE INFORMATION INTO THE DRUM MACHINE ONCE!

"We've got to stop meeting like this."

"Yeah, and we've got to stop having gigs like this," I replied.

Jamie just shook her head and blew out some air.

"This really sucks," I said. "Big-time."

"Yeah, tell me about it. I don't know what to think anymore."

"I think you do—you're a lot smarter than you let on."

"Yeah? Why don't you enlighten me?"

What could I say to that—that the guy she was hooking up with had turned into a flaming jerk? Because he's insecure about whatever? Good luck trying to get *that* across in one piece . . .

"Well, first I'm supposed to believe that suddenly I forgot how to play drums and need tutoring on how to keep time. And now Glenn Taylor, of all people, needs to be told how to control his dynamics onstage? Gimme a break."

"Have you tried talking to him about it?"

I snorted. "That's like pissing into the wind. Somehow it

always ends up all over you instead of him." I paused. "You should know that better than anyone."

She let it go and changed the subject. Or maybe not. "You're missing your friends, aren't you?"

I just nodded.

"You're serious about that girl—Kimberly—aren't you?"

"Yeah, I think I am."

"Good for you. She seems real sweet."

"She is." I paused for a second. This was one of those 2:30 a.m. things and I didn't want it to be misunderstood. "She actually reminds me of you. Quite a bit. She's smart as a whip." I grinned. "She just doesn't hide it as well."

"Um, thanks? Then you guys should be a good match. So do me a favor . . ."

"What's that?"

"Pay attention to her."

That's it? I nodded and started to say *Sure*, when she cut me off.

"I know it sounds easy, and you're going to say *Yeah, yeah, of course*. But it's *not* that easy. She's not a guitar or a microphone or whatever that you can just play with for a while and then put down. She wants to be a part of your life, and I'm sure you're cool with that. But she also wants *you* to be a part of *her* life. And that's a little different."

I nodded again, slower, and this time I didn't try to say anything.

She came around and gave me a hug, then surprised me with a kiss on the cheek. "I want you to be happy, Zach. Really."

35

"High on a Mountain Top"

Jackson Hole, Wyoming, is one big room with a view. I mean, you step outside the door anywhere in town and turn north and you're looking at the Grand Teton. (Yeah, the name is worth a grin the first time—I can imagine the report home from the explorer who originally discovered them: *Your Highness, today in this new land we have discovered a range of beautiful mountains, pointed and firm and well proportioned as no other. We have decided to call these majestic peaks . . . the Big Titties. Uh, the men and I have been on the trail a very long time . . .)*

And beyond the view, the town of Jackson itself is also very cool. There's this amazing square right in the middle, with giant arches on each corner made of elk antlers that you walk under to enter. At first the girls were freaked out, thinking that thousands of animals had been shot to make the arches. But after they found out that those antlers were actually *shed* by elk in the nearby preserve, they were good with going to the square. And shopping . . .

The place was a *serious* tourist resort—there were tons of good restaurants, and the club we were playing in was a great venue called the Wild Frontier, with a huge western-style bar that must have been eighty feet long and a big balcony that would hold a bunch of additional people on a busy night. So all in all, it was a first-rate club in a cool town in an absolutely amazing location.

But all of that doesn't mean squat if everything around you is falling apart.

It only took us three hours to drive down, but it was the longest trip of the summer. Talk about the silence just hanging there ... I probably said ten words the whole way, which was nine more than Jamie. And Glenn may as well have been a rock—he just sat there, staring out the window. Even Danny and Amber were subdued. But for some weird reason—even though he didn't really talk, either—Brad actually seemed kind of cheerful.

The club was part of this big complex that was a ski destination in the winter and a golf and tennis resort in the summer. When we got there, I helped unload the gear. Then I took my duffel to my room and got the hell out of there. I ended up at this great little place near the center of town that had a book-case running the length of one wall, a chessboard at every table, and interesting indie music coming from the speakers. They specialized in coffee and *chocolate*. I swear, Kimber would have set up residence and never left.

So I ordered a mocha in her honor, took a quick flick of the place, and gave in to a sudden urge to write her. . . .

From: Zach Ryan [ZR99@westnet.net]
Sent: Sunday, July 25 5:40 PM
To: Kimberly Milhouse [kimmilhouse@cencast.net]
Subject: Hanging in the Hole

Hey, Kimberina—

Check out this video clip. Yeah that's a huge bookcase along that wall, yeah those are chess pieces in the little bags hanging off each table, yeah that's Los Campesinos you hear in the background, and yeah on the table right in front of me is a big hot mocha featuring the house specialty . . . dark chocolate they make right here. So, ya wanna join me or what . . . ?

Seriously, I could use the mental-health break. You've been gone less than a day and already things are 180 from where they were. Every group has its issues, but the weirdness here is at an all-time high. There's some subtle triangulation thing going on, but instead of two guys fighting over one girl, it's more like one girl fighting over two guys. And I'm also getting the feeling that my joining this band wasn't exactly by unanimous consent. But I'm trying not to let it affect me (too much). My musical insecurities are getting better, thanks to you and a few other things. (Hey—I never told you about my late-night run-in with a burned-out old hippie dude who turned out to be anything but. Remind me sometime, k?)

But I know that sooner or later we'll turn this bus around and get it back on the right track. There's too much talent here not to.

In the meantime, it's amusing to consider . . . Toby Bates vs. Brad Halstead. Who wins? (In a perfect world, they'd charge across the ring at each other and explode into a giant egotistical fireball. But hey, maybe that's just me . . .)

Miss you already.

L,

Z

* * *

The next morning after breakfast I was setting up my gear on-stage when Brad and Jamie walked in. I didn't really want to talk to them, especially together, but I also didn't want to hang around all day just waiting for someone to finally call me.

"Hey, Brad," I said. "What time you wanna sound-check?"

"Don't worry your little self about it. We'll be fine."

Jamie shot him a confused look, then said to me, "We'll figure it out later and let you know, Zach."

I made some final adjustments to my drumset and left. I didn't know where I was going, but anywhere was better than there.

In the lobby they had a ton of brochures about all the different things you could do. Hmm ... Most of them were either pretty pricey or didn't really interest me, but there was this chairlift that went to the top of the mountain on the south end of town. During the winter it serviced the ski slopes, but in the summer you could ride up for a few bucks and take in the view or go hiking or whatever.

It was turning out to be a great day, weather-wise, so I changed into some hiking clothes, grabbed a bottle of water, and headed over to the lift. And the view from the top *was* pretty freakin' outstanding. There's the whole town laid out below you, like a pic from Google Earth or something. Beyond that is the Grand Teton, clear as a bell. And beyond *that* you can actually see Yellowstone in the distance. Wow—talk about a photo opportunity.

I got off at the top and started on a trail that wound along the ridgeline. I went out a few miles, then stopped and took more pics before I headed back. When I got back near the lift station, I found a tree and sat under it in the shade, just leaning against the trunk and taking in the scenics as I finished my water. I didn't know if it was the environment, the posthike lift, or just being up there by myself, but it felt great. I didn't really care *what* it was, I was just glad to feel human again. After a minute of this—or maybe an hour, who knows?—I took out my phone and punched in a number.

Hi. I can't answer the phone right now, but leave a message and I'll call you back soon. Beeeep . . .

I looked at my watch. It was before noon in California—she was still in class. "Hi. I have something important to tell you. I love you. Like crazy. That's all. Bye . . ."

✳ ✳ ✳

From: Dandy Don Davis [DDD@W107.com]
Sent: Monday, July 26 3:08 PM
To: Zach Ryan [ZR99@westnet.net]
Subject: RE: Song Entry

Hey Zach!

There's something I want to run by you—give me a call when you get a minute, okay?

Talk soon,

Don

"Hey, Don, this is Zach Ryan. I got your message."

"Zach! Hey, man, thanks for calling back."

"No problem. So what's up?"

"Well, I might have an interesting opportunity for you. But it depends—when are you guys getting back from tour?"

"Hang on a sec." I scrolled through my calendar. "Let's see . . . We finish up August twenty-first in Canada. Give us maybe three days to get back. So we should be home Tuesday, the twenty-fourth. Wednesday at the latest."

"Well, that's a little close, but it'll work."

"Work for what?"

"How would you guys like to open for Neverland?"

I about dropped the phone. *"What . . . ?"*

I could hear him laughing. "Yeah, I thought you'd say that. Here's the deal . . . Wild 107 sponsors the grandstand rock show that closes out the Golden State Fair—been doing that for the last four or five years. Well, it wasn't easy but this year we managed to score Neverland to headline—they're in the middle of a big US tour this summer."

"Awesome."

"Yeah, we're totally jazzed about it. And to make a long story short, we need an opener and we like to use local talent whenever we can. Out of all the bands on our *Best in the West* CD, Killer Jones is getting the most requests. And you guys just plain rock. So the question is, can you open the show on Saturday, the twenty-eighth?"

All kinds of things flew through my mind in the two-second pause before I answered. Like how KJ was mostly a figment of my imagination. And whether this was some sort of prank that

Toby or someone set up. (Which was stupid, because I'd called Don at the station, not the other way around.) But mostly, it was just a sense of unreality as my brain kept repeating, *Neverland? Never-freakin'-land???* But what else could I say?

"Uh, yeah. I mean yes. Definitely. Holy cow, are you kidding? Of course!"

"Great. I was hoping that was the case. The show starts at eight and it has a hard quit time of eleven p.m. due to noise restrictions in town, so your slot is forty minutes, max. We're talking maybe eight to ten songs, and we'd like most of them to be originals—this ain't no cover gig, believe me."

"I understand." I thought quickly . . . Glenn and I had maybe six tunes roughed out, but we should have no problem getting the band to polish them and help us work up a few more in the next month. Not with the incentive of opening for a huge act like Neverland to kick us in the ass. "That shouldn't be a problem," I said.

"Outstanding. I have to get going, but we'll be in touch."

"Thanks. The guys'll be so stoked to hear this—I can't wait to tell them."

He laughed again. "I'll bet. We'll talk details later. Take care."

"You too." I hung up and just sat there for a minute. I'd mentioned to Kimber about the bus eventually turning back around, but I had no idea it would happen this soon.

Or this way.

Wow . . .

36

"Drop the Bomb"

You ever have something inside that makes you feel like you're going to freakin' *burst* if you don't get it out? I felt this burning need to go tell someone right damn now, so I went looking for Glenn, but when I found him, the guy seemed so bummed that I didn't even feel like telling him.

I sat down on the corner of his bed. "I'm not sure what's going on, but if there's anything I can do to help, just let me know."

"Thanks. But I don't think so."

"Okay. God knows I'm no expert when it comes to women."

He cracked the tiniest smile. "You seem to be doing all right."

"So I've got one poor girl fooled. For now. You, on the other hand, could have a whole harem of groupies swooning around you." Actually, he could. I've seen 'em.

He laughed a little. "You know, I hadn't considered that option." He looked around the room. "What's the capacity in here? I'd say a dozen, easy."

"Well, I don't know about *that*. You seem to attract them big gals. I'm thinking more like five of 'em. Six, max. And that's if I leave first." I had to duck the pillow he threw at me. "Hey! That's no way to treat your wingman. Or whatever you call the go-getter."

"I'd have you *go,* all right, but I'm afraid of what you'd *get.*"

"Okay, so let's talk about something we *can* control. Like music. As in, original music."

"Yeah, great. So far we've played one original tune onstage one time, on a night when Brad was AWOL."

I held up my hands. "Hey, you've gotta start somewhere."

"We started and finished all in the same night!"

"So far," I agreed. "But what if we *could* do our originals—would you?"

"Of course."

"In front of *thousands* of people?"

"What kind of a question is that?"

I held up a finger. "Final question: How would you like to perform them while opening for one of the biggest bands in the country?"

He squinted at me, but behind the curtain I could see curiosity fighting with annoyance. "Exactly what are you getting at?"

I couldn't wait any longer—I just dumped it on him. "We've got a gig opening for Neverland at the Golden State Fair, a week after we get back. Saturday, August twenty-eighth. Eight p.m. Closing-night grandstand show. We get forty minutes to play—we're talking originals, of course. And don't even ask me about the pay, because I was so freakin' stoked that I forgot to ask."

He stared at me for a minute, then he said quietly, "My God . . . you're serious, aren't you?"

I nodded. "Yup. What gave it away?"

"That big-ass smile on your face. But back up a minute. How did we land this gig? There's no way Corey got it for us, right?"

"Not hardly. This isn't a Bad Habit gig, it's a Killer Jones gig."

"Huh . . . ?"

"Wild 107 is one of the sponsors for the show and they get to choose the opener. They want someone local and we got the best listener response from that *Best in the West* thing, so we won the slot. How freakin' cool is that?"

He reached out and we bumped fists. "This is amazing! So, we've got to bring the others on board."

"Yeah," I said, "they'll need to learn the stuff we've got roughed out, and we'll need a couple more."

"Have you told them?"

"Not yet. I wanted to tell you first, since it was your tune that got us this."

He shook his head. "Not even. It was you, man."

I shrugged. "It was a team effort. Anyway, I'm thinking we should call a band meeting and tell them all at the same time."

He suddenly stopped. "Uh . . . Brad . . . original music . . . *my* original music . . . ? See any issues here?"

"Look at it this way. God comes down and says, *GT, you can share the stage with Neverland. But you have to wear your underwear on the outside of your pants.* Are you in?"

I could see the lightbulb go on above *his* head. He nodded. "In a hot second."

"No kidding. And I think the others'll feel the same

way." I paused. "Smile, dude! I think this just might help end the weirdness."

He seemed genuinely happy for the first time in a long time. "You know, it just might."

I asked Glenn to set up the meeting since Brad and I weren't exactly best buds these days, so Glenn ended up calling him. After he hung up, he turned to me. "Well, that was weird."

"What's up?"

"He seemed only too happy to have a band meeting—he actually said it was a good idea. Only apparently tomorrow morning works better. And he wanted it at the club, too, instead of in one of our rooms."

"That's cool—he probably wants to sound-check. And after they hear the news, they'll probably want to start working on the originals, too."

"Sounds good to me . . ."

✳ ✳ ✳

As I lay in bed that night, it occurred to me that this was a time where maybe the ends really did justify the means. Okay, I'd invented an imaginary band for this Franken-tune, and then I'd stuck my neck out by telling Don Davis that we *were* that band and that *of course* we were ready to open for the biggest band in the land, no problem.

And if we couldn't live up to that fictionage, then I guess I deserved whatever I had coming. But if we could—if this was what it took to get us out of the trenches—then it was all going to be worth it.

I couldn't wait.

Q: WHY IS BEING A PROCTOLOGIST BETTER THAN BEING A DRUMMER?

A: BECAUSE YOU ONLY HAVE TO DEAL WITH ONE A-HOLE AT A TIME.

Walking through the resort to the club the next day with Glenn, I thought about how to tell the band the good news. I could tease them by stretching it out. Or we could play twenty questions. Or I suppose I could just tell them straight up.

I'd finally decided on having a game of *Celebrity Deathmatch*, as in *Bad Habit vs. Neverland on the same stage . . . who wins?* They'd say, *What the hell are you talking about?* and I'd say, *You're about to find out . . . bitches!* The thought made me bust up as we walked in, and then suddenly the laughter stopped.

Have you ever been in a situation where you can tell, instantly, that things are definitely not going to go as planned? Like the doorbell rings and you're expecting a friend, only you open the door and there's a policeman standing there instead. Or this really cute girl in class asks you to come over and help her with her homework, and you get to her house and her football-player boyfriend is there, too, and what she really wants is . . . help with her homework.

Well, this was like that. On steroids. For starters, Brad was the only one there. And he didn't act like he was expecting anyone else to arrive. He also didn't bother to ask why we'd called the meeting.

But the really subtle clue that I'd cleverly picked up on was that my drums were no longer onstage where I'd set them up. Instead, they'd been stacked off to the side. Holy backstab, Batman . . .

I was right back in that garage with Toby. And man, I'd forgotten what a totally shitty place that was to be.

"Who the hell's been messing with my drums?" I spat out.

Brad ignored the question. He was all calm, like he was the mature supervisor and I was some underperforming employee. "Zach, you haven't been very happy working with us lately, have you?"

I almost screamed, *No, really—I love dealing with all your shit.* But I realized that that was exactly what he wanted me to do. I could hear my dad's voice after I'd blown up at Chris: *No matter how mad you get, the way you win is to act professional.* I'd hated it when he'd said that, because he'd had a point. So I took a seat, willing myself to stay calm.

"Actually," I said, "I *have* been pretty happy overall. I think the band's been sounding better than ever."

That seemed to throw him off balance. "Uh, you do?"

"Sure. Yeah, we have little personality flare-ups now and then, but it's no big. Everybody has to deal with that stuff. Either you figure it out and move forward or you fall apart and no one ever hears from you again." I shrugged. "It's up to you . . ."

His eyes narrowed—he was back in familiar territory now. "Oh, so you're telling me how to run my band again?"

I shook my head. "That's your job. You're a smart guy and you've been doing this longer than I have. I'm sure you figured that out a long time ago, right?"

"Uh, right."

"So yeah, I think we've been sounding pretty damn good. I'm looking forward to us doing some original material, which is partly what we wanted to talk about."

"Yeah, I'm sure it is. Seems like you're always pushing your agenda."

God, I hated to admit it, but I was going to have to call my dad and thank him, big-time. This "professional" stuff was really working. The more we talked, the more calm and confident I felt. "My only agenda is wanting us to be successful." I looked at him and tried to imagine that I was the boss, interviewing *him*. "So, I'd be curious to know—what does *your* vision of success look like?"

He lost it a little. "Dude, this is *my* band. Why the hell should *I* have to tell *you* anything?"

I surprised myself by laughing out loud. I'd just realized that I *was* interviewing him, and for a pretty good promotion at that. And he was failing, miserably.

Glenn hadn't said a word the whole time. He was just sitting back and listening, like he was watching an interesting debate on TV. Finally, he leaned forward and said quietly, "Did it ever occur to you to ask why we called this meeting?"

Brad shrugged. "You want to do more originals, or some other bullshit. Whatever. It doesn't really matter."

"It might . . ."

I looked at Glenn and cut him off with a shake of my head. "Let's not even go there. I'd rather not do it at all than do it with his attitude. If you really want, I'll give you the contact info and you can work out the details by yourself."

He looked at me, then slowly shook his head. I could tell—he was watching the boat drift away downstream with some very big dreams on board. "Nope," he finally said. "Hard right over easy wrong." He managed a sad smile. "Right?"

"What the hell are you guys talking about?" Brad said.

"Never mind." I looked around. "Where are the others? I thought this was a band meeting?"

"It's a meeting about band business, but that doesn't mean they all need to be here. I still call the shots, remember?"

Okay, I slipped for a minute. "Oh yeah, how could I forget? You're the big fish. But your pond's really just a puddle on the sidewalk. Sooner or later the sun's gonna come out, and *poof*, it'll be gone."

That finally drove him to the punch line, although probably without all the little excuses he'd had in mind. "Why the hell am I wasting my time talking to you? You're outta here, man! It just ain't working. You're all paid up as of yesterday, so pack up your shit and get gone."

It's weird. I mean, I guess I was expecting it ever since I saw that my gear had been moved, but still, hearing him say it like that felt like a punch in the gut.

"Who's gonna cover the gig?" I finally said.

"Don't worry about it."

I just stared at him. I mean, what more was there to say? Maybe to the others, but not to him. He was a closed book.

Glenn broke the silence. "Well, in that case I hope whoever you found brought another guitar player with him."

"What?"

"You heard me. If you're seriously gonna let him go for whatever screwed-up reasons you've got rattling around in your brain, then I'm done with you."

Wow. "Hey, man," I said. "Really. You don't have to do that."

"Yes, I do."

"Whatever!" Brad said, clearly annoyed. "We'll be *fine* without you. And after tonight the manager's gonna know you're not in the band anymore, so you're out of a room starting tomorrow."

And with that, he got up and left.

37

"Imminent Bail Out"

"Hold on there, pardners—what's goin' on here?"

We were hauling our gear from the club back to our room when we ran into Danny. The band's rooms were spread out, and we'd planned on looking up the others after we'd regrouped.

"Uh, we're schlepping our gear?" Okay, I wasn't exactly in the best mood.

"Good answer. But the question is, why?"

"That would be a question for Brad," Glenn said. "I don't want to put words in his mouth, so you're better off getting it straight from him."

"Seriously, bro?"

"Seriously."

"*Okaaay* . . . I'll check in with you after I've talked to him."

After Danny headed out, I said to Glenn, "Man, that was pretty damn big of you. I was just getting ready to tell him what an asshole he was working with."

"You think he doesn't know? Plus, if you do that, then Brad

fires back about you, and we're off to the races. The way to avoid a pissing contest is to not piss."

I stopped and looked at him. "Dude," I finally said, "sometimes you are way too calm."

Jamie, however, felt a little more like I did. She showed up as we were loading the last of our stuff into the room, and believe me—she did *not* look happy.

"What the hell's going on around here? Danny just told me it looked like you guys were pulling out."

I glanced up from stacking my toms on top of my kick. "We're not pulling—someone's pushing."

"Why?" At least she didn't ask who.

"Maybe you ought to get that from the horse's mouth," Glenn replied.

"Or the horse's ass . . . ," I muttered under my breath.

Her eyes flashed. "Don't give me that crap, GT! This is *me* you're talking to. And I want to know what's going on. Right now. From you."

Whoa. I'd never seen her do that she-who-must-be-obeyed thing before. It was impressive.

"Brad just told Zach he's been replaced," Glenn said.

"But why?"

"He didn't say, so this is all conjecture," Glenn said.

"I'm listening. Conject away."

Glenn took a seat straddling his amp, and Jamie sat on the corner of my bed. I tried to look busy messing with my hardware, debating whether I should go.

"Okay, but remember—you asked," he said. "Brad's problems

with Zach—and with me, too, lately—don't have shit to do with the music, no matter what he says. It's important to him that he runs the show. Hell, it's *everything* to him. Before, Nate sided with Brad, and Danny was pretty much neutral. And you . . . well, you rarely voiced an opinion, for whatever reason. So Brad felt in control . . ." He paused. "But you'll remember he never wanted to do any of my songs. Because once you open that box . . ." He shrugged. "Anyway, Zach replaced Nate and that upset the balance of power. He had some new ideas—good ideas—but they involved playing originals. Including *my* originals. And he can't have that."

"So . . . ?"

"So Zach had to go. But Brad couldn't just say *I'm threatened because it feels like I'm losing control of the group, so I'm firing the new guy.* Hell, maybe he doesn't even know that's what he's doing. So he makes up these nonexistent issues as an excuse to get rid of the problem child."

"Interesting theory."

Glenn nodded. "Uh-huh." He paused. "And I'm sure Brad has a very different view." It wasn't really a question, but after he said it he just looked at her, waiting.

"Yes, he does," she finally admitted. But that's all she said about that, and *I* sure wasn't going to press. "But that doesn't explain why *your* gear's here," she said, nodding at his amp. "Did you get, um . . . let go, too?"

"No. I let myself go."

"Why?"

He jerked his thumb toward me. "I pushed to hire him, he signed on to do this, and he's been doing a great job. Hell, besides his drumming, he got one of our tunes on the *radio*. He's moving things forward. And now, through no fault of his own, he's been pushed out. I can't just abandon him here, a thousand miles from home. And I can't stay in a band that would do that to someone. . . ." He paused, then said quietly, "Things are changing. You'll be fine without me."

She didn't say anything for a long time. In fact, I had to look twice to make sure she'd even heard him, but then I saw that her eyes were watering. Finally, she kinda snorted and looked down, just shaking her head. I couldn't tell if that meant *No, I won't be fine without you* or *No, you just don't get it* or *No, I'm an idiot.* Maybe a little of each. But in the end it didn't really matter, because she walked out of the room.

Suddenly I wished I could disappear.

DID YOU HEAR ABOUT THE GUITAR PLAYER WHO LOCKED HIS KEYS IN HIS CAR?

HE HAD TO BREAK THE WINDOW TO GET THE DRUMMER OUT.

"Hey, look at this one," I said. "Chevy half-ton. Supposedly runs good and it's cheap. Body's a little beat up, but who cares?"

He shook his head. "Sorry, but a pickup won't work. What happens if it rains? Who watches our stuff if we go into a restaurant? And where do we sleep if we're tapped out?"

I turned back to the computer.

After Jamie left, we'd had a strategy session. I just wanted to get the heck out of there, so I'd suggested pawning our gear and flying home, but Glenn convinced me we'd be giving it away for next to nothing. Then we looked into renting a van, but that was expensive—for not much more we could buy some old beater. That way we could at least sell it when we got home and maybe get some of our money back. So we called up the local Craigslist and were looking at the prospects . . . which seemed pretty slim, considering our limited time frame and finances.

"Well, what about this one? An old minivan—got almost two hundred and fifty thousand miles on it but had the motor rebuilt at a hundred and fifty. Looks okay."

"Let's see." He looked at it. "Hmm. Six-banger . . . might get okay mileage." He looked at his watch. "No time to be picky. Let's go look at it . . ."

It turned out to be more beat up in person than it looked in the pic. This scruffy old guy was selling it—it had been a delivery vehicle for his bait business. The rear bench seat was MIA, and the slider didn't really latch, so it was held closed with the strategic application of duct tape. There were dents all around—mostly on the rear end, like his backing-up technique involved going in reverse until he heard a noise. And the paint was peeling pretty bad.

But we took it on a short spin and it seemed okay. I mean, it moved forward when you pressed the gas and it stopped (eventually) when you hit the brakes. The guy wanted $1,750. Between Glenn and me we had less than two grand.

"We've got to drive to the Coast," Glenn said to the guy, "and we have to leave tomorrow morning. If we pay that, we'll either go hungry or run out of gas somewhere in Nevada, because we're low on funds." He took out the envelope with our money in it and thumbed through it so the guy could see the green. "We can give you twelve hundred bucks, and that's it. Cash. Right now. Will that work for you?"

The guy looked at the money, then at Glenn. Then back at the money. He nodded. "Okay."

"Thanks."

As we drove away, I said, "So, is this thing now the *Bait Mobile?*"

He grimaced at that. "How about the *Worm Wagon?*"

I laughed. "Sounds good."

Q: WHAT'S THE BIGGEST LIE EVER TOLD TO DRUMMERS?

A: "HANG ON A MINUTE AND I'LL HELP YOU WITH THAT..."

In the morning we headed to the dining area to fill our tanks one last time before we hit the road.

The other guys were there. At least, all of them but Brad.

Talk about serious weirdness. Then I thought, *It's only weird because I think it's weird.* I mean, they were still the same people they were last week, right? Brad was still an asshole, Danny was still funny, Amber was still Danny's "humor soul mate," and Jamie was still . . . well, whatever Jamie was, she was still that. So I figured what the heck, and I got some food and sat right down among them at a big long table, just like usual. And Glenn joined me.

And at first it *was* weird. But I turned to Danny and asked how it was going, and he made some small talk about needing a new bass amp, then I started riffing on the Worm Wagon, exaggerating every little problem. And pretty soon he was cracking up, which got Amber going, and it was actually pretty *un*weird. At least for a little while, which was nice.

Then he leaned closer and spoke quietly. "Look, bro—this sucks big-time. It's not right." I tried to wave him off, but he wasn't interested. "Part of me really wants to get on the bus with you. Right now. But Jamie's staying because . . . well, because she's trying to make something work, I guess." He glanced over at her. "And Amber is her best bud, so she's staying with her. And I . . ." He paused.

"And you're gonna stay with Amber," I said, "which makes sense."

He nodded. "Yeah. And I've got bills to pay. This is my job."

I could tell he felt guilty. "This isn't *even* your fault. You've been great, man—I couldn't ask for a better road guide, onstage or off."

"Thanks, bro. It's been absolutely killer playing with you. We definitely need to get together and make some noise in the fall."

"That's a deal."

Amber leaned across Danny. "Take care of yourself, baby bro. And your baby girl, too. You're a first-class guy." She grinned. "And I still say you look sexy as hell with those whiskers."

"Thanks." I rubbed my chin. "That's all your fault, you know." I nodded toward Danny. "Keep an eye on the wild man, here."

I looked over toward Glenn. He was on the other side of me, and next to him was Jamie. I could only hear snatches of their conversation, but it seemed personal, so I looked around for somewhere else to be.

I wandered across the room to graze at the buffet. It was already a gorgeous day out and I was standing by the open double French doors when someone familiar walked by on the sidewalk outside. He stopped in the doorway and looked at me, too. It took me a second because it was so out of context. It was Nate, the guy I'd replaced. *Wow.* All of a sudden a few things fell into place.

I was about to say *How's it going* or something when he sneered at me. "Hey, thanks for subbing for me while I was on vacation, *man.*"

"No problem." I smiled and stuck out my hand. He took it, a little confused, and I pulled him in close and did that backslap-hug thing. Then I grinned like he was the funniest damn thing I'd ever seen. "You poor son of a bitch," I said, shaking my head. Then I turned and walked away.

The hell with the food. I walked over to the table and looked at Glenn, but he was still talking to Jamie. Finally, he looked up and I gave him a let's-go head tilt.

He nodded, but Jamie got up to see me first. "What can I say?" she said.

"Nothing. You don't have to."

"Take care of yourself." She glanced over at Glenn, who was saying goodbye to Danny and Amber. "And take care of him, too."

I thought that was weird, but I said, "Sure." Then I hugged her and said quietly, "Thanks for everything, Cupid. And hey . . ."

"Yeah?"

"You deserve to be happy, too. . . ."

* * *

Finally, we were all loaded up and good to go.

"Well, you ready?" I asked Glenn.

I guess a door was open somewhere, because we could hear the guys in the club across the resort, loud and clear, working through a few tunes with Nate. Listening to them, I couldn't imagine it would take him too long to get back in the groove. With just Brad on six-string there wouldn't be many solos until they found another guitarist, but they'd manage.

"Yup. What about you? You wanna go say one last goodbye or anything?"

"Nope," I said. "I've already done it, except for Brad, and I've got nothing to say to him."

He nodded. "I hear you."

The band started playing "So Far," our usual opener. Suddenly I felt like crap, hearing them do that with another drummer. And they totally killed it, too—Brad really was a great singer.

Glenn must have read me. He turned to me and said, "That *sucks* compared to that night when you sang it!"

That made me laugh.

At least for a minute.

38

"Going to California"

SALT LAKE CITY—146 MILES.

I can remember seeing those signs before, only I'd been driving north instead of south. Amazing what a little change in direction can mean, huh?

Anything new is an adventure. At least for a while. But then the novelty wears off and you're stuck dealing with whatever's left, good or bad. In this case, what was left was the simple fact that I'd been fired from my band. Again.

And no matter how hard I tried to rationalize that it wasn't my fault or that it had nothing to do with me or my drumming, there was no getting around it. And this time it double-sucked, because getting in *this* band had kinda redeemed me from getting kicked from *that* band.

And okay, I'll admit it—I'd had hopes of maybe getting somewhere with these guys. Especially after I'd worked with them for a while and seen what they could do. Things had started to turn around. And then . . . the bus drove right off a freakin' cliff.

"What are you thinking about?" Glenn asked, interrupting my thoughts.

"Food," I said.

"Yeah, *right*. Your knuckles are white on the wheel and you've got death and destruction in your eyes. That must be one hell of a hamburger you're thinking about."

"Okay, here's what I'm thinking . . . I'm thinking this sucks. I'm thinking it sucks big-time. I know it sucks for you, too, and I really appreciate you backing me up, but that doesn't hide the fact that I just got canned from the best band I've ever been in . . . not three months after getting canned from my *last* band. Which totally sucks." I looked over at him for a second, then I turned back to the road. "That's what I'm thinking. So, what are you thinking?"

"I'm thinking it's about time to get some food. . . ."

* * *

A few minutes later my phone rang. Kimber. Oh God. I let it roll over to my voice mail and I listened to it maybe half an hour later, after we'd stopped and gotten a bite in Logan.

Hey, just wanted to check in with my drummer boy—I hope everything's going good for you. You're probably working on some new songs or something before your gig tonight. From what you said earlier, it sounds like a beautiful place. Let's put it on our list, okay? All right, I'll let you go. Just wanted to say have a good gig tonight, and I'll talk to you soon. Bye!

God. I had some calls to make, and I was totally dreading them.

The first was to Don Davis about the show. I mean, I had

to let him know. I sure didn't want them printing up posters or whatever with our name on them. Well, hopefully he'd contact me first for specifics or maybe a picture before he did something like that, but still, he'd need time to find a replacement. But I was going to feel like *such* a freakin' chump, making that call. I mean, I'd full-on promised him that we could cover the job, and now I had to tell him that I'd been full of crap and that the band that played that song didn't really exist. God, what a loser story *that* was, huh?

And then there was Kimber. Man, she'd just been up here and heard us and everything. And I'll admit, it felt pretty cool to have her see me playing with such a good band in such a nice venue. It's like it validated all the supportive things she'd been telling me all along. So to have to tell her I'd been kicked *again* . . . Well, in some ways that was even worse than calling Don.

Oh yeah. And my parents. Well, that could keep until I got around to it. Or until I rolled up to the house. Whichever came first. Man, there was almost too much wonderfulness here to handle at once, huh?

Anyway, Kimber wouldn't expect to hear back from me until tomorrow. Except she'd be in school until after noon. Of course, that way I could conveniently return her call in the morning and get away with leaving a message. But that was a little too chickenshit, even for me. The other option was to wait until tomorrow afternoon, but that meant I'd have all night and half of tomorrow to think about it. . . .

We'd swapped in Logan, so Glenn was driving. It was dark out, and there was music on.

The hell with it. I took out my phone.

"Hi, Zach!" she answered, really cheerful. Which only made me feel worse.

"Hi, Kimber . . ."

"What's wrong?" she immediately asked.

"Nothing" was my automatic reply. *Way to go, Mr. Honesty.*

"I figured you'd be playing by now. It's after nine there, right?"

"Uh, right . . ." *Brilliant, dude. Keep it up and you might make it all the way to moron.*

"Did something happen at the club? Did they cancel the gig?"

"Well, not exactly . . ."

"Okay. So what's going on?" She was being patient with my stumbling, but I could tell that the long, slow buildup wasn't going to work.

I took a deep breath and held it, then let it all out at once. "I got fired. From the band."

"What? I can't believe that! Why? Where are you now?"

"I'm in northern Utah, on my way home—I should be there in a couple of days."

She sounded happy at that, which kinda threw me. "Oh God, I can't *wait* to see you!" Then she got serious. "Sorry. Self-ish. I just miss you. Tell me what happened."

So I told her pretty much everything from the time she'd left Yellowstone until now. Except for the Neverland gig—that could wait until later. But I didn't want to get too deep into the internal politics of the band—especially the whole Brad/Jamie/Glenn thing—because Glenn was right there, and even with the music playing, I was pretty sure he could hear. Heck, it was weird enough just talking about the stuff we *did* discuss. So when she asked, I told her I'd give her more on that later.

She seemed okay with letting it go, but when I mentioned about Nate being my replacement, she wasn't about to let *that* go. "So Brad's been planning this for a while . . ."

"Yeah, I guess." Hell, I don't know *when* he first started talking to Nate. Looking back on it, there were several places where he might have been motivated to replace me, all the way back to that first week in Bozeman. Man, I can read a crowd of five hundred from behind a drumset, but I can't seem to see what's going on right in front of me. "I guess I just didn't pick up on it at the time. Hindsight's twenty-twenty, right?"

"Yeah, but you didn't know he was like that." I could hear the anger coming out in her voice. "Either way, he knew about this way in advance. That's so wrong."

"No argument here."

"What about the other guys . . . did they know what was coming?"

"Naw, they were pretty surprised, too. And not exactly happy about it, either. That's another long story that we can go into later if you want. But at least this time I have some backup."

"What do you mean?"

"Glenn left with me."

"Wow! He did? What happened?"

So I told her all about that, too. When I was done, she asked me to hand the phone to Glenn. Weird, but I passed it over. "Hey, man, Kimber wants to talk to you."

He took it. "Hello?"

She talked to him for a few minutes. He didn't say much, just the occasional *yeah* or *thanks,* or *maybe, we'll see.* Then he handed the phone back.

"Hey," she said softly.

"Hey."

"How're you doing?"

"Better now."

"Good. I just want to tell you one thing before I go. I know you feel really bad over this, but it doesn't have anything to do with you or your playing."

"Thanks."

"You'll land on your feet—you're smart and you're talented and you know how to make things happen. It's their loss—they've lost a great drummer and a great guy, just because their leader has an ego problem. So the hell with him." She paused. "I love you, and I can't wait to see you. Keep your chin up, okay?"

"Okay. I love you, too. Bye . . ."

I put my phone away and Glenn said, "She seems real nice. You're lucky."

"Yeah, I think so, too."

"She wanted to thank me for sticking with you. She told me a little about how bummed you were when you got fired from your old band, so she was glad you had someone with you on the way home." He looked over at me and raised an eyebrow. "She also joked about setting me up with her older sister."

I laughed. "Cool. You could be like my brother-in-law-in-law. Or something."

"I don't think I'm really going there anytime soon."

Hmm . . . "Remember that stuff I said back in West Yellowstone when we played basketball? I still think it's true—you and Jamie'll figure it out, sooner or later."

"I think she's *already* figured it out," he said casually. "She's figured out that she likes someone else better, that's all."

I turned to him. "Dude, sometimes you're too in control for your own good! Plus, I happen to know you're full of shit on this one." Oh God, there goes my indie mouth again. "She's freakin' *crazy* about you, but she doesn't want to be second fiddle to a guitar, excuse the pun. In my dumb-ass, uninformed, unasked-for opinion, I think she's settling for something that she thinks she might actually be able to have."

"She tell you all that?"

"Hey, I can read between the lines."

He snorted and shook his head. Just like you-know-who . . .

"But I can tell you this," I went on. "I've seen her in tears over you more than once. And late one night she happened to let slip that she thought you were incredibly sexy—God, I can't believe I just said that. . . . But don't gimme that she-likes-someone-else-better crap. No, she actually likes *you* better, but she needs to know where she stands. And it better not be before the Marshall but after the Strat." I caught his look. Uh-oh. "And I've said *way* too much, dude. Signing off now . . ." And I leaned back in the seat and closed my eyes.

He didn't say anything. After a long time I heard "Hey . . ." I looked over, but he wasn't talking to me. I closed my eyes again.

"It's me," he said. "I'd like to talk to you sometime after you guys get back. Pretty funny, huh? All this time, and *now* I want to talk? Yeah, I thought so, too. But there are a few things I'd like to clarify. About all the reasons I love you. I'm not always the best at that, but I'd like to try. I know you've got your hands full right now, but maybe after you're in town, we can get together and sort some stuff out. Or maybe you're happy where you are and . . . If this all sounds stupid and pointless, then please just delete this message and get on with your life. But I hope . . . I hope I'll see ya, JD-girl. . . ."

There was silence for a few minutes, then a voice in the dark.

"Hey, Zach, you awake?"

"Yeah, what's up?"

"You were right. Even if you were wrong, you were right. So thanks for the push."

"No problem."

"So, what are you thinking about?"

"Food . . ."

39

"Burning Down the House"

I spun my computer around so Glenn could see the screen. "Hey, check *this* out . . ."

We were having breakfast at a Bean & Leaf in St. George, Utah, after crashing in the Worm Wagon. I remembered what I'd been thinking yesterday—about the posters—so I went to the Golden State Fair's website. I was relieved to see that all it said was "And Special Guest" in small print down at the bottom of a full-page blast about Neverland. Whew . . . I resolved to call Don before we got back to California.

Anyway, I ended up clicking on Neverland's tour schedule link, just because. And sure enough, they were all over the United States, mostly working from the East Coast out to the West. The Golden State Fair show was wedged in between multiple-night stands in L.A. and San Francisco as they worked their way up the coast toward Seattle. And in the meantime, they were playing places like Dallas and Albuquerque and Denver and Salt Lake and Phoenix . . . and Vegas. As in Las Vegas. As in tonight.

Glenn looked at it. "Mandalay Bay, huh? That should be a great show."

"I guess. Somehow I can't see them playing a casino."

He laughed. "I can't, either. But they've got a couple of cool venues there. A House of Blues and a really nice arena. They'll be in the arena for sure—it holds, like, ten thousand people. I saw a big festival show there last summer."

"That makes more sense."

"Yeah." He looked up from the monitor. "So, you want to go?"

"Huh?" That took me by surprise. "Uh, it's sold out."

"We could probably get tickets. If you want to spend the money."

I thought about it. We were low on bucks. And we needed gas and food to get home. And I hated to come home stone-broke—that would be extra fun when it came to talking to my parents, and . . . The hell with it. "Yeah. Let's do it."

Q: HOW DO YOU GET A DRUMMER OFF YOUR FRONT PORCH?
A: PAY HIM FOR THE PIZZA.

It had been warm enough coming down through Utah, but that was nothing compared to Vegas in the middle of the day in the middle of summer. Holy freakin' smoke—it was like a hundred and twelve degrees or something. We hopped off I-15 a little farther north so we could cruise through town on the Strip, but that might have been a mistake. I mean, the Worm Wagon didn't exactly have functioning AC. The best option was to roll the windows down and try to keep moving—when it got hot, the past life of the vehicle began to seep out of the floorboards, if you know what I mean. Plus, whenever we had to idle too long, the temp gauge started to head for the hills, threatening to turn this thing into the flaming bait-bucket from hell.

So I fired up "Highway to Hell" and crankèd it as we slogged down the Strip toward our destination. Glenn looked over at me with a wild look in his eye and did this demonic wicked-ol'-witch thing.

"I'll get you now, my pretty! *Ahh-haa-haa-haa* . . ."

I leaned back in my seat so I could get my feet up in the air, then closed my eyes and banged my Converse together. "There's no place like home, there's no place like home, there's no place *like freakin' home!*" I opened my eyes and looked around. "Damn . . ."

Finally, we pulled into this massive parking structure next to Mandalay Bay, which had to be ten times larger than the one at the mall back home.

"So, what now?" I asked.

"Now we go inside and cool off. Maybe see about those tickets."

When we got out of the van I was struck by how darn hot it was, even though we were in the middle of a structure where the sun never shines. But when we walked inside, all was forgiven. It was like sixty-eight degrees in there. And huge. And nice. And smelled like food. And *coffee.* I was just about to nudge Glenn and point him toward where the good smells were coming from when he turned right and headed through the enormous building like he knew what he was doing. As we walked along, I started seeing posters for the show and I could feel myself getting excited. We ended up at the entrance to the arena and Glenn walked up to an open window.

"Hi," he said to the bored-looking guy inside. "Do you happen to have anything for tonight's show?"

The guy shook his head. "You kidding?"

"How about all the will-call tickets? What if no one picks them up—do you sell them after the show starts?"

"They're paid for, so they stay here until someone comes to get them, or until the show's over. Sometimes people'll be having a winning streak at the tables and they'll finally show up fifteen minutes before it's over." He shrugged. "Hey, it's their money, right?"

"Thanks . . ." Glenn turned away and I followed him, totally bummed.

"So that's it—we're not going?"

"No, we still have a shot. We just need to be back here by eight, cash in hand."

We spent the afternoon cruising around. We probably walked ten miles and never went outside once. Mandalay Bay was like this long mall-ish thing and it connected to the Luxor—which was another casino, shaped like this huge black pyramid. Man, you could literally shop until you dropped.

At first I thought it was cool. But after several hours of it I was craving something more . . . organic, I guess. Anyway, after we got a bite in a place called the Burger Bar, I was overloading on the plasticity of the whole scene. Luckily it was after seven by then, so we headed back toward the arena.

There was a crowd already forming, mostly standing around

waiting for the doors to open, but there were merch stalls set up and they were already doing great business. We found a space off to the side of the lines. "This is good," Glenn said. "Let's wait here."

Sure enough, after a while this guy shows up and starts waving something over his head, calling, "Tickets! I got tickets to Neverland. . . ."

Glenn waved at him. "How much?"

The guy walks over. "Great seats. Only four hundred each. You'll catch the sweat off the stage. That's a deal, man . . ."

Glenn held up his hand like, *You can stop now.* "Thanks."

The guy just shrugged and turned away. You could tell he did this all the time. Another guy arrived, pretty much spouting the same story and the same price. I was getting nervous, but just a few minutes before eight a man in a suit came walking fast up the ramp to where we were, looking pretty stressed. Instead of broadcasting, he was going around asking individual people if they needed tickets.

"There's our dude." Glenn started toward him, and I followed. "Where are the seats?" he asked the guy.

The guy took out the tickets and looked at them. "Section one-thirteen," he said, looking at his watch. There was a seating chart on the wall—Glenn and I went and looked at it. They were maybe halfway back.

"They're behind the mix position—they'll sound great," Glenn said to me. "Plus, the room isn't *that* huge . . . those aren't bad seats."

"Okay."

"Give me eighty bucks."

"Huh?"

"The price printed on those tickets was seventy-nine bucks each—I saw when he took them out."

I gave him the money and we went back to the guy. "Looks good," Glenn said, holding out my money and four twenties of his own.

The man looked at us for a minute, like maybe he wanted more for them. Just then the doors opened across the lobby and people started pouring into the arena. He finally nodded. "Okay. My girlfriend overdid it, and she's in no shape to party anymore tonight. So what the hell—at least I'm not out of pocket." He handed them over.

"Thanks a lot, man," Glenn said. "They won't go to waste, believe me."

Now *that* was an understatement. . . .

✱✱✱

"We're from New England," Jeremy, the lead singer, was saying to the cheering crowd near the end of the show. "That's a long way from Nevada. I love being here, but I love my home, too. And that's what this next song is all about."

I turned to Glenn with a big-ass grin on my mug and yelled over the noise, 'Long Walk Home,' man!"

He just grinned back and nodded.

It was a killer show. In fact, I'd say it was the best concert I'd ever seen, period. We weren't front row or anything, but there was a big screen above the stage if you were interested in seeing close-ups. Which I wasn't all that worried about. I was more into watching the whole band thing, how they filled the stage and interacted with each other and the crowd. They were really good at what they did, no doubt about it, but it wasn't like they were putting on an act. I think your eyes and ears have like this built-in lie detector, and mine was telling me that these guys were telling the truth.

Plus, the sound was freakin' awesome. The room was full and the seating went up at the back, so that helped absorb the big echo you sometimes get in large venues. The mix had that thump-you-in-the-chest-with-a-hammer effect, but you could still hear every word. God, what I'd give . . .

Anyway, we'd been guessing songs all night. And getting a fair amount of them right. Including this one.

"Long Walk Home" was an early hit of theirs, and everyone sang along. Including me. Everybody in the room was on their feet, fists in the air, bellowing out the words. And please don't tell anyone, but when they finally broke it wide open during the chorus, I actually took out my cell phone and waved it.

I looked over at Glenn and he was doing the same thing, waving his phone and singing away at the top of his voice. At first I was surprised, but it actually made sense. He liked music more than just about anyone I knew, and how can you really love something if you're too cool to publicly enjoy it?

They got two solid encores after that, and the crowd would've definitely brought them back a third time if the lights hadn't come up.

As we were walking out, Glenn asked me, "So, what do you think?"

"I was blown away, man. That was absolutely awesome."

"Yeah, me too. Everything. The band, the mix, the lights . . . amazing." Then he looked at me kinda funny. "So, what do you think?"

Same words, different question. Hmm . . .

As luck would have it, when we entered the immense restaurant-shop-casino area, there was a Starbucks to our left, just inside the entrance. He tilted his head toward it. "We need to talk."

"Okaaaaay . . . ," I said. "So, what are *you* thinking about?"

"Not food . . ."

PART IV
HOME

40

"Rock 'N Roll Fantasy"

Our preflight was pretty damn brief—three words. "Let's do it!" I yelled as we ran onstage.

I picked up my sticks from my floor tom, clicked them in time, and counted. "One . . . two . . . One, two, three . . ." On the *and* of *three* I hit my kick, and then rimshot my snare with both hands right on the backbeat of *four*. Not too shy about it, either. Like, *ka-slam*.

And it wasn't just any old *ka-slam*, either. The kick drum sounded like the freakin' cannon of doom, just about collapsing my lungs as it pounded back at me from the huge drum-fill monitors on either side of my kit.

So away we went, pounding out "End of the Day" as our opener, which we'd put together over the last few weeks. Okay, full disclosure. The first tune was actually a little . . . well, I won't call it rough, because that's not really fair, but I could tell he was nervous. Not that I could blame him. I mean . . . the venue, the crowd, the sound, the lights . . . let alone the freakin' *headliner*. Major whoa-age.

And it wasn't that he was making mistakes or anything, but he was kind of tentative. I'm sure it sounded fine to anyone else, but I could tell he wasn't having much fun. And fun is the key to an outstanding groove.

I waved him over with the old low-profile head tilt. "How we doing?" I yelled when he'd gotten closer.

He shrugged, and nodded.

He stood there, playing his bass until the song ended, then I spoke quickly during the applause.

"We good? You sound fine."

"Thanks. I'm a little nervous."

"God, are you kidding? I'm ready to puke on my snare drum." That got a laugh out of him. "Hey!" I said. "Let's just play like we're back in the garage."

"Back in the garage?"

"Yeah. Screw the crowd, forget who we're playing with, just lay it down like when we used to jam in the garage."

"Back in the garage . . . ," he repeated, like it was a mantra.

"Yup, back in the garage—fat, dumb, and happy."

I nodded across the stage to Glenn, and we went into our only cover song of the set. Glenn started playing his own unique version of "Are You Gonna Go My Way?" while I pounded out that snare and hi-hat groove, and after four bars the bass slid down the neck and joined in with a very simple but solid pattern. So far, so good.

I kept it fairly sparse with no flash, concentrating instead on just locking in with the bass. Our little chat seemed to have helped. He was still playing it smart at the top, basically hitting the root on the quarter notes to define the pulse. And that worked great. But as he got more comfortable with it, he added more grace notes on the bass and made the whole thing drive along even better. And by the end, when we had the breakdown section where Glenn usually played the opening riff by himself again, the bass played along with the guitar riff in absolute unison. It was smoking hot, and Glenn looked over at him with a huge grin.

That broke the tension, and from then on it was a total pocket party—just slammin' away in the groove and busting out a cool fill once in a while when appropriate, but never losing track of where the almighty *one* was.

The next song was that slower minor-key thing Glenn and I had first worked on back in West Yellowstone. It pulled the energy level back a hair, but that was perfect—you can't keep everything turned up to ten all the time, or pretty soon ten becomes the new five. I was actually able to relax and look around a little by then, and as I gazed out at the huge crowd, the thought that went through my head wasn't *Oh-my-God-look-at-the-crowd, I don't know whether to crap or go blind.* It was actually something a lot simpler: *This is where we belong. . . .*

* * *

It wasn't the easiest thing I'd ever done, making contact with him when we got back, but somehow things were different now. (Hell, three months ago I wouldn't have even bothered.) And it had nothing to do with the gig. In fact, I didn't even discuss it at first, because that would have been too easy. It's like some guy approaching a girl he likes and mentioning right off the bat that he's a multimillionaire. Yeah, she might agree to go out with him, but was it him or his wallet? He'll never know for sure. . . .

Anyway, at first it wasn't even about music at all. We had some unfinished business as friends, and that was the priority. If we could get along, I knew the music would be fine. And if we couldn't, then I wasn't really interested in working with him no matter how well we played together.

***

He answered the phone. "Hello?"

"Hey, man, it's Zach. How's it going? I'm back in town."

"I'm good. Yeah, I heard. From Kimberly. What's up?"

He didn't sound real excited. But oh well . . . at least I had to make the effort. "Nothing much. I just wanted to see if maybe you'd like to get together. We haven't talked in a while." *No kidding . . .*

But he actually surprised me with his enthusiasm. "Hey, that'd be great! What about this afternoon?"

"I don't know. Let me check my calendar. Hmm. I've got band practice, and . . . Oh yeah, I forgot—no band. But then there's my job . . . uh-oh, looks like no job, either. What do you know—I'm free."

He laughed. "Your calendar sounds just like mine. . . ."

***

We met down at Land of Lights. Which might seem kind of weird, considering, but he picked it and I went along. What the heck—shouldn't really matter to me, right? At least that's what I thought, until I went inside and saw the Sock Monkeys' gear on the stage. But then I looked at it and realized that without Kyle's amp up there, it was now completely different from what we used to use. Different drumset, of course, and Justin's new stack and that big JBL sound system. And now there was a new Ampeg SVT bass rig up there, too. With the massive 8 x 10 cab and everything.

"Holy shit," Kyle said when he walked in and saw it.

"You're drooling, man," I said. "But don't feel bad—that was the same thing I said back when I first saw Josh's new drumset."

"That's about three grand worth of bass amp sitting up there," he said.

I had to laugh. "And that was pretty much the *second* thing I said." I thought for a minute. "I noticed when I saw you guys with Josh that everyone had shiny new gear. Except you."

"Yeah. They offered to buy me a rig like that, but I told them I just wanted to use my old stuff." He shrugged. "I don't know. I didn't want to feel like I owed them."

"Good for you" was all I said about that. "Did Kimber tell you why I'm back early?"

"Are you kidding?" He laughed. "Dude, you're all she talks about!"

"Is that going to be weird? I mean, that Kimber and I are going out . . . ?"

"Man, so many weird things have happened lately that that's no biggie." He shrugged. "And when you think about it, she could be going out with someone like Toby or Kevin. So actually, I think it's pretty cool that you two are together." He grinned. "And now we know why she wasn't into anyone we tried to set her up with. . . ."

"Hey, thanks. So, what happened with you and the band?"

He glanced at the floor and shook his head. "It just wasn't doing it for me anymore. We spent a ton of time in the studio, but everything ended up sounding like some really well-recorded demo. The production quality was amazing—man, you should see that place—but if it's not played right . . ." He let it hang there. "And the gigs were the same deal. There was no pocket to our party."

"Well, I saw Josh do a couple of pretty technical things at that backyard gig. I couldn't have played those licks."

"That's just SARKS," he said.

"Huh?"

"Spoiled-Ass Rich Kid Syndrome. You have the best toys, and all the time and money in the world, so you just stay home and get really good at doing some show-offy crap. And then you get with a band, and you can't actually play *music*." He laughed. "Trust me, I know all about it." Then he got somber. "Look, here's the reality—it's sucked since you left."

"I didn't actually leave," I said quietly. "I was, uh . . . invited to go."

"Yeah, and that sucked, too." He paused. "Look. That whole thing was wrong. I don't care if Josh's dad was Sir Dave Grohl or something, it doesn't matter. I should have gone with the right vs. wrong angle with those guys, instead of just insisting that you were better than Josh. Because even if you weren't, it was still wrong."

I held up my hand. "Hey, it's okay. . . ."

But he shook his head. "No, it *isn't*. You don't know how many times I've wanted to go back in time and tell those losers, *Hey, if Zach goes, then I go, too.*"

"But you did leave. And now you don't have to deal with them anymore." I held up my coke. "And neither do I. So, cheers."

He stared at his glass but he didn't raise it. He went on like he hadn't even heard me. "You know, that's what I told them when I left—that I should have walked the day they canned you."

God, he really did feel bad about that whole thing. "Thanks. Really. It's okay." And it was. "We're good, man. Seriously."

"Really?"

"Really."

He looked at me, then let out a deep breath. "Good." He seemed hugely relieved.

"Besides," I said, "it was all for the best, anyway."

"You serious?" He seemed doubtful.

I thought about everything I'd learned being on the road. And the people ... I thought about Glenn. And Jamie. And Danny and Amber, and even Brad. And Kimber. Especially Kimber. To say nothing of all the music that came from it—and all the music yet to come from it.

"Yeah, I'm serious." I held up my glass again, and this time he returned the toast. *Clink.*

I grinned at him. "You'll see. . . ."

✱✱✱

"Woo-hoo, that drummer's *hot*!" a *Girls Gone Wild*–type voice yelled from the crowd between songs. But I didn't let anything get too big, because I was pretty sure who it was. Sure enough, there was Kimber, smiling and waving. I waved back.

Probably the best part of the whole thing was that we'd each gotten four killer comp seats, front and center. I gave mine to my parents and Alicia and Kimber, and I'd joked that Glenn and Kyle ought to give theirs to Bad Habit and the Sock Monkeys. God, wouldn't *that* be funny . . . ?

And actually, Glenn sort of did—Danny and Amber were right there, next to Kimber. I'm also pretty sure he offered one to Jamie, but I sure wasn't going to ask him about it now. We'd see how that played out soon enough. Kyle gave his tix to his parents and Sarah, as well as Ginger, who was on the other side of Kimber.

So yeah, it was nice to have our own little cheering section right up front, but we were getting pretty good vibes from the whole crowd. And that picked up when we did our one "hit" near the end of our set.

"Hey, how about a shout-out to Wild 107 for sponsoring this!" I said into my mic. There was some applause. "Here's one you may actually have heard before, thanks to them. It's called 'Every Day.'" At the mention of the song title, the applause actually increased. Okay, so it wasn't a standing ovation or anything, but hey, that was the first time that'd ever happened to us, on any level.

We dove into that tune and just tore it up. This was only the second time it had been played in public, but if anything, the response was even better than when we did it that night back in Butte. The song may be totally unknown elsewhere, but it was getting pretty good airplay on the Central Coast, and it showed. And the loudest of all was Danny, on his feet, waving and screaming wildly when it was over. Yeah, he's a clown, but what a guy, huh?

There was only one song left, and now it was my turn to be seriously nervous. And not just because I carried the primary vocals, although that was bad enough. Have you ever set something up that seemed like such a great idea at the time, but at the moment of execution you had major second thoughts?

But here we were, and there was no going back now.

"This is our last song," Glenn said to the crowd. He looked back at me and grinned. "Here's a number that Zach wrote this summer when he was suffering from a serious lack of love out there on the road. So let's all show him a little love. . . ."

As the applause died away, he went into the quiet, hypnotic intro, and Kyle joined in on the bass after four bars. I was supposed to come in on the drums and vocals after four more bars, but instead I just played that little *chick* sound with my hi-hat pedal and waited. I didn't hear anything at first and I was beginning to get worried, then finally I heard this haunting female voice creeping up in the mix and filling the stadium. Man, it gave me chills just hearing it. . . .

> *Pray for rain . . .*
> *Pray for rain . . .*

She kept singing as she walked up from backstage and clipped her mic into the waiting stand, next to my drums. Once the mic was in place, she played tambourine on the backbeats along with my hi-hat as she sang, and I joined in, singing under her part. I was too busy playing and locking in with her to be looking around at that point, but I heard Glenn's voice in my monitor doubling my part, just like it was supposed to. So whatever was going through his mind at that moment, he was still a total pro. It sounded great to have both of them behind me, as well as the percussion, as I went into the verse. . . .

> *You want her with you*
> *But she's miles away,*
> *Don't know if she's coming back.*
> *You reach the station*
> *And you're out of breath,*
> *But the train's already down the track.*

And then all three of us hit the chorus strong just as Glenn's big guitar part busted loose.

> *Pray for rain . . .*
> *Pray for rain . . .*
> *Pray for rain . . .*
> *Pray for rain . . .*

Wow. In a perfect world I suppose I would have arranged for Jamie's keyboard to be up there, too, but this was enough.

Totally. Our three voices, on top of the massive groove Kyle was laying down, just sounded huge.

The next two verses were just as strong, if not stronger, then we went into this extended instrumental ending we'd come up with, which built higher and higher each time we went through the chord progression.

Rhythmically it was mostly driving eighth notes, at least for the bass and drums, but Kyle and I made the most of it as we just locked in and freakin' *slammed*. By the middle of that section he was back by me, and he had his foot up on my kick drum so he could feel the pulse as well as hear it, and we drove that bus all the way home.

✱ ✱ ✱

"Whoa," I said to no one in particular as we stood backstage during the gear change-out. When we'd finished that last song, we'd gotten some serious applause.

Kyle was excited, too. "Did you hear that crowd, man?"

"Pretty damn good," I agreed. "Especially considering they came to see Neverland. They didn't even know who we were. . . ."

"Well, they sure do now," someone said. I looked over. It was Jeremy Castille, the lead singer for Neverland. He stuck his hand out. "Great show, guys. You rocked."

"Wow . . . thanks!" I took his hand, and he gave me that rock-star-hug thing. I couldn't help it—I was grinning like a fool. And so was Kyle.

"Hey, do you guys know 'Long Walk Home' . . . ?" Jeremy asked.

I almost said, *Are you kidding—I've played it every damn night on the road this summer, and we just saw you do it in Vegas last month*. But I didn't want to come off as more of a fanboy than I already was. "Sure do," I said.

He nodded. "Awesome . . ."

***

There was a spread set out in a big pavilion tent backstage between the motor homes, and I found Glenn and Jamie at a table, deep in conversation. They glanced up as I approached.

"Hey, man," Glenn said. "From now on I expect to see you with a bare ass, wings on your back, and a little bow and arrow in your hands."

I winked at Jamie. "I learned from the best. But actually, I'm here with some bad news. For both of you."

They looked up, serious. "What's the matter?" Jamie said.

"We're not done yet. . . ."

***

Watching a big concert from backstage is way different from being out front. For one thing, you see that there's a lot more than just the band involved. Man, people are *everywhere*, tuning guitars, mixing monitors, even diving low across the stage behind the drummer to rescue a fallen floor-tom microphone right in the middle of a song. And every one of them is wearing a black T-shirt.

And the sound backstage is better than you might think, too. These guys had huge side-fill monitors that were basically a PA just for the stage and the wings.

By the time their set was over, all fifteen thousand people in the audience were on their feet, singing along, with their hands in the air—just like in Vegas. As the band came offstage, the crowd noise only got louder, if that was possible. Underneath the general roar a chant was building. *Ne—ver—land!* . . . *Ne—ver—land!* . . .

After he'd grabbed a water bottle from a nearby cooler, Jeremy turned around and looked at us. "You guys ready?"

We nodded.

"Cool. No need to get fancy—just sing the melody on the choruses."

Kyle raised his hand, like a kid in class who has to use the restroom. "Uh, I don't really sing. . . ."

"No sweat," said Zeke, their drummer. He tossed him a tambourine. "Just stand back from the mic and mouth the words and hit this on the backbeat." He laughed. "If something sucks, our sound guy'll pull you out of the mix. No harm, no foul. But don't worry—you guys'll sound great."

They kinda hung for another minute while the crowd roar got even louder. I was trying to figure out how they could be so relaxed when this skinny dude with a headset came up to us and said, "Time."

"Thanks, Nigel," Jeremy said.

The band took off for the stage with us close behind, but Nigel grabbed us and said, "Not yet. You four wait here until I give the word."

We just nodded, and I guess he could tell we were pretty nervous. "There's one critical thing you absolutely *must* do onstage for this to work."

"What's that?" Jamie asked.

"Smile, dammit." He demonstrated with a big toothy grin. "How often do you get to sing onstage with Neverland . . . ?"

That loosened us up. The roar from out front hit a peak, then stopped. Jeremy's voice came booming over the PA. "We've only got time for one more . . . Zeke's been smelling that meat all night, and if he doesn't get some soon, he's going to hunt something down and kill it!"

The crowd roared at that—this was like the barbecue capital of the free world, and the smell of wood smoke was thick in the air.

"You guys have been awesome," he continued. "Awesome! So thanks for giving it back. We're going to get a little help on this one from our new friends, Killer Jones." There was a little applause at that, then he went on. "Here's one I think you might know. . . ."

As the slow opening chords to "Long Walk Home" rang out, the crowd recognized it and went crazy, and Nigel gave us a push toward the stage. "Now get out there . . . and smile!"

He didn't have to tell us twice.

41

"Right Here, Right Now"

"Venti half-caf three-pump white mocha. Nonfat, no whip, extra-hot. And a venti Americano, with room . . ."

I'd gone half of June and all of July without saying that once. (Well, unless you count my Freudian slip back at that little indie coffee joint in Butte . . .) And there were times in there when I thought I'd never be ordering that again. Ever. So yeah, it still felt good to be giving that goofy order. Especially tonight.

I got our drinks and headed back to the table.

"Thanks," Kimber said. "So, have you come down yet?"

I laughed at that. "Honestly? No. Give me a few more hours. Or maybe a few days."

She took a sip of her drink. "Mmm . . ." Then she swapped to this gossip-girl-from-hell voice and leaned forward. I swear, I could almost see her ears flare out. "*So . . . what did GT think about Jamie coming onstage? Are they, like, an item now? Is she, like, in the band now? Are you guys going to make a record? What was it like, meeting the guys in Neverland? And how about—*"

I held up my fingers in a cross like you'd do to drive off a werewolf. Or is it a vampire? Either way . . . "Stop. Stop-stop-stop. Oh God, *please* make it stop!"

When she smiles, she has this little dimple on her left cheek that's just about cuter than anything. I'll have to tell her about it sometime. "Sorry," she said. "I just had to get that out."

"I understand." And even though she'd never admit it, there was probably a little truth behind the act. So why make her beg? "Let's see . . . Glenn was really stoked that Jamie was up there, and if anything, she was even happier about it. So who knows what's going to happen with them?" I shrugged. "But anyway, being onstage with Neverland was freakin' awesome . . . those guys are so cool. I hope someone got video, because that whole thing almost didn't seem real. And yeah, we're definitely going to do some more recording, and—"

I stopped. She was looking at me. Her eyes were bigger and deeper than ever. Whoa. All that stuff I'd just mentioned was great. And it would all still be there tomorrow. But right now, it was tonight. . . .

I reached across the table and snagged her drink out of her hands and took a sip. I swished it around in my mouth, like I'd seen her do a hundred times. "You know, this tastes like I'm at Starbucks, hanging with Kimber Milhouse. Right here. Right now. And nothing tastes better than that."

Acknowledgments

There are three women in my writing life without whom this book would not exist as such:

Nancy Siscoe, a gifted editor who possesses that rare combination of a great work ethic, a wonderful intuition for getting at the heart of what a writer is attempting to say, and the creative and technical skills necessary to bring it out in the best way possible. (All this, and she's a wonderful person, too. How lucky can one author get?)

Ginger Knowlton, literary agent *par excellence.* She has an amazing way of being a strong advocate for her writers while remaining warm and gracious to all parties at all times. Thanks so much for your wisdom, support, and understanding.

Wendelin . . . Best friend. Wife. First reader. Trusted confidante. *Partenaire dans le crime.* And lest we forget, Chief Harvester of Corn. You're the absolute best!

Special thanks to Ed, Rosalyn, Leslie, and Eric. I'm beginning to realize how rare it is for one to grow up and not only still love but *really like* all the members of their original family. Thanks for all the support, feedback, and validation.

Colton and Connor (our boys . . . our monkeys . . . our band!) read early drafts and provided valuable insight and support. I love you!

There's nothing like enthusiastic, insightful early readers to help you believe you're on the right track, and two of the best have been Caradith Craven and Tricia Owen. Hugs!

Here's a toast to all the musicians (yes, even lead singers) I've shared the stage, studio, and road with over the years, from those first school dances to last week's gig. Also, I'd like to acknowledge the killer crew at *Modern Drummer* magazine, which has been carrying the torch for drummers everywhere for nearly four decades. Rock on!